C000125856

DESCENT
INTO CASEY
HARPER
DOUBT

Descent into Doubt

Copyright © 2023 by Casey Harper

ISBN (Paperback): 979-8-9890053-1-4
ISBN (Hardcover): 979-8-9890053-3-8
ISBN (eBook): 979-8-9890053-0-7
ISBN (Audiobook): 979-8-9890053-2-1

This book is a work of fiction. Names, characters, places, and incidents are either the product of the author's imagination or are used fictionally. Any resemblance to actual persons, living or dead, events, or locales is entirely coincidental.

Edited by:
Lena Rabinovich
&
Caitríona Crowley

Cover design:
gamdesignbooks.com

PROLOGUE

*F*ortunately, freedom is not a necessary condition for writing a book. *Unfortunately*, I sit here writing these lines as a suspect in a rape case under house arrest. How the hell did I end up in a situation like this—just four weeks after my initial encounter with Jade?

I remember the look on her face so well. Lying on her stomach underneath me, she turned her head, flashing a smile. That image is etched in my mind now. It was an innocent smile, and under different circumstances, there would have been nothing seductive about it. At that particular moment, however, it only hastened the inevitable.

You read these stories all the time. You fill in the blanks, imagine what might have happened, and decide who you believe: rape suspect or suspected victim. But when it's you and not someone else, those terms take on a whole new meaning. Things can go one of two ways for me: At best, the State Prosecutor decides to close the case against me and gives me back my life; at worst, I'm indicted and stand trial. The State vs. Cayden Chase. Charged with rape and sodomy.

Before house arrest, I spent a full 24 hours in a police detention cell. Under the laws of my country, the penalty for the crime of rape is 16 years in prison. Another 140,000 hours. A small cage, an orange jumpsuit, and a one-hour daily walk in the yard. I'm 33 now, so If I'm found guilty, they'll throw me in prison, and I won't walk free until I'm 49.

Except, I won't do the time. I won't! I'll kill myself first. Death, a funeral, a grave, an annual memorial. Or maybe I'll donate my body to science. I'm single, and I don't have any children, so I won't be leaving a family that depends on me to its own fate. Yes, it will be hard on the people who love me, but I don't have a choice. I simply won't go to jail. How can you spend years behind bars when you know you're an innocent man? It would be a different story if you had committed the crime, any crime. But in my case? And what's the point of life after prison, branded a sex offender, unemployable, unlovable, unfuckable, all for something I didn't do?

—

Meanwhile, my belief in the power of the truth makes me feel that everything is going to be okay. I have to believe that the police investigators, the State Attorneys, and a court of law will come to this conclusion once exposed to the evidentiary material in full. But, of course, that's just my belief—reality doesn't always fall in line. Surely there must be at least one innocent man currently serving a lengthy prison sentence at one of the detention facilities around the country, despite his clean slate. I'm sure that he, like me, also told himself that everything was going to turn out just fine, that he hadn't committed a crime, and that the truth would finally come to light and justice would prevail. That's exactly what he must have said to himself, and now he's doing time. And he can't be the only one; there must be many who have suffered the same fate. That's just the way it is. Doctors, engineers, technicians, waiters, techies, celebrities—everyone makes mistakes. State attorneys can also get it wrong. And the same goes for judges and juries. So I'm readying myself for anything that comes my way, all scenarios, including the real possibility of a terrible error.

I can't be left alone for even a second. On the day I was released from police custody and placed under house arrest, two of my closest friends, Anna and Megan, reported to the court and posted bail of two months' salary each in my name. They're supposed to ensure I abide by the conditions of my release and confinement. I'm not allowed to leave my apartment, I'm not allowed to contact anyone, and I'm not allowed to receive visitors. If I violate any of these conditions, I'll be thrown back into the detention cell, and my friends will forfeit their financial commitment to the court. They do alternating 24-hour shifts. It can't be easy for them, imprisoned in my place: a two-room apartment in the center of town. I've given them my bed, and I've been using the couch in the living room. I go to sleep long after they do, usually around five in the morning. I have a lot of time to myself, to think.

—

Friends are bombarding Anna and Megan with countless calls and messages for me. I, meanwhile, remain cut off from my social circle. I'm not allowed to use the phone; the police have seized it and my laptop anyway. The messages are touching, but they don't help.

I'm smoking again after not having touched a cigarette for almost two years. I broke the moment I learned Jade had filed the complaint against me, and went straight to the nearest store. Not just a single cigarette, as people do when they don't yet realize that they're done with their current attempt to quit smoking. I had no illusions. No, I bought five full packs, a grand total of 100 cigarettes. I knew right away that my stumble wasn't a fleeting crisis in my attempt to kick the habit. I simply took it up again then and there.

I've been on almost two packs a day ever since, puffing my way through one after the other, clenching my fist around an empty pack, crushing it, tossing the small ball of cardboard into the wastebasket, reaching for a new one, opening it, and attacking the next 20. I'll often light one cigarette with another, and sometimes I'll forget I already have one burning in my other hand or even between my lips, and I'll light a second.

Not all of my new habits are unhealthy. Physical exertion provides relief, and I make an effort to exercise whenever possible – weights, press-ups, pull-ups, and stomach crunches. I'm working out, but I'm not eating much and my calorie intake is low. I've lost several pounds already; I have no idea how many. But I'm sure my body fat percentage has never been as low as it is now. More muscle and less fat. I'm tanned too. Confined to the apartment, I spend most of my days on the balcony in the sunshine. By all outward appearances, I must appear to be a healthy and happy man.

Being accused of rape is every man's worst nightmare. So far, it couldn't be worse, and this is just the beginning. I don't know what awaits me or how much worse it might get.

Megan said I'd lose my shit completely if I kept it all in. I've written every day since she said that, but telling my story isn't pure catharsis. My story is the truth and, whatever happens to me, it means there will be a factual record of the events. You can accompany me on my journey in real-time. But first, let's go back a few weeks—we have some catching up to do.

CHAPTER ONE

*J*ade messaged me just moments after I confirmed her friend request. I responded politely. I always do. I have to. Not only online, but out on the street too – a smile, a handshake, a quick chat, and only then will I apologize, explain I'm in a hurry, and leave. When a stranger approaches me on the street with the words, – "Hey, it's you from Channel 3 News! Boy, have I got a scoop for you," – I listen. And sometimes there really is a story to hear. I've reported on stories that originated in just this way. So I responded to Jade.

It only took a few exchanges for me to realize she wasn't trying to interest me in a news story. No, what Jade wanted was to get to know me, personally. To meet in the real world. I looked at her profile. She was an attractive young woman. Nevertheless, I declined her first suggestion that we meet.

I consider myself a B-list celebrity, but even we, the

B-list members and under, have an aura of sorts around us. We're household names, certainly those of us who appear on television, with all due respect to social media platforms. Every unattached television reporter becomes a desirable catch for women who like the attention they get when they hang out with celebrities. It's not a bad thing, I guess, but I do feel like some kind of human accessory sometimes. I get offers like Jade's all the time, and I usually decline the first suggestion, as I did with Jade. I know that some of them won't try again, so I never hear from them again, but I don't mind, and from my experience, the fact that I don't mind is what makes many of them try again.

So I allowed myself to flirt with Jade. A couple of messages on Facebook, and even a few compliments on some of her photos. A few days after her initial approach, she tried again:

Jade: Maybe I'll get an interesting date offer one of these days . . .

Me: Maybe . . . ;-)

Jade: I wonder if you've got the balls...

That was the moment she managed to persuade me. *Okay, we'll get together for a drink*, I wrote, without a specific where or when. I left things open, but she had swayed me. A slight questioning of my manhood and there I went, lured right into her trap. All because someone I didn't even know, but who was attractive online, dared to suggest I might not have the balls.

CHAPTER
TWO

*J*ade and I met at Yassou, a Greek restaurant on the beach near my apartment. It was her idea, a place she frequented often and liked. I had suggested the Hilton Bay or Loullie, my favorite places, but I didn't argue.

We live in the start-up capital of the start-up nation. It's famous for its 13 beautiful beaches, but to be honest, the city itself is not beautiful. However, the people who live here definitely are, both the men and the women. And, not only are they good-looking, they're pretty rich as well, at least a lot of them are. There are more millionaires here than in Abu-Dhabi or Riyadh, about one out of ten people. It could be any of my neighbors, but sadly, it ain't me.

Jade couldn't have known that I lived two buildings away from Yassou; we had never talked about it. It was a coincidence, I guess. Or maybe fate, who knows? We ordered zucchini balls served over eggplant yogurt in olive oil, roasted peppers and goat cheese spread, shrimp and fried calamari with lemon cream, and tzatziki.

It was nearly eleven when I suggested we order dessert and eat it at my apartment. I don't know what would have happened if we had met somewhere else. But as it was, it felt almost stupid not to make such an offer—we could literally see my balcony from the restaurant's window, and Jade commented on what a great view I must have.

Jade was pretty. She was a second-grade teacher, and I had no doubt that many boys in her class had a crush on her. She was three years younger than me, 30, but looked younger. Her Facebook photos aligned well with her real-life appearance; actually, she was even better looking in person. Her green eyes were the first thing that caught my attention. After a few seconds, I took the rest of her in: long blond hair, full lips, elegantly dressed. Maybe too elegant. She was wearing tailored slacks and a blouse with a modest-but-not-prim neckline, and I was wondering if she had tried too hard. But one thing I knew for sure: sometimes, when you finally met someone after a long and flirtatious exchange online, it doesn't work face-to-face. With Jade, this was definitely not the case.

By 10 p.m., we were sitting at the bar that divided my kitchen from my living room after coming in from the spectacular view-but-too-cold balcony. Jade was playing with her long hair, gathering it above her head and then letting it fall loose again. The gesture flattered her, exposing a long and lovely neck. I offered her something to drink. We both had beers at the restaurant, but now she asked for a whiskey. I poured two regular shots, and we sipped our drinks and started chatting. The minutes went by, and we flirted happily and touched each other lightly, my fingers caressing her cheek, her hand brushing against my knee – the kind of things that sometimes lead to sex and sometimes don't.

We were sitting pretty close to one another, but far enough that one of us would have to move closer if real physical contact was wanted. Finally, Jade moved closer. We kissed. It was a good kiss. With our lips still pressed together, I for some reason, opened my eyes to look at the clock hanging on the wall above the bar. Maybe because things were happening so fast? It was eleven-thirty. Jade had walked into my home only 30 minutes earlier. I responded willingly, of course. I felt lucky.

Jade got to her feet and leaned forward against the bar. I stood up and moved behind her, wrapping her in my arms and caressing her hair. She pressed back against me, her butt pushing into my crotch, and the waistline of her slacks slipping down a little below her tan line to reveal the initial rise and curve of her ass. We rubbed up against one another. It was time to move to the sofa.

She wanted another drink. "Whiskey?" I asked, assuming she'd like to stick with the same drink as before, but she opted for a Vodka Red Bull.

"You're going to wind up with a headache if you mix your drinks," I said.

"It's okay daddy, I'm a big girl," she replied.

After undressing pretty fast, each of us our own clothes, Jade lay on her back and motioned for me to approach, then guided my head down between her legs.

She was pretty indecisive, or that's at least how I felt.

It made sense, though. I mean, it's pretty unusual, isn't it? After all, it was our first sex, or at least potential sex, not to mention that it was also our first date. And indeed, a few seconds later she said:

"I'm not trying to make you go . . . you know. I'm just . . . Let's just say that I really like small kisses around it, you don't have to actually . . . you know . . ."

"I didn't know, but I know now."

Right after the first kiss, a zephyr of fresh soap hit my face. It was a different kind of soap than the one she used for the rest of her body, and the combination of this one and the smell of the perfume from her hand was so good that it made me move on. I touched it with the end of my tongue, over her thong. Jade moved gently the piece of fabric that separated sex and not sex. Her taste was totally synched with the smell, and the look was definitely the result of a laser hair removal treatment.

I was hoping to bring her to climax, but unfortunately, I could see that it wasn't going to happen, and I stopped a few minutes later. For her part, she didn't choose to respond in kind, and I didn't ask.

I stood up, wiped her wetness off my lips, and reached for a condom, which took me three attempts to put on successfully. On my first try, it refused to unravel, and I assumed I had put it upside down; for my second try, it was indeed upside down, and I realized I should have persevered the first time. I flipped it over again and got the job done. Jade giggled, and I felt embarrassed.

With the appropriate protection finally in place, I entered her gently. "It's a little big for me," Jade gasped. It's hard to tell if a woman is being honest when it comes to flattery of that kind. "You'll get used to it," I said with a wink.

After a short while, with Jade still lying on her back and me on top and inside her, I lifted from my torso slightly and pushed myself up onto my hands, locking my elbows and holding myself above her, our bodies still joined from the waist down. I could see more of her in this position and kept my eyes fixed on her face while sliding back and forth inside her. And then I looked at her breasts. They were really beautiful. Pretty big, actually, but small enough to make me wonder if they were natural. It was confusing because they didn't stick out like silicone breasts, they kept a reasonable relationship with gravity. And then, as if she read my mind the moment I entered her, she said:

"Silicone. I know that you're trying to figure it out now."

"You got me."

"Even though, from a health correspondent like you, I'd expect you not only to recognize it by yourself, but also to figure out who the plastic surgeon was."

She smiled at me. I guessed it was her sex smile, since it was different from her usual smile till that moment. Her usual smile, which appeared at the end of her laughs, looked happier and decisive, but her sex smile looked timid. I'd seen it only once till that moment, when I warned her not to mix her drinks, and she said: "Don't worry Daddy, I'm a big girl." I didn't know then, about an hour ago, that it was her sex smile. But I know now. It really turned me on. I was lost in the moment, inside the pleasure and the fun. And then, she slapped me across the face.

It came out of nowhere. I didn't see it coming, and my

position wouldn't have allowed me to parry it anyway, with my arms supporting my weight, my elbows locked. Even Bruce Lee himself wouldn't have been able to block that slap.

I pulled out, sat up on my knees, and just looked at her. "What the fuck?!"

She didn't respond, just giggled and reached out toward me, motioning for me to come back.

"Don't do it again," I said, though my words sounded wimpy and ridiculous, even to me.

She didn't respond, just kept smiling and gesturing back toward her. It took a few seconds for me to convince myself that the incident had been a one-off, and then I entered her again.

—

The second slap came fairly soon after the first. This time, however, I was ready for the hand that flew at my cheek, and I blocked the blow.

"What the fuck, Jade?!"

Perhaps I should have ended things right then, but I didn't. Instead, we went on in this strange manner for a while longer: One moment we'd be kissing and caressing, and then a second later she'd lash out and try to slap me again. Whenever I noticed it coming, I'd grab her hands and pin them to the sofa until the "danger" had passed. Despite her ever-present smile, I felt uncomfortable every time I grabbed her hands.

"Am I hurting you?" I said.

"Don't be a pussy!"

And so it went. I'd "neutralize" her, she'd laugh, we'd go

back to normal sex, and then the same ritual would begin all over again.

During the course of our long, protracted encounter we took a few breaks, sitting naked next to one another on the sofa and talking, snacking, drinking, and laughing. She was cute and funny. She said that the slaps were my punishment for making her initiating everything here – the date, as well as the sex.

Then we'd return to sex. I lay on my back and Jade lowered herself onto me and started to ride me gently. She didn't try to slap me from her new vantage point. I caressed her breasts, hips, ass. She lay flat on my chest and showered me, in kind, with soft kisses on my lips, cheeks, and eyelids. She was gentle; in fact, I completely forgot about the slaps.

Then she rested for a minute, relaxing all the muscles in her body as she lay there on top of me, my body supporting her weight, and me still inside her. She stayed in that position for a while, and I took advantage of her closeness to caress the back of her neck with my fingertips. I ran them down either side of her spine, all the way from the top of her neck down to the rise and curve of her behind, imagining that my fingers were a paintbrush.

I could feel tremors running through her. They pleased me. I felt her tighten herself around me, firmly gripping my penis. I wanted to give her more, so I grabbed her hips and pulled her down even tighter against me. She began lifting herself up into her riding position again, doing so slowly and deliberately, sweeping her breasts across my chest and then stopping and raising herself a little so that they swayed in front of my face, pausing for another second, and only then sitting up straight again. I slipped one hand between her legs and started to stroke her. She moaned and picked up the pace of her riding, before pausing to adjust the angle of my hand, and then picking up the pace again until she climaxed. Or faked it.

CHAPTER THREE

*A*fter dismounting, Jade lay face down on her stomach, turned her head towards me, and smiled. I suggested moving to the bedroom, but she said she was fine on the sofa. I sat down on top of her, gently across her legs, and caressed her back, sliding my hands upwards and gathering her hair into a ponytail, then stroking it between my fingers. And as she lay there under me on her stomach, arched her back a little to push her ass slightly upward in my direction, and said, "Hey Cayden, guess what? It's your lucky day."

I raised my hand to my mouth, wet my palm a little with saliva, lubed my penis, and then pressed it against her ass cheeks. I didn't try to enter her yet, just placed it there to see if she would recoil or exhibit some interest. She was interested. I started pressing into her, slowly and gently. This turn of events was a bit surprising, but not shocking. In my experience, women sometimes initiate this kind of sex, even on a first date. Jade wasn't the first woman, nor the second, to do so. Some, like her, acted as if it were some kind of special prize they awarded to me. Others actually seemed to like it and didn't try to hide it as a prize in disguise.

An additional benefit: There was no slapping this round. I continued to push slowly into her.

"Fuck me harder," she whispered.

I picked up the pace and penetrated deeper, but gently— life isn't a porn movie.

"Should I come?" I said.

"Soon," she said, "but not yet."

I changed positions. I slid my forearm under her, around her neck, and leaned on her beneath me. I stopped when I felt her press her neck against my forearm; afraid she'd choke. After a few more seconds, I asked her again if I should finish, and this time I was given the green light.

Jade stood up and asked if she could freshen up. It was jarring how quickly she moved; evidently, she had no interest in lying on the sofa with me for a while, relaxing together. I went to my bedroom, retrieved a clean towel from the closet, and then led her to the bathroom, where she ensconced herself, closing the door behind her. When she emerged, it was my turn.

The bright, bathroom light knocked me out of my post-coital stupor. I had mixed feelings about what had just happened. I didn't like the whole slapping thing, that's for sure. On the other, her funny explanation that it was my punishment for making her initiate everything, made some kind of sense to me. And she was very pretty, and I guess that most men tend to open their minds even wider when it comes to pretty women.

When I walked back into the living room, I saw her clothes still lying there on the sofa, but Jade wasn't there. Instead, she was in my bedroom, lying underneath my comforter. I must have exhausted her, because she had turned off the lights and was now fast asleep.

CHAPTER FOUR

*M*y apartment was a bit of a mess: empty glasses, bottles, clothes tossed haphazardly on the sofa, and a few dirty dishes in the sink. I connected my iPhone to the portable Bluetooth speaker and chose a random song from a random playlist: *Stay*, by the Kid LAROI and Justin Bieber:

> *I do the same thing, I told you that I never would*
> *I told you I changed, even when I knew I never could*

I paused the song. It made me feel like I had promised something to Jade that I might regret, like a relationship, even though I hadn't. I scrolled through my phone, found a techno set by DJ Jenia Tarsol, and started tidying the place.

Shortly thereafter, the phone rang: it was Karen. I hesitated for a moment, maybe it would be better to get back to her tomorrow, but Jade was fast asleep when I left her, so I answered.

"What's up, my favorite worm?"

"Worm" was a nickname I'd given Karen a while back, ever since I'd found out about her participation in Operation Olympic Games, about 12 years before. Together with the CIA and NSA, her national cyber agency, Unit 8200, used a weapon named Stuxnet, a kind of malicious computer worm, to attack the nuclear Iranian facilities in Natanz. Karen had never admitted her part in it, of course, but I could tell by her smiles.

"Well, I just got a very tempting job offer from a private cybersecurity company. Again. It's not a seven-figure number, but it's getting closer and closer every time."

I held the phone to my ear with my shoulder, scrubbed away, and chatted with Karen about the potential new job.

That was when Jade showed up, standing at the entrance to the kitchen, and catching the tail-end of my phone call with Karen. I mouthed a "hello" to her.

She looked at me for a few more seconds and then moved towards me. I said a quick goodbye to Karen, placed the phone on the bar, and then – when I sensed that Jade was right behind me – I turned around. It was a good thing I did: a slap was heading directly for my face. I blocked her blow with my left hand, which was holding a sponge soaked in dishwashing liquid. The slap didn't make contact, but I lost hold of the sponge and it splashed against my face, leaving me holding her wrist, our faces inches from each other, and mine covered in soap.

"Jade, enough already," I said, trying to keep my tone in check as I wiped my face clean.

She didn't respond; she just looked at me and smiled that damn smile of hers. Then she reached her hands out towards my waist. I pulled back.

"I'm serious, Jade. I'm done."

"Oh, really?" she said. "That's it? The rules have changed?"

"Yes," I said. "We can watch a movie if you want, but–"

"Gotcha."

I had no idea what she was really thinking, but for the time being anyway, she hung out with me, uncomplaining – accompanying me back and forth from the living room to the kitchen – until I was done straightening up. She asked if she could help me feed my cats, Ian and Amy. She stroked them while they ate, a gesture that pleased me. I have a fondness for people who love animals. A few minutes later, she started flirting with me again, hugging me from behind while I was washing the cat's bowls, kissing me gently on the back of my neck, and grabbing my waist. I wasn't in the mood, but at least this time she didn't try hitting me. Eventually, I gave in. A male ego thing, I guess. Had I known she would want another round, I wouldn't have climaxed during the previous one.

The second round was much shorter than the first, and she made no attempts to slap me. I pulled out of her and pleasured her with my fingers until she came. It was a weaker orgasm than her first, based on short vibration in her thighs and her soft moan at its peak.

"I am pretty sure you faked that now."

"Well, I didn't, so it's your word against mine, I guess."

I got up and got dressed. She asked if I didn't want to come too. I said I was fine.

Jade stayed the night. I remember her giving me a kiss in the morning before she left, and I remember her saying goodbye. When I woke up fully some two hours later, I found a note on my door:

Thanks for having me over, Jade.

CHAPTER
FIVE

*T*he next day I returned home from work in a great mood. I had put together a good story for the evening news: the health authorities were going to dramatically change their medical cannabis policies in a way that would make getting a prescription much easier. I could think of quite a few people who would greet this news with great joy.

I made myself a cup of coffee, and sat down at the computer. *Ten minutes and that's it*, I said to myself. I had planned to take a nap for an hour on the sofa, and then go out.

I was pretty satisfied with my life in general up until that point. If anything was worrying me, it was the state of my State, which was becoming more and more religious and conservative. Ironically, as I would find out soon, the feeling wasn't mutual—the State wasn't worrying much about me.

When you're a suspect of a crime, you might discover that the State can be pretty brutal.

I opened my Facebook messenger and saw that I had a new message.

Cayden,

I need to share something with you and I want you to know up front that it may not be very pleasant. Don't get me wrong; I'm not blaming you. But I didn't come to you yesterday for sex. I wanted to get to know you – the person. But for some reason that small shot of whiskey and the Vodka Red Bull really wiped me out. I was tired beyond reason, couldn't speak, think, or resist, the way I would have been able to if I had been sober. I've never been like that before. I know you didn't force the alcohol down my throat, but I trusted you. I thought I deserved to be allowed to decide with a clear head if I was into it. And it hurt a lot. It may not have seemed so to you, it may come as a surprise to you, but the things you did, and the way you wrapped your arm around my neck with me on my stomach, and all the other things you did that hurt me (and of course I tried to resist but couldn't), left me with bruises on my skin, and with pain. You could see I was totally out of it and you even spoke to me as if I didn't know what I was doing, and it didn't bother you. I'm sure you're a good guy. But please, the next time a girl comes to visit you and wants to sleep with you, it would be best if she was 100% lucid. From the little I saw when I was clear-headed, you have so much to offer without the need for drugs and alcohol. And again, I'm not blaming you, only myself. But I wanted to get it off my chest and share it with you.

Jade

I read the message six or seven times to ensure I wasn't imagining things. The words *and of course I tried to resist but couldn't* weren't typed in bold print, but they may as well have been: My whole body went into full panic mode at the sight of them. I had heard about men who faced false sexual assault complaints, but I'd never even imagined that something like that will happen *to me*. Just like car accidents, I guess. If driving was dating, then I guess I felt like I'd been driving fast towards a brick wall, and had just found out that the brakes weren't working. Maybe it wasn't too late to stop? I responded immediately.

Hi Jade,

I have to tell you I'm very surprised by what you've written. There was nothing about your behavior that indicated that you weren't thinking straight or were "tired beyond reason."

And we didn't drink that much. But if you're saying now that you don't remember what happened, let me remind you: you slapped me across the face, even though I told you I wasn't into that kind of thing. Then, when I worried I was misinterpreting your signals, I asked if I should stop. And you responded, "Don't be a pussy!"

I have never taken advantage of a woman under the influence of alcohol, and I didn't do so yesterday. Not at all. You didn't appear out of it to me, Jade. To me you looked to be very confident and determined, sexually speaking. In short, I could go on and on, but it's best I don't. It's best we don't discuss the fact that you turned to me and said, "Fuck me harder!" Yes, you asked me to. How was I to know that it would hurt you? I strongly reject any attempt on your part to accuse me of taking advantage of your condition, or to even imply that I did so. Strongly reject.

Cayden

I sent my message and remained fixed in my chair,

frozen, staring at the computer screen, reading Jade's terrifying message over and over again. I tried to tell myself that our current dialogue reflected some kind of misunderstanding, but the terrifying words "and I tried to resist but couldn't" were driving me insane.

Jade didn't answer. I checked every few seconds, but nothing came. And then suddenly I realized what I had to do: I had to call her and record our conversation. Immediately. First, I called my lawyer friend, criminal defense attorney Marcel Beto, and gave him the lowdown. Marcel's response was swift and unequivocal: "Call her and record it. Just in case. Better you should regret recording her than the opposite."

CHAPTER
SIX

"**J**ade?"

"Hi," Jade said. "What's happening?"

"Uh, listen, I have to tell you; your message really took me by surprise. I mean, what? What? Tell me. What?"

"What what?"

"Look," I said. "You aren't even close to being someone who loses control or isn't aware of what's happening. At least you weren't like that last night."

"Ok, first of all, that Vodka Red Bull and mixing drinks seems to have had a bad effect on me."

Was she kidding me?! "I had specifically warned you not to." And then, just to make sure we were on the same page, I added, "Mix your drinks, that is."

"That's true," she said, "you did say that. Listen, it's not like I'm accusing you of doing anything to me."

"But it seems like you *are* accusing me, Jade."

"I'm not. I just wanted to share my feelings. I was simply out of control; you need to understand that."

"Out of control? That's an interesting way of expressing it."

"Why are you putting me in such an uncomfortable position, Cayden?"

"Because I was shocked by what you wrote, and I want to understand it. Anyway, I think you have it backward, Jade. Do the words *fuck me harder* sound familiar?"

"I may have said that. People say things like that."

"Yes, they do sometimes. On that, we can agree."

"Maybe I should have told you what I was feeling, every step of the way, because you weren't looking at my face, so you couldn't know I was in pain."

"Give me a break, Jade, you never said a word about pain. If anything, you made it clear that things were a bit too tame for you."

"Listen – really . . . Look, this isn't a battlefield; I'm not going to war with you. And I'm not a sex-crazed nymphomaniac who's trying to make trouble for you."

"I didn't say you are. But you're no shrinking violet either, Jade; you're no timid little girl." And then I brought up just one of her many non-timid little girl behaviors. "How about when I was washing the dishes and you came up and slapped me?"

"Yeah," she said, "I vaguely remember doing that; somehow I splashed you with soap. I don't even know how we got to that point. All I'm saying is that sometimes, when someone drinks . . . that drink, it wiped me out. There was something wrong there; I relied on your judgment. For some reason, I trusted you. If you had been a true friend, you would have noticed and said: 'Yes, this girl is drunk.' You would have seen a girl who'd had too much to drink. I was a mess."

"No. You weren't a mess, and you weren't drunk, Jade."

"Cayden, I know what I'm like when I'm thinking straight and having sex. I'm a thousand times more fun that way than when I drink."

"Then don't drink."

"You don't need to sound so defensive. I told you it's not your fault. You didn't force the alcohol down my throat."

"I didn't force anything anywhere, Jade."

"True. But . . ."

"But what? What exactly is it that you're accusing me of, Jade? Frankly, I think it's you, yourself, that you're so angry with, and you're just taking it out on me."

"I'm not taking anything out on you. But I am angry about one thing: that I couldn't make the choices that I'm capable of making when I don't drink."

"And I'll say it again: Then don't drink next time."

"Cayden, I think you think I'm trying to make trouble for you."

There she went again. What was up with her? Why did she keep saying this? *Was* she trying to make trouble for me? And if so, why??

"Cayden, you don't have to get angry with someone when they want to share something with you. It's not like I'm blaming you for anything."

"It definitely felt as if you were blaming me," I said, noticing my use of the past tense. "At least until we had this talk now."

"Well, I'm not. I think you're cool and interesting, and, umm, I mean, I assume you meet a lot of women in your life. And I'm just another one. So that's how I see it. Here I am, just another one."

"You're not just another one, Jade," I said, calming down a bit now that it seemed things might be okay. "You're special, you're surprising, you're stormy, you're wild, you're unpredictable, okay? Obviously, there was just a big misunderstanding between us, but I like you."

"I guess it's good you called," she said with a sigh, as if she'd given up some kind of battle, thank God. "I'm happy we spoke."

"Me too."

"So, we're still friends?" she said. "We're going to get together again?"

I was so relieved by this turn of events that it was all I could do not to blurt out something completely inappropriate, like: *Thank God you're not accusing me of rape, I've been slowly losing my mind, we can be whatever the hell you want!* Instead, I very calmly said, "Well, sure, of course."

I saved three copies of the recording – in my email inbox, on a flash drive, and on my laptop's hard drive.

CHAPTER SEVEN

*T*he next day, Jade messaged and then continued doing so almost daily. She wanted to get together again, but I made my best efforts to hold her off. The truth was, I was afraid of her, despite our "friendship." I was still reeling from the shock of her words: "And I tried to resist but couldn't." I continued dodging her efforts and waited hopefully for them to stop.

At one point, I considered asking her if she wanted to go out to a nightclub. A one-on-one date would have been too scary, so I thought about asking her to bring a friend along, and suggesting I do so as well. I was hoping that maybe this way she would let me go if she actually saw me one more time, and that this kind of going out, to a nightclub, amongst a group of friends, would be something I could handle.

The start-up capital is known worldwide for its vibrant

nightlife scene. Ibiza is the party capital of the world, then my city was definitely the party capital of the whole region, not only of my State. So I considered the plan: asking Jade if she wanted to meet a bunch of us, in a new nightclub that had just opened called John Doe. Actually, I was hoping to *become* a John Doe for Jade after hanging out there together. The best part was that two DJs I liked, who collaborated under the name *Hard to Tell*, were going to be there that Friday. But eventually, I didn't go for it. I guess my fear of her made it difficult for me to think straight. Big mistake? Huge mistake? Hard to tell.

A week later, Jade called. I didn't record the conversation. She got to the point: she wanted to meet again. For a drink, a cup of coffee, anything, she didn't really care.

I decided to put an end to my evasion tactics and tell her the truth: I was afraid of her. I said it was difficult for me to trust a woman who'd implied I'd forced myself on her when she was drunk. I explained that the things she'd written had really thrown me, and I hadn't yet recovered.

She seemed surprised. She told me she thought "we had talked it all out" during our previous phone call. She insisted she wasn't accusing me of anything, that it was all just a "misunderstanding," and that she thought we'd cleared things up. It was a polite conversation, but one that, in the end, did not yield the result she was after. Despite her best efforts, Jade was unable to get me to meet with her. That was all she wanted, and I wouldn't give it to her.

CHAPTER EIGHT

*T*he following day, I woke up to another message from Jade. My iPhone's battery was very low, only 1%, and when I opened it, the phone shut down. While I plugged it in and waited, I thought about the women in my life. I'd had four long relationships, all between six months and two years long each, and all of them ended by me. In addition to those, there were two women who had broken my heart, both because they didn't want to be more than friends with benefits. It was very painful, and the recoveries were pretty long, about a year each. But it was also a good experience for life, I guess, because I am usually on the other side, and I remember the pain.

The iPhone got back to life. I could read Jade's message.

You're good, Cayden. You almost got me thinking that I was the one at fault the other night. Up until yesterday I really believed that maybe I was to blame. But fortunately, I've come to my senses. Here's how things actually happened: When the alcohol suddenly hit me, you moved in and started kissing me and leading me to the sofa and feeling me up and undressing yourself. And there's no way I would have gone along with you if I had been sober. Although I was drunk, I resisted and struggled and slapped you, and you gripped my arms tight, and you said to me, and I'll never forget: "Never mind; you'll get used to it." I remember going to the bathroom and finding it hard to stand up. I'm stupid because I wanted to believe that this was all a misunderstanding. But then on the phone yesterday you just pushed me and my feelings aside. You made it clear that you really don't care at all about me, and that your main goal is to not get into trouble. Don't worry, Cayden, I'm not going to file a complaint or try to hurt you. But you'll have to live with the fact that you hurt me. You made fun of me, and you humiliated me. You made me feel ashamed of myself. I don't want a response from you. From now on I'll keep my distance, and as of now, I'm ending all contact with you. You win! I hope my wounds heal and that I never again meet another person like you, and I'll leave it up to God to settle the score with you. Let him be the one to forgive you.

I decided to answer her immediately.

Listen, Jade, I didn't do anything forcibly. You've already said you were sorry for accusing me, you've already apologized for that, more than once. I don't get it. What's changed since then? You're only proving my point: that my instinct to stay far away from you was right.

Jade replied within a few hours:

What's changed? I already told you: I came to my senses. Your true colors were revealed to me, and I'm not going to let you step all over me. No. Go look for another sucker. I don't want anything to do with you, I don't want to remember being with you or knowing you, and I don't want to hear from you! I've heard enough; please don't message me back.

This time, I decided to respect her request. I didn't contact her, and she didn't contact me. And then, eight days later, I got another jolt. A notification popped up, saying she'd commented on one of my Facebook photos:

Love the backdrop.

Hope springs eternal. I actually thought her public comment might indicate some regret on her part, and that it might presage an apology from her.

A fool is born every day.

CHAPTER
NINE

*I*t happened three weeks after I met Jade. I was just beginning to hope that this scary episode in my life was behind me, but I guess in my case, life is what happens when *someone else* makes other plans for you. I was getting ready to go out to a party at the Jimmy Who nightclub, located right next to the Facebook corporate office headquarters. When I think about it now, I wonder if a date like mine with Jade could have happened in the pre-social media era. I had never used dating apps like Tinder or Bumble, would she have been able to contact me if it hadn't been via Facebook? Just as I was heading out, to a party, my phone rang. My friend Sharon, an actress and TV presenter, was on the line.

"Is everything okay?" she said, sounding worried.

"I'm fine," I said. "Why wouldn't I be?"

"You're not keeping anything from me, are you?" she

said.

At that point, my heart began to pound. Still, I told her no, I wasn't keeping anything from her, and I found myself praying that this was true. Because if I was, then I was in deep shit—it could only be one thing. I prayed my little head off during the brief silence on the line. But like many other prayers that have been uttered over the course of human history, this one didn't work.

"The city's flooded with rumors that someone's filed a rape complaint against you."

I swallowed. A terrible taste of bile came up into my mouth.

"Where did you hear that?" I said.

"People talk, Cayden. Do you really not know anything about it?"

"I haven't heard a thing."

"Really?"

"Really," I said making up an excuse for why I had to hang up.

My cell phone rang again a few seconds later. A journalist this time—a crime reporter from one of the newspapers. He asked for my response to reports that someone had filed a rape complaint against me.

My life flashed before my eyes. I know, another cliché, but this actually happened. Literally: I had a video clip running in my mind, providing a kind of overview of my life experiences—scenes from school, my hometown, and university. It wasn't chronological, as one might have expected. One minute I was ten or eleven, playing with friends in the neighborhood; a second later, I was a bit older, falling in love for the first time; a second after that, I was younger again, a five-or-six-year-old who had lost sight of his mother on the beach. I suddenly had access to memories that I had long ago forgotten.

I lost track of time during this mysterious replay of my life. I couldn't tell if it had been five seconds or five minutes, but when it was over, the bile-tasting saliva in my mouth had dried up. I stood up from the bar stool and felt so dizzy that I almost toppled over. So I sat down again and called Marcel, but he didn't answer. Fuck! Where the hell was he? I tried seven or eight times, but to no avail. I went over to the kitchen sink and drank some water straight from the tap. I hadn't drunk like that since I was a little boy. I felt like a little boy.

I switched on my laptop and inserted the USB stick attached to my keychain. I turned up the volume on the computer. Jade's voice filled my apartment wall-to-wall. The recording was saved and intact but, still, I couldn't breathe.

I picked up my keys, stuffed my wallet into my pocket, and ran downstairs. I checked again to make sure the flash drive was firmly affixed to my keychain. I decided I had to keep it on my person at all times, even if I was only taking out the trash. The police could show up at any moment, and it was vital for me to be in possession of the recording so I could play it for them.

I walked to the convenience store and spent almost all the money in my wallet on five packs of cigarettes. My hands were shaking, I lit one even before I left the store. The dizziness hit me again. When I braced myself against one of the refrigerators, the guy behind the counter asked if I was okay.

"Fine, fine," I said, but I could barely hold it together enough to open the refrigerator, retrieve a bottle of water, and pay.

I hadn't smoked for almost two years. Indeed, the toxic vapors that filled my lungs caught my body by surprise, but it quickly got used to them again. The dormant nicotine demon inside me awoke in an instant, stretched a little, and was soon quite at home. I knew how easy it was to wake the demon; I knew all about that demon from the Allen Carr self-help book that got me to quit in the first place. And I had no doubt that my personal demon was in for a very active period. I walked back home, lighting one cigarette after another, and trying repeatedly to get ahold of Marcel, without any success.

As I was coming around the bend of my street, there was a middle-aged man standing outside my building. I braced myself. What fresh hell could this be?

He appeared to be waiting for someone, and I wanted to believe – though of course I didn't – that he was just innocently waiting for a tenant to come down, any tenant other than me. His face looked exceedingly familiar, but I couldn't place him. And then, just as I was walking towards the stairs, he produced a large camera out of nowhere and said, "Excuse me, I'm sorry," and started taking pictures. It was then that I recognized him as a photographer from one of the large national dailies. He managed to snap several pictures of me in quick succession. Instinctively, I raised my hands and covered my face. *Fuck! Big mistake! A typical image of a guilty man!*

I raced upstairs at breakneck speed, leaping four or five steps at a time – a total of 68 up to my apartment. I went in and slammed the door behind me, panting and coughing. And then I collapsed on the floor. I tried to get up but couldn't, so I remained there, just as I was. My body had yet to adjust fully to the nicotine again, and I had hit it with three or four cigarettes in a row, not to mention the effort it took to race up to my fourth-floor apartment. Too much at once. I remained in a heap on the floor and tried to think. My cats, Ian and Amy, approached and stared at me inquisitively. Amy brushed up against me, trying to coax a caress out of me or perhaps trying to cheer me up.

I began breathing deeply – inhaling through my nose and exhaling from my mouth, slowly, several times. After a few deep breaths, I gripped the door handle and pulled myself to my feet. Great, I was up – a good start. Then I locked the door from the inside and tried calling Marcel again. Still no answer! I had to keep the panic at bay, but how? The cops could show up at any moment to take me in, and I had no idea what I was supposed to do. *Should I answer their questions? Why not, in fact? I've nothing to hide! But hold on a second; perhaps it would be better to invoke my right to remain silent until they allow me to speak with Marcel? I know I'm entitled by law to speak to a lawyer before police questioning. Everyone knows that. But what do I do if they tell me that my very refusal to cooperate only incriminates me? After all, who invokes their right to remain silent? Someone who has a reason to want to remain silent – that's who! Real criminals! And me?*

Marcel didn't answer so I turned to Google to solve

my dilemma, and after a brief review of some of the results, I learned that in the event of my arrest and immediate questioning, I should tell the investigators that I would answer all their questions, as I had nothing to hide, but only after speaking with my lawyer. Okay, okay, now I could think straight.

I sat at the bar and read through my correspondence with Jade. I began talking to myself: *Cayden, you need to calm down and think straight! You can't lose your cool! You're as hard as nails, you're tough, you're a fighter. You're going to be okay!* It helped. I tried Marcel again. No answer. *Fuck.*

I placed my phone on the countertop. I had to talk to someone, someone I trusted. I picked up my phone again and called my closest friend, Eddie, a Channel 3 cameraman I worked with. A woman answered.

"Is Eddie there?" I asked.

"Who?"

"Eddie."

"Sorry, but there's no Eddie here. You've got the wrong number."

I called again. The display on the screen of my phone read *Dialing Eddie.* The same woman answered – in a less friendly manner this time.

"I told you – you've got the wrong number!" she said, hanging up abruptly.

What the hell? Was it possible that my phone had been tapped? Why else would I keep getting the wrong number? Maybe the police were listening to me? I had, on occasion, filled in for the Channel 3 crime reporter over the years, so I knew how these things worked. On the other hand, maybe

I was just being paranoid.

I reached for the handset of my landline and dialed Eddie's number. This time he answered. So, I guess I hadn't been paranoid after all – my cell phone might indeed have been tapped by the police. Or maybe they were spying on me by using one of those cyber-attack techniques, and my phone was already infected? The battery had actually been running down pretty quickly recently, and I knew this was one of the signs of being under a Pegasus cyber-attack. They must have Pegasused me! The bad-tasting saliva in my mouth dried up again. I needed more water.

"What's up, bro?" Eddie said. "What time do you want to start heading to the party?"

"Eddie, I'm not going to any party. I'm in trouble." I took a deep breath. "Someone's filed a rape complaint against me."

Total silence. And then: "What?" The word came out in a horrified whisper.

"Yeah," I said. "You heard right."

"Fuck," he said. "I'll be there in five."

"Please," I pleaded. "Come." If I'd ever had any pride, I had none now.

"Hey, listen – when we hang up, call Marcel."

"Believe me, I've tried. And I can't reach him. Anyway, please come ASAP; I'm going crazy."

When Eddie arrived, I filled him in on the bare bones of the story and gave him a job: Go home and print out my Facebook correspondence with Jade. I had saved it through screenshots in my phone of course, but I felt it would be better if I had printouts as well. Just in case.

And then, finally, finally, *finally*, Marcel called.

"Marcel!" I cried. "Where have you been? Do you have any idea how many times I've called you?"

"Apologies, my friend. I was completely caught up in the Johnny Depp-Amber Heard news. Actually, my head's still spinning. It's fascinating. Have you seen the news? He won the case! I've never seen anything like it before: the court deciding in *his* favor! *And* finds *her* guilty of defamation! Honestly, in this day and age, this kind of verdict is like something out of science fiction."

I hadn't heard. I'd been a bit preoccupied with other things, you could say.

"Talk about timing," I said. "One man gets his life back; another man loses his." And then, before he could ask, I broke the news. My news.

When I finished narrating my tale of woe, Marcel said a lot of things, but the truth is, I could barely take them in, I was in such a state.

"Listen," Marcel said. "I do believe that eventually, all will end well. However, I also have to say this: By the time this whole thing is over? You'll have been through the seven circles of hell."

He said that I could of course be arrested at any point now, but it probably wouldn't happen this evening—if they had wanted to arrest me today, I'd already be locked up by now. He asked me to meet him the next morning in his apartment and instructed me to turn off my phone when I left the house.

"This way you'll already be with me, at my home and unavailable by phone, in case the cops try to come for you at some ungodly hour."

A few calls came in while I was talking to Marcel, calls from friends who were going to the party. I needed to fill them in, but not just yet—there was someone else I needed to call first. I took a deep breath and dialed.

CHAPTER
TEN

"**H**i, honey. How are you?"

"Mom, listen, there's something I have to tell you."

"Is everything okay?"

"Everything will be fine; let me start by saying that. But I need you to promise me something before I go on. I need you to promise that you trust me and that you believe me when I say that everything will be all right. Okay?"

"Okay," she said, sounding tentative, "I promise."

"Mom, someone has filed a rape complaint against me. But everything's going to be okay. Really."

Unsurprisingly, her promise was for naught. "What?" she wailed into the phone. "Oh my God!" And then she started to sob. But I mean sob. I hadn't heard my mother cry like this since I was a little boy. Actually, it wasn't just crying; it was a complete and utter breakdown. I allowed it for a bit. I had to. And then I tried to reassure her.

"Don't cry, Mom; it'll be okay. Listen to me, please! I didn't rape anyone, that's the main thing, and at a certain point that will become obvious to everyone."

But she just kept crying.

"I have proof, Mom. I've got our Facebook messages and a recording of a phone conversation I had with her. The conversation proves she only flipped out on me because I rejected her. A recording like that can be a game changer, Mom, believe me!"

My mother was a very rational person, but she wasn't buying into any of this. And her sobbing was killing me.

"Mom, the police and State Prosecutor aren't fools. They'll investigate, they'll examine the evidence, and the truth will prevail. They'll have to come to the conclusion that there was no rape; there won't be any other option."

Her nonstop sobbing threatened to awaken old demons inside me.

"Mom, I'm about to begin a battle for my life, but I'm tough, I really am. And I know that everything's going to be okay because I haven't done anything wrong."

But still, she wouldn't stop, and I was sinking. It was the demons; they were rising up and threatening to pull me down. I knew that I had to stop her crying. Enough was enough. We didn't have time for this shit now. This was not a telenovela.

"Mom, really, you need to calm down and listen to me: I have a battle on my hands. I'm stronger than you can imagine, but I need you to be level-headed here. I need to know that you're strong too, that you have faith in me, and that you understand that everything's going to be okay. If I sense that you're weak, it'll weaken me. Do you understand what I'm saying?"

I guess my words finally got through to her because, after a last sniffle or two, the sobbing stopped. "Yes," she said quietly, trying to stifle a little hiccup, "I understand."

"Thank you, Mom. Think of it like this: We're at war now. I'm on the battlefield, and you're on the home front. The soldiers on the battlefield have to know that the home front is safe and well-protected, so they can fight an all-out war. Do you get it?"

"Yes."

"Great. So repeat after me: I know that everything's going to be okay, and I promise to be strong so that you can be strong too."

"Okay, it'll be okay."

"No, Mom! I want you to repeat my exact words: I know that everything's going to be okay, and I promise to be strong so that you can be strong too."

"I know that everything's going to be okay, and I promise to be strong so that you can be strong too."

"Thank you, Mom."

"But, Cayden, honey, why is she doing this to you?"

"Revenge, I guess," I said.

"But she knows you didn't rape her, so how can she –"

"Ah, well. I don't know about that, Mom; at this point, I don't know what she knows, what she doesn't know, what she's talked herself into believing. And to be honest, none of that's really important right now. The important thing is that you keep your promise. Okay?"

"Okay, Cayden. Okay."

"And Mom, I love you very much, even if I don't tell you enough."

"I love you too, Cayden. God knows how much."

"I'm hard as nails, Mom, just remember that."

My mother and I were very close. My father died when I was six when he fell from our balcony. He had gone out there for a smoke, even though he knew he shouldn't have: The railing wasn't secure. That was why my mother had locked the door in the first place: because she was afraid I would go out there. My father had been drunk, as always. But this time he was too drunk to go up to the roof, the way he usually did. So he asked my mother for the key, and though eventually she gave it to him, she also argued with him, and tried telling him why it was a bad idea. He didn't like that. He slapped her across the face, hard, something that was not a rare occurrence in our family. But this time he did something else too, something he'd never done before: He grabbed her by her earring and yanked it. I remember a lot of blood on her white shirt. It was a big mistake. He should have gone up to the roof. Our apartment was only on the third floor, but he stumbled backward, hit the ground, landed on his head, and broke his neck. In the local newspaper the next morning, this is what it said: "Horror on the balcony – the railing was broken, a young father was killed in front of his six-year-old son."

Every family has dark secrets. At least one. If you know nothing about it, it's probably because you never tried to find out. If you did, and still discovered nothing, then someone in your family decided you shouldn't know. I know my family's secret, that's for sure. I was only six years old, but I know what I saw. My father didn't stumble and fall because he was drunk. He was drunk, of course. But it wasn't the alcohol that pushed him—it was my mom.

CHAPTER ELEVEN

I hung up and looked at the display on my cell phone. Eight missed calls. Maybe the police? I checked. No, only my friends from the party. Okay then, I needed to tell them too.

I tried to calm down a bit after my conversation with my mother. Several deep breaths, two more cigarettes, and a lot of scary thoughts. Do I know someone who faced a false sexual assault, and managed to get away with it? I mean, Johnny Depp did, of course. But he wasn't really facing the option of being thrown to jail, it was a defamation trial, he was "just" trying to clear his name, and restore his career. My case is much tougher. And, in more ways than one, I'm not Johnny Depp.

I picked up my phone again and called Megan.

"Darling," she said. "Where are you? I'm on my way to the party, everyone is already there!"

"Megan," I said, and since there was no way to soften the phrase, and no point in doing so, I just came out with it: "Someone's filed a rape complaint against me."

"What?" she screamed into the phone. "I'm coming over!"

Within 20 minutes, Megan was knocking on my door – dressed up as a fairy for the costume party I should have been at. She looked deeply alarmed. She hugged me tight and said: "Cayden, another two or three cabs are on their way over here. The entire gang, everyone's on their way. Now tell me what's going on."

"I will," I said. "I promise." I wanted to tell the story only once, properly, to everyone. Less than 10 minutes later and my living room was filled with concerned faces in costume. Eddie, too, had returned, armed with a printout of my correspondence with Jade.

I told them the story. I had never before spoken to such a captive audience. I read them the messages, and when we got to the point where I had recorded our phone call, I simply connected my laptop to the stereo system and played it for them. Ben was the first to speak when the audio file ended.

"Oh man, what is this bullshit?" he said. "The cops are gonna release you the minute they hear this recording. Totally."

I looked at Tony, the head of security at a big hi-tech company, who'd served in the police force until about two years before. I was curious to know what he thought. Despite Ben's words, Tony shook his head. I knew right away what he meant, and my heart sank. No, it wasn't going to be that simple – even with the recording.

A discussion ensued. Everyone spouted words of encouragement: It's going to be okay, the police and prosecution will realize you've done nothing wrong, you're a good guy and don't deserve this, and it'll be over a lot quicker than you think. When the discussion died down, my visitors began talking among themselves, but not only about my predicament; small talk too. Eddie put out refreshments from my kitchen. For a moment it looked like just another get-together of the gang. All of us together in someone's house, music in the background, snacks, alcohol. As if my entire world hadn't been turned upside down.

I opened a beer for myself, went out to the balcony, and lit a cigarette. I needed some quiet. One of my female friends approached.

"It'll be alright," she said, hugging me.

"It'll be alright," I repeated back, robotically, to her.

She went back inside, and then a male friend came out. Our brief exchange was an exact replica of the previous one. When he went back in, another friend took his place. And then another. Like an assembly line. And this little dance continued once I was back inside too. And then it occurred to me: We were at a wake. Yes, a veritable wake. People had come here because they wanted to, of course, but also because it would have been bad manners not to. Light refreshments were on offer, but nothing more. People were engaged in conversation, and there was even a little laughter here and there, but in general, the mood was doom and gloom. One by one people were coming up to hug, kiss, and encourage me, and to promise that everything would end up being just fine – even though they had no way of knowing that.

And after an hour or two, some of them clearly wanted to leave, but didn't, out of guilt. The whole thing was exactly like when you made a condolence call – the exact same. In this case, I was the bereaved, but I was also the deceased, and they were consoling me.

My apartment finally emptied out at midnight. I turned off the stereo and sat down in the living room. It was quiet. Really quiet. I opened a fresh bottle of beer and listened to the silence. Then it hit me: No matter how much support I got, at the end of the day, I was alone in this story. Completely alone. I tried to cry but couldn't. I kept telling myself how sad and fucked up my situation was. Above all, it was fear of prison, of course. But that was just the main course. The appetizers were shame, embarrassment, and losing my career. And of course, there was also the dessert, after 16 years in prison: the life of a convicted rapist.

It didn't help. Nothing; my eyes remained totally dry. I tried to keep my eyes open without blinking, hoping that maybe this would trigger my tears, but again, nothing. I tried to reconstruct the distress I had felt during difficult situations in my past, but also to no avail.

Apparently, my body was telling me that there was no time now for nonsense. What good would tears do? It was time to fight, not to cry. I couldn't afford self-pity. There was no point in thinking things such as: Why is this happening to me, why me, what have I done to deserve it? That kind of thinking could distract me from more important concerns. I told myself that weakness was for the weak, and I was a strong man. From now on, no more wasting energy on anything that wasn't vital for my fight for survival. Not even thoughts.

I turned on my computer and emailed my boss. I wanted him to hear this news from me, and no one else, if such a thing were even still possible. After explaining the situation, I told him I'd be taking a leave of absence starting now, indefinitely.

When I was done writing the saddest email of my life I opened a new document, listened to the recording of my phone call with Jade, and transcribed every word. Marcel had asked me to do this for our appointment the next morning, with as much precision as possible. Our objective was a quick and efficient investigation, and if the investigators only received an audio file, it could hold things up; it was best to provide them with a printed transcript of the recording at the same time. Marcel explained that the police would still make their own official transcript, of course, but it takes time, and providing them one of my own can be helpful at the very early phase of the interrogation, *as long as it's accurate*, he warned me. So I transcribed it, not leaving out a single comma or period, and inserting them when necessary. It took me almost four hours, so there was only one hour left for sleep. Finally, ready for my six a.m. assignment, I headed to bed for 60 minutes of shut-eye.

CHAPTER
TWELVE

I couldn't sleep. My body was beyond pumped up. In fact, I was convinced that if someone had measured my adrenaline levels, they'd have found them to be like skydivers the minute he leaped from an airplane. But with skydiving, those levels dropped to normal after a few minutes; mine had been off the charts for the past eight hours straight. I could actually feel the hormone, the neurotransmitter coursing through my veins and arteries. I know the effects of adrenaline – the heart palpitations, increased blood pressure, dilated pupils, and tremors – I'm a health correspondent, after all. I went to the bathroom and looked at myself in the mirror. I looked terrible. Terrible and pale. Something in my facial expression had changed. I simply looked like a different person.

At 5:30, I threw on some clothes, dashed down four flights of steps, nervously looked over my shoulder for the presence of cops, got on my motorcycle, and sped over to Marcel's. The city was just waking up, but I had never been to sleep. I viewed my surroundings through my sleep-deprived brain and my helmet's tinted visor, with the sense that I was now a visitor to a different planet. A tourist, traveling through a world of which I had been a part, just moments ago, but no longer was. I was still here, but not really. I was in a twilight zone.

Marcel opened the door and threw his arms around me, something that might have made me dissolve in tears if I hadn't been so busy freaking out. As always, he looked like a tough criminal, not a criminal lawyer. What can I say? It's what everyone who sees him for the first time says. If he was an actor, his charm would get him a lot of work, but his looks would keep him in criminal roles. He actually gets offers sometimes, when casting directors see him on television talking about a case.

Once, about 5 years ago, he said yes to one, and took a small part in a movie as a senior boss in a big criminal organization. It was nothing in particular in his look; muscular, tall, bald, brown eyes. That could describe any cop or lawyer. But it was the way he walked, the way he talked, and the scar on his cheek that looked like it came from a knife fight, that made him seem like a criminal.

He grew up in a very bad neighborhood in the south of the city. He was proud of his poor childhood and tough background, and how far he'd come, but he never lost his native way of speaking and carrying himself. Marcel took the right turn at the end of the road he grew up on and ended up a huge success. The scar he got in a yoga class a few years ago. Another student, a 70-year-old woman, scratched his face with her ring while moving too fast from one position to another, in a too-crowded class.

I immediately gave him a copy of my Facebook correspondence with Jade and played the recorded conversation for him. He ushered me inside and we sat in the living room before reading and listening twice, making notes for himself while I watched anxiously. Marcel owns his apartment in one of the best neighborhoods in town, close to the national theater. He doesn't rent like me. Good criminal lawyers make much more money than news correspondents, and Marcel is the best. At 42, if he cared to, he could have his pick of women in the start-up capital.

When he was done reading, he explained that my biggest advantage was that I was telling the truth and that I had nothing to hide. It was a huge advantage, he said: I wouldn't have to concern myself with concealing details from the police, I wouldn't have to bother trying to construct a credible story with no holes in it, I wouldn't have to worry about my storyline crumbling in a heap of lies, and perhaps most important, I'd have nothing to fear when it came to taking a polygraph test. Always a big plus in a police investigation, Marcel added – a privilege of sorts for the innocent. Suspects who had something to hide would reject a polygraph; but as explicitly instructed by Marcel, I was to demand one the moment I was arrested.

Our objective, Marcel reminded me, was to get through this mess without an indictment at all.

"Cayden, you've got to do exactly as I tell you. I mean, to the letter. You're going to do exactly as I say. Got it?"

I nodded solemnly, trying to match the stern expression on his face with one of my own.

Frankly, I'd never seen Marcel this way before: so serious, so forbidding. In the past, when the two of us would meet for a Friday afternoon coffee, or go out for a drink, it would be all laughs and jokes. But now I was a suspected rapist, and Marcel was my defense attorney. My life depended on him. I had no idea what I was supposed to do or how I was supposed to act, so of course I would do whatever he advised. And if he asked me to clean his house so he'd have time to review the documents? Gladly. And if he instructed me to slash my wrists and then regret it and call for an ambulance, because that was the kind of thing an innocent man did when he found out he was a rape suspect? No problem. I would probably feel no pain anyway, because of all the adrenaline pumping through me.

"I'll do whatever you say, Marcel," I added for extra emphasis.

"Cayden, I'm not only telling you what to do, I'm telling you what *not* to do. Listen up: From now on and until further notice, you don't do a thing at all without my consent. I mean it. You don't talk to anyone, you don't contact anyone, you don't go anywhere – unless I say you can."

"As I said, I'm putty in your hands."

"Just so you know, a criminal attorney spends a lot of time trying to minimize the damage caused by his client's foolish behavior, and you're a definite candidate for problems."

My antennae went up. "Me?" I said, "Why?"

"Because you're not a criminal and you've never been

interrogated by the police, that's why."

I nodded.

"And there's something else you can do: work out. Continue your life as normal, going to the gym as usual, and you're running too as if nothing's happened. Got it?"

"Got it."

"Oh, and one more small thing: No more calls to me from your cellphone. Get yourself another phone that isn't registered in your name, and call me only from that one. But call me; don't text me. Is that clear?"

As our meeting progressed, I learned that the media hadn't released any report about my predicament yet, because immediately after Jade's complaint, the police had asked for a sweeping gag order on all the investigation's details, including the fact that an investigation was even underway. The court granted the request, and Marcel found out about it from one of his friends, a crime reporter who got the notification about the gag from the police spokesman's office.

So the media were banned from saying or publishing a word about the case, not even that a media personality, who could not be named, was suspected of rape. I told Marcel what a relief this was, because it gave me hope that I could fight this war without the shame and embarrassment that comes with media coverage. But he said we shouldn't get carried away: The reason they'd asked for the gag order was not because they wanted to protect my good name; they just wanted the investigation to go ahead discreetly for now, and that was also why they hadn't arrested me yet. Marcel explained that from their perspective it was the smart thing to do, since this way they could keep track of me from afar, tapping my phone to see if I made contact with Jade or tried talking her into retracting her complaint. If I did that, I'd be guilty of interfering with a police investigation, and then I'd be in even deeper shit: In addition to 16 years in prison for rape, I could also get another three years for the additional offense. A total of 19 years behind bars.

So, there it was: The day before, I'd been pretty sure the police had tapped my cell phone, and it seemed that I'd been right. You know what they said: Just because you're paranoid doesn't mean they aren't after you. Or, in my case, I should say: Just because they're after you doesn't mean that you're not paranoid.

I left Marcel's house, hopped on my motorcycle, and headed toward my apartment. What a beautiful day. I was traveling down one of the city's main streets, a wide and tree-lined boulevard, with a café in the center, where I spotted friends and acquaintances from across the way. What a nightmare. I lowered the dark visor of my helmet and pressed on the gas.

I got home. And now what? Maybe I would make something to eat? I hadn't eaten anything since yesterday afternoon. But no. I wasn't hungry. I opened a beer, lit a cigarette, and went out to the balcony. My head was swimming. When were they going to arrest me? The waiting was killing me. I felt like the American soldiers in *Saving Private Ryan*, on their way to Normandy to fight the Nazis. They knew they were cannon fodder, and that many of them wouldn't come home, but right now they were making their way across the fucking sea, smoking cigarettes, against the backdrop of a deceptively pastoral landscape.

But it wasn't going to be today. After all, today was Sunday, and Marcel had said they wouldn't take me into custody over the weekend; the police deserved a day of rest too. Tomorrow perhaps? Tuesday? When the fuck were they going to do it already? Hey, you there: I'm a rape suspect, I'm a dangerous person! Why aren't you coming to get me?

I decided to go to the gym to work out. If I wasn't eating or sleeping, at least I could try to stay fit, as per Marcel's instructions. Things were going to be tough for me, particularly in detention. Marcel said the cops were probably going to hold me for at least 24 hours. And if things didn't go well in court, perhaps even longer. Maybe even a week, two weeks, a month. God only knew. Being in detention was no laughing matter. You've heard the stories and the jokes about bars of soap falling in the shower. Maybe those comments were amusing in the abstract, but not funny when I imagined myself as the one picking it up.

So I had to stay in shape, get stronger, and keep up with my running too. Cardiovascular fitness was critical when you were involved in a physical fight. The loser in a fight isn't always the physically weaker one, but sometimes just the first one to run out of air. I put on my trainers, grabbed a towel, and headed to the gym. Afterward, when I got home, I still had no appetite, but I took a can of tuna out of the kitchen cupboard anyway and ate. Just like that, with a fork, and with nothing on the side. I had no appetite, but I wanted to get some protein into my body, to strengthen the muscles that I had just worked so hard at the gym. It disgusted me because I wasn't hungry, but I forced myself to finish the entire thing. When I threw the empty can into the garbage, I took a vow that if I won this war and got my life back, I'd become a vegan.

At eight o'clock, when I was done, I knew I had to try to sleep. A quick bit of mental arithmetic told me I hadn't slept for 25 hours. I brushed my teeth and got into bed.

Fuck, who could fall asleep in this situation? I tossed and turned for half an hour before trying the one thing that always helped. I gave it a go, I insisted, I fought with myself, I tried to be clever, I delved into recollections of intense experiences and passionate encounters from my past, I took a trip down memory lane and immersed myself in thoughts about all my ex-girlfriends – but there was no point. Jade's smile flashed across my mind. I gave up.

CHAPTER
THIRTEEN

*A*nother day went by, and still no sign of the police. I packed a bag for my time in detention, as Marcel instructed, and put it aside: a sheet, a change of clothes, a toothbrush, toothpaste, and deodorant. When I was done, I put on my exercise wear, grabbed a towel, and went to the gym. I left the building cautiously, glancing around. Maybe the cops were out here somewhere waiting for me? Then I went back upstairs to get the bag I'd packed, just in case they were here when I returned. I decided then and there that I wasn't going anywhere without that bag, from that moment forward. I even gave it a nice name – my "Custody Kit."

Later, on my walk home from the gym, I noticed that the weather had turned a bit cooler. I walked by a woman who turned to the friend next to her and said there was the smell of rain in the air. But I couldn't smell any rain. I smelled gunpowder. A war was about to break out.

No cops standing at the entrance to my building when I arrived, thank God. I went upstairs, took a shower, and polished off another can of tuna. And now what was I supposed to do? I decided to try to sleep. It had been more than 40 hours since I had. Again, I tried the natural sleep inducer that had always helped me in the past, but again: no luck. It simply wouldn't happen. Just like the time before. I downed four whiskey chasers. I was turning into an impotent alcoholic.

Even so, I must have eventually fallen asleep, because a few hours later, the phone rang and woke me. It was Marcel, and he wanted to meet. I asked when. "What do you mean, when?" he said. "Now!" I would quickly learn that "now" was his favorite time for meetings.

This time, Marcel wanted to go through all the material again and stressed several issues. Well, "stressed" isn't really the word for what he did. He had instructions for me, strict instructions. We focused on particularly tough situations that would be coming up, and he coached me on how to deal with them: what to do when my interrogators yelled at me or tried to humiliate me; how to respond to accusations of "acting in a criminal manner" by recording Jade without her knowledge; how to deal with allegations that I had tried to undermine the investigation before my arrest. Each issue required clear responses. I needed to know how to act. I needed to practice.

Just as Marcel excused himself to get us some fresh coffee from the kitchen, Karen called, my friend whose nickname is "Worm". I was too exhausted to answer, but a text message from her appeared a second later:

Get back to me, Cayden. It's to do with the mess you're in, and it's important.

Not thinking too deeply about the implications of calling, I went out to Marcel's balcony, lit a cigarette, and dialed. It turned out she had a snippet of interesting information from the police, something she wanted to share with me.

"'Listen, you won't believe this," she said. "My colleague's father happens to be that woman's boss, and he said ...'"

Fortunately, my brain snapped back into place just in the nick of time. "Don't, worm!" I said, shutting her down before she could go any further.

If the police had tapped my phone, and she had passed on the information, it could have been tantamount to obstruction of justice. Marcel had explained it to me and warned me to be careful. I asked her not to tell me anything even if we met in person, explaining that obstruction of justice was a criminal offense.

I went back inside and told Marcel about the conversation.

"You'll be happy to know that I acted against my instincts. I told her not to tell me anything, that I didn't want to hear, when the fact is that I really do want to hear. Oh, did I say that I want to hear? How about: I'm *dying* to hear!"

"Nice," Marcel remarked drily. Then, almost proudly, he added, "Just FYI, that's the behavior of a criminal."

We reviewed the documents and listened to the recording one more time, and then I went home. I felt emboldened by Marcel's energy and insights; I could almost say I was even itching for a fight.

At home, I did some stare-down practices with Ian and Amy. Anyone who has a cat knows the drill: we're dealing after all with creatures who can sit and look you straight in the eye without budging, for 10 minutes at a time, until you're the one to break your gaze. It takes a fair amount of determination and willpower to come out on top in a stare-down with a stubborn cat. It's an amusing game, as well as a very effective way of showing the cat who's boss, because cats tend to get a little confused sometimes. Now, over the past few days, the same amusing game had assumed an operational purpose: as a dry run ahead of my interrogation. According to the various cop shows I'd always watched on TV, I could expect to be up against a hard-ass interrogator, one who would fix me with a menacing look and stare at me in total silence. I practiced my not-looking-away-abilities mostly with Ian, who was usually tougher than Amy. He looked tougher than her too: he was bigger and jet-black all over, whereas Amy was almost all white except her black tail and nose. He seemed to have picked up on my recent interest in our stare-downs, and he had even started to initiate them himself. In the mornings I woke up to a huge pair of eyes gazing at me just a foot or so from my face, waiting for our morning standoff.

—

The next morning, a phone call from Marcel woke me at eight, a pretty normal time, I suppose, around the time that other people, who aren't sitting at home waiting to be arrested, are getting up for work. But me, with my newfound screwed-up sleep patterns, had to take what I could get, and what I could get was a few hours in the early morning. Marcel sounded pissed off.

"I'm on Facebook now," he said. "I just opened Jade's page. Why the hell didn't you tell me about the pictures of her with the leather whip?"

"What? I didn't – "

"You didn't what? You didn't think they would be important?!"

Marcel was referring to one of Jade's photo albums, an entire collection of pictures showing Jade in skin-tight black leather outfits with plunging necklines, and a black leather whip in her hand.

"But Marcel," I said, "we can still... "

"We still can, thanks to me!" Marcel said. "Do you realize that she could have erased those pictures? It's a damn good thing I saw them when I did. I saved them in my phone by screenshots for now, so we have a backup. But I want you to print them as soon as possible. Big color printouts, highest quality. Got it?"

"Got it. But I have to ask, Marcel, what does this have to do with my case? I mean, the fact that she posted a few provocative pictures doesn't prove anything. It doesn't mean that she's lying, that's for sure.".

"Cayden Chase, my friend, with all due respect and love, we've seen where your fascinating understanding of women has got you so far, haven't we? So please, let me do it my way, okay? I hope that I won't need to use them, but I want them asap, just in case. So, do you have any more insights about women's behavior? If not, just print the fucking pictures."

—

Almost five full days had passed since I first learned of Jade's complaint against me. My phone didn't stop ringing. I didn't take the calls and mostly read the messages without responding. I answered only the people who could help me; I had become more self-centered than I had ever before dared to be.

Marcel called at nine in the evening. He told me I wasn't going to be taken in for questioning. Not today, not tomorrow, and not the day after. It was going to take a few more days. I asked how he knew all this, and if he was sure, and he said I could bank on it, but he wouldn't elaborate. He asked me to trust him.

"Cayden," he said. "You need to get a good night's sleep. I know you're not sleeping well these days, and that's not a good thing for us."

"You're right. I'm not sleeping well at all."

"So go to bed, turn off your phone, and get up tomorrow afternoon as far as I'm concerned. Got it?"

I read through the documents and the transcript of the recording one more time, making sure I knew the significant sections by heart; two shots of whiskey later, I was in bed. It was 11 by then. I turned off my cellphone and was out in an instant, for my first truly proper sleep in five days.

CHAPTER FOURTEEN

*T*he doorbell rang. A long, loud, chilling ring. I shot straight up and glanced at my alarm clock as I rushed out of bed. 10 in the morning. I took a quick look through the peephole which, ridiculously, offered me a sense of security. After all, the cops were sure to show up, and when they did, I would be opening the door for them, I wouldn't be running. But the peephole gave me a few extra seconds to ready myself, to regulate my breathing and focus my thoughts before opening the door to my fate, to hold onto one more moment of freedom, to fill my lungs with one final puff of my previous life.

Standing there were several men, none of whom I recognized. So this was it; it all started now. I opened the door. There were three of them, dressed casually in jeans, sneakers, and t-shirts that did little to conceal the handguns tucked into their belts. One was wearing a leather jacket, another was wearing black fingerless gloves, and the third – a pretty scary-looking thug – was wearing a hoodie.

"Good morning, Cayden," Leather Jacket said. "Police. You know why we're here."

Yes, I knew. After giving me his name, Leather Jacket flashed a police ID card that identified him as a chief inspector.

I remembered Marcel telling me the night before that there was no chance the police would be turning up this morning. *Nice one, Marcel!* I thought to myself. *Your inside information is spot on!*

They walked in and immediately began to look around. Leather Jacket looked at me.

"Cayden," he said, "we've come to take you in for questioning at the station on suspicion of rape and sodomy. We have a warrant that allows us to conduct a search in your apartment."

The search began. The cops were courteous, but the search was rigorous. From time to time, they asked me questions.

"What's this passport in the name of Maurice Chase?" asked Fingerless.

"It's my grandfather's."

"What's it doing here?"

"It's a keepsake. He's dead."

"There's another passport here – Paulina Chase. Your grandmother?"

"Yes."

"Dead?"

"In a nursing home."

They searched through everything, and they searched everywhere, finding things I had lost way back when and had long since given up on. In other circumstances, I might have been amused.

The search went on for a little more than an hour, and the whole time they engaged me in small talk, as if they were just workmen who had come to repair a broken air conditioner.

"How many cats do you have?"

This question came from Thug. He was definitely the most intimidating of the three. He resembled one of those special forces cops: like someone who beat up criminals daily.

"Two," I said. "Ian and Amy."

"Cool names. I have a dog," Thug said.

"Me too," Fingerless added.

"Me too," Leather Jacket said, making his own little contribution. "I have two dogs."

"I thought so; you don't look like cat people."

I acted friendly, but in my head, another narrative was running: *They aren't your friends, they're cops. Questioning is already underway, even if not officially. They're taking note of everything you say. And maybe even recording everything.* So I didn't take my eyes off them while they were searching for god knows what in my apartment.

Can I leave some food and water out for Ian and Amy before we go?"

"Of course!" Leather Jacket said.

For a moment, it made me feel good to know that the cops cared for my animals, maybe because I expected people who loved animals to be compassionate human beings. But then I remembered the way Jade fed my cats during her visit on that infamous night and realized that, on the other hand, someone who loved animals *was the reason* that the cops were here in the first place.

I filled the cats' water and food bowls, and we left the apartment. Before closing the door, I took one last look inside. I knew it might be a while before I was back. I closed the door and locked it, before figuring out, what the hell, and picking up the newspaper that was lying on the mat. I stuffed it into my Custody Kitbag.

We drove to the police station in the northeast of the city.

"Tell me," I said. "Will there be photographers outside the station?"

"No, Cayden, there won't be any photographers," said Leather Jacket.

I had been advised not to believe them so I persisted.

"If there do happen to be any, can I duck down in the car so they don't see me?"

"You can duck, but there won't be any photographers there. Don't worry."

I was worried. How could I not be? I knew this field – the reporting field – inside and out. I was used to being on the other side of reporting, the camera side, but still – it was the same system. Who hasn't switched on the news to see the stunned face of a well-known figure being led out of his house, surrounded by police officers, and straight into a sea of flashes? And who do you think invites the photographers?

"Tell me," I said, feigning calm, "will you be the ones questioning me?"

"No," Thug said. "It'll be a different team. We're from the Criminal Investigation Department; we're the ones who do the fieldwork. You'll be questioned by the interrogators."

I stared out the window and tried to digest my change in status, from a free man to a captive. I was in the back of a police car, surrounded by three cops. I may not have been in cuffs, yet, and from a legal perspective I had yet to be arrested, but these were mere technicalities that did little to soften the blow: For the first time in my adult life, I was no longer the master of myself. I had been stripped of the ability to make personal decisions and carry them through without asking permission first. Not even to pee. Breathing seemed to be the only thing I was allowed to do now.

It turned out that leather Jacket wasn't lying; there were indeed no photographers outside the police station. Well whaddaya know? I reminded myself that even a broken clock was right twice a day, and even a blind chicken found a seed once in a while. My good friend, Ronny, Channel 3's senior military correspondent, used to say these things to me whenever I had a good and exclusive news story. He'd been joking, of course, and it had always made me laugh. Now I only wondered when I would get my life back.

We went up to the fifth floor, to the Interrogation Division. I noticed the fuss I caused as we walked in: looks, a hum of conversation, quiet whispers into cell phones.

"He's here."

"He's arrived."

Fingerless asked me to follow him. We entered a room along the corridor: an interrogation room. He closed the door behind us and asked me to sit down. We were alone there.

"I want to warn you, Cayden, that everything you say during your questioning could be used against you in a court of law. You have the right to remain silent if you wish, but you must know that a failure on your part to cooperate could serve to strengthen the evidence against you – and the stronger the evidence against you, the more likely it is that you will be charged. In addition, you may consult with a lawyer ahead of your questioning."

Exactly like the movies. I was prepared for it, but it still hit me hard when I heard it aimed at me. My stomach cramped up, and for a moment I thought I might vomit. It passed, but I asked Fingerless's permission to use the bathroom anyway.

When I emerged from the stall, I saw a familiar face in the corridor. He looked at me, smiled, and winked. *Marcel!* God, I so needed him right here and now.

Fingerless led Marcel and me to one of the rooms further down the corridor, where he left us. Marcel reminded me not to trust any of the police officers, and again explained what I already knew: that every one of them would be happy to be the one to put a television reporter in prison, and that I should be especially wary of the ones who were nicest to me. They were likely the most dangerous ones. He reminded me that my strategy should be simple: I should answer all the questions, as embarrassing as they might be, and tell them everything, truthfully.

Marcel gave me a hug, wished me luck, and left. My self-confidence, which had been shaken ever since the police came to get me, returned; Marcel had done that for me. I felt strong and determined again. So, bring it on: Let loose your toughest and meanest interrogator. I was ready. I had been waiting a whole week now, and I was eager to do battle, to fight the war that had been forced upon me. I was a gladiator. Yes, a gladiator. Like in the battles of the days of yore, it was a matter of life or death. I do not exaggerate. If I lost the battle and they will throw me in jail for many years, I would die, and I mean that literally: I would kill myself before being incarcerated for a crime I didn't commit. That was my plan B.

And just like those battles of yesteryear, mine too would attract an audience. And, although the spectators wouldn't be sitting on stone benches and cheering, and although I wouldn't even be able to see them, I would know they were there. When the interrogation began, they would be sitting in an adjacent room – three, five, maybe even more cops – and they would watch everything on a monitor.

Do you ever think about death? I do. Not often, but sometimes. And I really do understand and accept the idea that death is inevitable because it's a part of life, but only when I'm thinking about *other* people's deaths. When I think about my own, I find it intolerable, unacceptable, and outrageous. I guess many people feel this way. But right now, at this moment, death served exactly the opposite purpose for me: It was, in fact, a backup plan that inspired and strengthened me, a moment before waging the battle of my life.

Fingerless began asking me questions and typing my responses into the computer. The questions focused on personal details like my name, address, phone number, and other things I knew they already knew. While Fingerless was typing, I scanned the ceiling and walls to try to find the hidden cameras, but I didn't succeed. How could I? The room was almost empty: One table, one window, two chairs, a fingerless' laptop, fingerless, and me. Where could they hide the cameras? I turned my gaze back to him and, oddly enough, noticed only now that he was missing a finger on his right hand. Fingerless actually was fingerless – something I hadn't realized until he'd removed his fingerless gloves in order to type. Whaddaya know?

Fingerless was being nice to me, and I didn't care what Marcel said, nice was better than not nice, even if it was fake. Maybe this interrogation thing wouldn't be that bad after all. I was thinking that by then the police had already listened to the recording of the phone call and read through the transcripts of my correspondence with Jade – and that they probably believed me by now.

An officer in a well-pressed police uniform with an impressive array of metal on his chest stepped into the room. He had it all: swords, stars, stripes. It was almost as if his ranks had ranks of their own. He approached me and held out his hand.

"Hello, Cayden," he said. "I'm Chief Superintendent David."

I stood up, shook his hand, and flashed him my most winning innocent-man smile. "Hi, Chief David, nice to meet you," I said.

I was so pleased! The senior officer had come to make sure I was being treated well.

I was such a fool.

CHAPTER
FIFTEEN

*C*hief Superintendent David nodded slightly at Fingerless, who seemed to have no trouble picking up on the tiny gesture. Immediately, he rose from his chair, left the room, and closed the door. He didn't even finish asking me the question he'd been in the middle of.

The senior investigator sat down in front of me. He held a metal cup with the police logo on it. It looked heavy. It was steaming. I could smell the coffee. He ignored me and looked at the screen of the computer for a while. I looked at him. Where else was I supposed to look? Anyway, I needed to come up with a name. It was easy this time. The heavy metal ranks on his shoulders and chest; the heavy metal cup that he was holding. There was no doubt about it: He was definitely Heavy Metal.

Heavy Metal looked me straight in the eye for some time. I stared back. This went on for a while, neither of us lowering our gaze, neither of us moving. Unlike Fingerless, Heavy Metal didn't smile. I didn't either.

"So, tell me, Cayden," he finally said. "Tell me about your sexual preferences. What kind of sex do you enjoy?"

I cleared my throat, then told him bluntly that I had experienced and experimented with a lot of things, other than S&M. He asked me to elaborate. I did. I told him that sometimes, but not too often, I find myself in bed with two women. Sometimes they touch one another, and sometimes they don't, they just focus on me, together. I added that the women in the start-up capital are very confident in their sexuality, and it feels that many of them don't care about what other people think. If they see you as nothing but a friend with benefits, they can surprise you and ask you to help them to fulfil a fantasy of having sex with two guys together. Heavy Metal asked if the two men are expected to touch one another in a situation like this, and I said that answer was absolutely not. It was fucking embarrassing. I wanted a cigarette.

"Can I smoke?"

"No," he said. "Maybe later, if I feel like a cigarette too – then you can smoke as well. Got me?"

I nodded. I certainly did.

"And you understand why you're here, Cayden, right?"

I nodded again. "Yes," I said. "Because someone is trying to kill me."

"What do you mean trying to kill you?"

"Kill, kill," I said. "When a woman falsely accuses a man of rape, she's killing him. Or at least trying to."

"You know, Cayden, it's not easy for her, for any woman,

to go to the police and file a rape complaint. The exposure, the shame, the intrusive questions, and then after all that – to stand up in court and have to answer humiliating questions. That's why there are a lot of women who don't file complaints, because they know they won't be able to handle the whole process."

I tried to control my fury; I knew it would do me no good. As calmly as I was able to, I said, "She knows she wasn't raped, but as far as she's concerned, she got exactly what she wanted the minute she entered this place and tangled you up in her lies. It's the perfect revenge."

Heavy Metal waved me off, noting that Jade hadn't waited ten or even five years to file her complaint.

"And not even a year for that matter," he went on. "It took her less than three weeks. That's not much time at all. That doesn't really play into your hands – the time thing. Do you understand what I'm saying, Cayden?"

"But I'm telling the truth, and there's evidence to prove it! And of course, she's not the first woman to lie about such a thing. If you'd let me explain and show you the evidence I brought with me, you'd see that I'm telling the truth; that I didn't rape her. Have you listened to the recording?"

"Yes, I listened to it," he said.

"Okay, great! So do you want me to show you where you can see a hundred percent, without a doubt, that she's lying?"

"Not now."

The cops had confiscated my phone, of course, so I took a peek every so often at Heavy Metal's phone, just to see the time. We were already into the second hour of questioning, and Heavy Metal now returned to the subject of my sex life.

He wanted to know who I was having sex with, and how often. While I answered him, he lit a cigarette and leaned back in his chair. I asked him if I could smoke too. He said I could. I lit a cigarette. From then on and until the end of the interrogation, we smoked nonstop. He smoked a lot, and me— about twice as much.

"Tell me, Cayden," he said. "When this story breaks, what are the chances other women come forward to file a complaint against you?"

"Pretty much zero."

"Pretty much zero, Cayden, isn't good."

"Zero!" I said. "I meant zero! No chance at all."

"Are you sure?"

"Yes!" I said. "A million percent."

I hadn't considered this. What if a woman from my past suddenly did turn up – someone angry, disappointed, frustrated, or even heartbroken – and took advantage of this perfect opportunity to get revenge? What the hell was I going to do then? I didn't have records of correspondence, I didn't have recordings of phone calls, I didn't have anything. All I had was my word, and it was becoming pretty clear to me that my word would not be enough.

"I don't understand where you're going with these questions," I said. "I really hope you're not going to give my story to the media for no reason at all and ruin my life."

Heavy Metal leaned back in his chair and looked me in the eyes again. I stared back into his polygraph eyes, making sure not to be the first to lower my gaze.

"Besides," I said. "What kind of interrogation technique is this anyway – publicizing my story to see if anyone else comes forward? What's that all about? I have no history of sexual offenses, no criminal record at all, and along comes someone who says I raped her. Well, I say I didn't. Yes, I could be lying. But so could she. Two possibilities – either she's lying or I am. Figure out who's lying, that's your job. But releasing the story to the media, just to see if other people come forward? And what if there are no other people, and it turns out in the end that this complaint was also false, which it is? It'll cause me irreversible damage! And then what are you going to do? What are you going to say to me: Oops, sorry for ruining your life for no reason?"

Unsurprisingly, Heavy Metal didn't bother to respond.

"Okay, Cayden," he said. "So tell me first of all: How did you find out that a complaint had been filed against you?"

I settled back into my chair, accepting that this was my fate for now. "I got a call from my friend Sharon," I said. "She told me that the city was abuzz with rumors. About a minute later, I got another call, this time from a journalist, a crime reporter. He asked me if I had anything to say about the rape complaint. It was then that I realized–"

"That journalist – did he say anything else to you?"

"No," I said.

"Are you sure, Cayden, that nothing else was discussed in the conversation?"

"Yes, I'm sure. It was short and to the point."

Up until that moment, Heavy Metal had been leaning back in his chair. But now he suddenly moved closer to the table and raised his voice.

"You're lying to me now, Cayden!"

For the first time since the start of the interrogation, I

looked down. Fuck. He was right. He was right! I had lied. Yes, the conversation with the journalist had touched upon one more thing: He had offered me his wife's services. She was a criminal defense lawyer, like Marcel. The thing was that I had been pretty sure, in real-time, that he shouldn't have made the offer, and so in my efforts to keep the journalist out of hot water, I had now landed *myself* in hot water. Boiling hot water, actually. Steaming fucking hot water. My heart was pounding fast, and I broke out in a full-body sweat. I was so angry with myself. How could I have been so stupid? I couldn't afford to make mistakes like this!

"Listen to me, Cayden," Heavy Metal continued. "I'm trying to assess your credibility now. Do you understand what I'm saying to you? I'm testing how credible you are, and this test is going to influence the entire interrogation. Do you understand?"

I understood; of course, I understood. I apologized in my heart to the journalist, and then related our entire conversation to Heavy Metal, explaining why I had lied originally. My hands were shaking. I took them off the table and pressed them against my thighs.

Heavy Metal continued looking at me, straight into my eyes and right through to my mind, reading what was written there. Everything was laid bare to him; I was transparent. I began to find it hard not to be the first one to look away. So I focused on his pupils, looking into the black holes in the center of his eyeballs, staring at them. I wasn't merely staring, though; I was delving into them, focusing further inside, as if I were looking at the wall behind him, through him. It worked. When I finally focused hard enough, the face around the pupils blurred and looked like a picture taken by a bad photographer. As a blurry figure, Heavy Metal seemed less intimidating. And then, after a fairly long silence, he went back to asking questions. The exercise that had allowed me to blur his image shattered, and Heavy Metal appeared before me again – sharp and frightening.

When I finished telling Heavy Metal about my conversation with the journalist, he allowed me to present the documents I had prepared – the transcript of the recorded telephone conversation with Jade, and the printouts of our Facebook correspondence. We focused on the conversation, the sheets of paper resting on the table between us, with me reading, and pausing at the points that I felt were solid proof that Jade was lying. But he clearly had one goal; to trip me up.

"I don't get it," he said. "Why didn't you stop the sex if you hated the slapping so much?"

"I thought about it," I said shrugging. "I guess I felt that maybe it would have seemed unmanly or something. Anyway, when it happened, it was always pretty short-lived, and then things would go back to normal, so . . ."

"If I were you, I'd have said, 'Take your things and get the fuck out of here.' And tell me, with all of this slapping going on, why did you agree to sleep with her again? How come?"

"Because she kept trying," I said, hating the way I sounded, realizing that all of this was probably coming across as lame, as supremely unimpressive, but continuing nevertheless, much the way I had continued with Jade, actually. Path of least resistance. "I told her I wasn't into it, but she kept coming over and trying to turn me on, so in the end I said to myself: Maybe the reason she keeps wanting more is because I didn't satisfy her earlier; not a very good thing for a man's ego."

"Do you know what I think? I don't think that was the reason. I think it was because your cock was hard and you couldn't control yourself."

"No!" I said. "That's not true at all!" Then I stopped momentarily because something important occurred to me. "Hey, wait a minute," I said. "We're talking about the second time, right?"

It seemed like he was making an effort not to go completely postal on me with exasperation. "What difference could that possibly make, Cayden?"

"It makes a big difference!" I begged. "It makes all the difference in the world! We're talking about the second round, right? After I had already come the first time?"

"Yeah, fine, whatever. So what?"

"Because I almost never go on to a second round!" I explained, ridiculously, way too happily, as if I had just achieved some sort of victory. "I'm simply not into it," I continued. "I'm satisfied. So I prolong the first round as much as I like, but when it's over, it's over. There is no second round, or third, or anything. That's just me!" This whole thing was absurd, and yet I had no choice but to humiliate and expose myself. "Honestly, you can question any girl you've found on my Facebook, WhatsApp, Instagram, whatever – anyone you believe I've slept with – and you can ask her. I promise you won't find anyone who says I went for a second round. And if you do, you can say: Cayden, you lied. You can't be trusted."

"You know what, I may just do that."

"Good!"

But I felt uneasy. I started thinking of all the women I'd had sexual relationships with over the years, and how they'd feel about having a police officer show up at their door and pry into their sex lives. It was a horrible situation to put them in, and yet I couldn't see any alternative.

We were more or less four hours into the interrogation now.

"So, Cayden, why do you think she filed the complaint against you if you didn't rape her?"

"I have my theories," I said.

"Let's hear them. Tell me your side of the story."

"In a word?" I said. "Revenge." And then I went on to tell him everything, in detail, things that he really should have known already, if he'd actually listened to the recording. All about how in my opinion everything that happened stemmed from her being embarrassed about her behavior, needing to pin that behavior on me, and then, in the end, feeling so insulted by my not wanting to see her again that she decided, essentially, to kill me.

Heavy Metal heard me out, but that was about it. I had given him a ten-minute detailed description of my "theory," and he hardly even acknowledged it. "The bottom line, Cayden," he said, "is that within less than 24 hours of your encounter, she accused you of forcing yourself on her. Do you understand that, Cayden? She didn't claim it a month later, or a year later, or 10 years later – she claimed it the very next day. You hadn't rejected her at that point. So why would she make something like this up?"

"But I just told you why!" I said. "Listen - why would she want to meet up again with someone who had raped her? And by the way, have you ever heard of a rape victim who worries about the impression she made on someone while being raped?"

"Rape victims, Cayden, sometimes want to get together with the rapist again. It happens sometimes, and it doesn't mean they weren't raped. Women who are raped, Cayden, are sometimes in emotional turmoil, or depressed, and that causes them –"

"Depressed!" I said. "My God, this woman was posting crude jokes on her Facebook page in the midst of her depression!"

"So she posted a crude joke, so what? People do all sorts of things when they're traumatized."

It took a lot of restraint, but I did not respond to his use of the word "traumatized." Instead, I said, "And what about the other things she said in the recorded conversation? For example, she remembered me warning her not to mix her drinks. What rapist is concerned about his victim getting drunk?"

"There are all kinds of rapists. Haven't you heard of the well-mannered rapist?"

"There are all kinds of complainants too. Have you ever heard of a rape victim who asks the rapist to fuck her harder?"

"She may have been in a state of shock because of the rape, and that's why she said these things. The fact that you have an answer for every question, after preparing yourself for almost a week, doesn't mean that you're doing well here right now. What can I say, Cayden? This is just the beginning, you know, and in the meantime – how can I put this gently – it doesn't look good for you. You need to understand that we have more evidence in our files, evidence you're not aware of, and that this evidence isn't exactly working in your favor. Do you understand what I'm telling you?"

Yes, I understood. I understood that he was trying to fuck with my head, and I needed to remain calm. Marcel had prepared me for this moment, the moment at which they'd claim to have evidence I was unaware of. He'd told me not to worry; even Jade couldn't manufacture evidence for something that hadn't happened.

"Cayden, she says that you put a date-rape drug in her drink."

"Oh, for God's sake, what the hell? Did she *see* me put anything into her drink? No, of course she didn't, because there was no such thing to see."

"She didn't see it, Cayden, but she says she has no other explanation for what went on there. She says she was completely wasted, that she had lost all control."

"Wasted my ass. She was completely in control, and by the way – she seemed to enjoy herself very much. I'm pretty sure she came, and if she didn't, then she's an even better faker than I thought. Faking orgasms just like she fakes evidence, what can I say? In any event, don't try to mess with my head; I didn't put a date-rape drug into her drink."

At this point, we were likely into the fifth hour of questioning, and I was getting agitated.

"Would it be okay if I stood up for a while?" I said. "I need to get my blood circulating."

He indicated with a nod that I could, so I did.

"Tell me," he said, "why did you record her?"

"I told you already," I said. "I got scared."

"That kind of behavior, Cayden, is criminal behavior."

"Criminal behavior?" I said. "Why?"

"Because it's the behavior of someone who knows he's committed a criminal offense, and now he's trying to cloud the evidence. I've listened to the call, Cayden. You put words in her mouth."

"No, I didn't! What's putting words into someone's mouth anyway? Can someone force someone else to say something she doesn't want to say?"

"You led her to say things that worked for you. Cayden, I'm sorry to tell you, but that's classic criminal behavior."

"I spoke to her about the issues that were troubling me. What was I supposed to talk to her about? The weather? Anyway, I don't care what you think of what I did, because I know it was the right thing to do. When I sit here in front of you now and try to imagine what would have happened if I hadn't recorded her, it makes me shudder."

Heavy Metal shook his head and seemed about to laugh. Then, changing tactics, he leaned forward, boring into me with his eyes, and shouted, "I'll tell you why you recorded her, Cayden. You recorded her because you raped her, and you panicked."

Until that moment, I was actually under the impression that Heavy Metal had, little by little, been starting to believe me.

"I see what you're doing here," I said, changing tactics as well, remembering Marcel's precise instructions. He had prepared me for just such moments and told me all about the scare tactics they would try to use. He said the best thing for me to do in this situation was to respond immediately and to use a very specific word, "humiliation." And he reminded me that even if I didn't see the video cameras, they were there, getting everything on tape. If God forbid, the State Prosecutor indicted me, we would receive the full video file of my investigation, and it might help us in court.

Ever the good student, I said to Heavy Metal now, "I see that you're trying to use humiliation on me. Why?"

"I'm using humiliation on you? What exactly did I say to humiliate you?"

"You said I raped her," I said. "Have you completed the investigation? Have you reviewed and analyzed all the evidence?"

"This is a police investigation, Cayden, and you're suspected of rape and sodomy. That's the way things work. Deal with it."

"In any event," I said, "as I started telling you before, I've never in my life drugged or taken advantage of a situation with a woman who was drunk. Please – go ahead and ask the women who've had sex with me to come in for questioning, and see what they say."

"Maybe we'll do just that."

I don't think I realized that some of them would actually be called in for questioning. Did I actually want that? I had no way of knowing which of them and when. How many women needed to testify that I wasn't a rapist in order to establish my innocence? Two? Five? Ten? What would be the extent of this horror show – for them and for me?

"Tell me, Cayden, is that word starting to creep in a little – rape?"

"I am well aware of the severity of the charges against me," I said, sounding like something out of a textbook, because at this point what choice did I have, nothing else was working. "But I know that I didn't rape her, and that if I tell the truth, everything will turn out okay."

I'd responded to Heavy Metal's question confidently, without taking my eyes off him, but I was angry. What was the point of his evil question? How exactly did it add to the progress of the interrogation? How does one answer such a question anyway? So I responded by saying that I knew everything would turn out fine. But how could I know? I knew nothing. I didn't even know the time of day.

"Can I pour myself a glass of water?" I said.

"What can I say, Cayden?" he said, granting my request with a nod of his head. "Perhaps it's a combination of everything – you were bored, you were mad at her for not wanting to have sex with you, you were pissed off because you weren't going to get any sex…"

"There's no such thing as no sex," I said. "There's no lack of sex here, in the big city. Just a lack of parking spaces."

"Tell me, Cayden, how do you know what evidence the police have in the investigation against you?"

"What do you mean?"

"Cayden, listen carefully. I'm not asking you if you know what evidence the police have. I'm asking you *how you know* about the evidence. My questions are very precise, unlike your responses.

"My responses are precise too," I said, like a petulant

little boy. That's what this investigation was turning me into. "And yes, I understand your last question perfectly. May I take a minute to try to remember? I may have missed something."

"Yes, go ahead."

I lit a cigarette, leaned back in my chair, and allowed myself to disengage from the lie-detector eyes facing me. I looked up at the ceiling, closed my eyes, inhaled the smoke, and exerted my memory. I assumed his question was another test of my credibility, and I knew I couldn't afford to fail. The penny dropped a few seconds later.

"Okay, I remember something you might be referring to. I got a call a few days ago from a friend who said: 'Listen, you won't believe how crazy this is. I have a colleague at work whose father happens to be Jade's boss, and he said . . .' But I swear I interrupted her immediately and told her not to tell me anything more; I knew it could be considered interference. If you were tapping my phone during the week that I spent waiting for you to arrest me, you'd be able to hear for yourself that nothing else was said."

The interrogation was entering its seventh or eighth hour. I was hot. I was wearing the shirt I had prepared for the ordeal, a long-sleeved white shirt with a collar and buttons. I could have taken it off – I was wearing a t-shirt underneath – but I decided against it. Even I get a little intimidated sometimes by people who have a lot of tattoos, before I remember that I'm that kind of person myself. There are three rings tattooed on three of my fingers, one small cat on another finger, and a small pirate skull on the finger next to the cat's. I also have two stars on my hands, one small eagle, and a pretty big design that looks like the one Mike Tyson has on his face. There are more tattoos on my arms, most of them are tribal variations of cats, tigers, and lions. Most of them are pretty small, I don't have a sleeve or any tattoos on my face— nothing radical like that— but I'd guess I'm still probably the most tattooed news correspondent in the country.

So I took into account the fact that somewhere down the line, a video of the interrogation could find its way to the media, and it wouldn't look good with all of my tattoos. It wasn't going to look good even without the tattoos.

"Okay, Cayden, we'll take a break," Heavy Metal said suddenly.

He stood up, walked out without looking in my direction, and closed the door behind him. I was left there alone with so many questions in my head: How long would the break last? Was I supposed to stay there? Could I leave the room? Had I done okay so far? Did he believe me? Was I under arrest? Was the interrogation over? What was the time? Was it a food break? And if so, where was the food?

—

A few minutes later, the door opened. A woman walked in and looked at me. I stared back at her, waiting for her to say something. She was thin, muscular, and pretty tall. She looked like a ballet dancer in a police uniform. Her kind of royal posture included an elongated spine, shoulders down and back, and a lifted chest. Her head was held high, creating a sense of elegance and poise.

"Cayden, you need to come with me now," she said.

"Chief Inspector Lara," she added.

"I know who you are," I smiled. "Everyone knows who you are. Supercop."

She was a celebrity. It was only about a year ago that she'd beaten the shit out of two men who'd tried robbing a convenience store. She'd had a gun. She could have shot them. They didn't have guns themselves: One of them had been holding a large knife, and the other had had an axe that he'd used to break in. But Supercop didn't even need to take her gun out of the holster. She approached them, dodged their blows, and quickly overpowered them with kicks and punches. It was a fascinating show of martial arts skills, and it had been broadcast live on Instagram by a kid who'd been hiding inside during the robbery attempt. Millions had seen the footage. Naturally, there'd been tons of media coverage, and a few days later everyone could see these two screw-ups on national TV, in the court hearings for the guys' remand extensions. One of them was using crutches, and the other had an enormous bandage on his head.

"Let's go, Cayden," Supercop said. "We've got some food for you."

"I'm not hungry."

"Don't argue."

I wouldn't have argued with this woman even if I hadn't been a suspect and she hadn't been a cop. Supercop led me to a small and windowless room with a table and chair in the middle. She told me to sit down, and she placed a tray of food in front of me. I suddenly realized that, actually, I *was* hungry. Ravenous, even. I asked her if I could begin eating and she nodded. On offer was a slice of roast turkey in sauce, pasta, and beans.

The door stayed open and Supercop sat on a bench in the corridor, directly opposite me. She glanced up at me from time to time: at me chewing and swallowing. Since the search at my apartment, I had spoken to a total of four detectives and investigators, but never to a female cop. A woman, a police officer, involved in a rape investigation, sitting and keeping an eye on the suspect. Just the two of us. What was she thinking? *Yes, this guy really did rape Jade?* Did she want to clobber me, just like she'd clobbered the two would-be robbers? Did she hate me? Did she hope I'd end up behind bars?

CHAPTER
SIXTEEN

While I ate, Supercop texted. Actually, she wasn't really texting, she was recording voice messages. I assumed she was using WhatsApp, based on the way the notifications sounded. People seemed to be using voice messages more than they used to, maybe because you could listen to them at high speed now.

When I was a free man, I would read the newspaper or watch TV while eating. I was never just eating; that's boring. But now those options were closed off to me, God only knew for how long, so I listened carefully to Supercop's voice messages, catching enough snippets to understand the conversation. She was talking to a friend by the name of Alina – an actress who was preparing for an audition for the role of protagonist in a new film:

"So, let me just make sure I got this right: The role of a TikTok star, who discovers one day that she can make all the magic she does on her crazy TikTok clips come true in real life?"

Supercop was waiting for her friend's response, and I was waiting too. I mean, she didn't know this, I guess, but her chat with Alina was serving as my mealtime entertainment.

After a few more seconds, I could hear the sound of an incoming message. I hoped it was Alina's response because I was curious, and indeed it was, but it was a text message, not a voice message this time. I couldn't read it, of course, but I could figure out its content by listening to Supercop's fast and excited voice message reply:

"Oh my God, Alina, this role was literally created for you! You're so perfect for it! It's like you don't even need to act since you are indeed a TikTok star, and you're also a kind of superhero, after everything you've been through in life. I mean, growing up without parents and all that. Anyway, let's talk later; I'm still at work."

This was interesting. I looked at Supercop and said:

"Funny. Supercop has a superhero friend! Well, wish her good luck at the audition!"

I didn't know what had gotten into me. I guess I'd forgotten where I was for a minute, but Supercop reminded me:

"Shut up Cayden."

A few minutes later, I asked Supercop if I could smoke somewhere. Much to my surprise, she smiled at me.

"So," she said, "how did you like our food?"

"Pretty good. Quite tasty."

"Well, you're the first interrogation subject to say that. Come with me; I'll take you for your smoke."

Supercop handed me over to Thug and Leather Jacket, and they led me back to the interrogation room. I lit a cigarette.

"How's it going, Cayden? Surviving?" Thug asked.

"In a manner of speaking, I guess."

"How's the interrogation been until now?"

"Well, you would know. You've been sitting in the room next door watching everything live."

"No, we're not up for interrogations; we don't deal with questioning," Leather Jacket said.

"Okay then," I said. "I answered all the questions; I've got nothing to hide."

"Have you eaten? Had something to drink? Did they let you smoke? Go to the bathroom? Do you need anything?"

Their solicitousness was making me suspicious. "I'm good, thanks," I said.

"Great. So tell me, Cayden. Why do you think she did what she did? Why would she file a false rape complaint against you?"

And, indeed, here we went. "Come on," I said. "I'm sure that you were following the whole interrogation from the next room."

"No, Cayden, honestly we weren't. We work the streets around here; we're not into interrogations," Thug said.

I answered them, but I assumed that Thug and Leather Jacket were lying. What they were doing obviously didn't amount to a "tough interrogation," like the one I'd had with Heavy Metal; in fact, to the outside observer, it might have seemed like we were just having a friendly conversation. But of course, there were no outside observers around here, in the Interrogation Division on the fifth floor. If you were here and you weren't an employee, you were probably in some kind of trouble.

The "conversation" flowed. I played the game, chatting as openly as I could. Unlike Heavy Metal, these two – Thug and Leather Jacket – just let me talk. I opened up about everything I hadn't had the chance to say during the long hours spent with Heavy Metal, just as Marcel had prepped me to do. He'd advised me to picture a scale, with Jade's testimony on one side, and mine on the other. To tip the scale in my favor, I needed to add everything I possibly could. It was good advice. At that moment, I understood something else Marcel had advised me to do, something I had originally thought was bad advice: to not let the cops try shaming me. Indeed, when I'd asked Heavy Metal to cut it out, he'd basically said, 'You're a rape suspect, deal with it,' but the truth is, he hadn't done it again. He hadn't resorted to his humiliation tactics. My request had obviously been effective.

So I took advantage of the freedom they were giving me and steered the conversation in the direction I wanted it to go, loading my side of the scale with everything I hadn't said earlier, like a selection of Jade's exact words from the recorded phone call that I had memorized while preparing for the questioning. I spilled it all.

I knew that a decision to either send me home or hold me overnight was being made at that very moment. I felt I was doing a pretty good job, actually, and that the officers were beginning to believe me. Maybe they'd already seen my interrogation with Heavy Metal in real-time on a screen. The more I spoke, the more my confidence grew in the really strong sense that they were coming around to my side. Even Supercop, the only woman on the team, smiled at me. Would she smile at a rapist?

And then the door opened, and Heavy Metal walked in.

"I've decided to book you, Cayden," he said. "Tomorrow morning we'll take you to court and file a request to extend your remand, in order to further our investigation."

CHAPTER
SEVENTEEN

I sat there, stunned, until the door opened again, and Fingerless entered.

"Take him down for photographs," Heavy Metal said, without looking up. "Then fingerprinting and a DNA sample. No dilly-dallying."

"Let's go," Fingerless said to me, and we went.

"So," I said as we arrived at the elevator. "Aren't you going to start questioning me now, while also telling me that actually you're not really questioning me, because you're not into interrogations?"

"No, actually, unlike the other two, I *am* into interrogations," he laughed. "But I'm not going to ask any questions right now."

We sat outside the fingerprinting room, or whatever it was called, and waited our turn.

"A few more minutes, and they'll let us in," Fingerless said.

"More time here means less time in the cell," I shrugged.

Fingerless laughed again. And then, I just had to ask him.

"I'm curious, you know, I'm a health correspondent: what's the story with the missing finger?"

"Ah. I see. Well, in my case, it's not a medical thing. Let's just say that in my job, sometimes the bad guys win."

About an hour later, it seemed we'd come to the end of my official welcoming ceremony. There was nothing about me that hadn't been exposed – they had searched my house, picked through my cellphone, computer, email, Facebook, WhatsApp, and Instagram accounts, and now my biology had been laid bare for them as well. My thoughts were all that remained my own.

I was going to be their "guest" for the night. Twenty hardened criminals in a foul-smelling room: Yes, that's what I was picturing. My God! I couldn't help remembering an article I'd read about an innocent man with no criminal record, a case of mistaken identity, who was violently raped by three detainees. The following morning, he was taken straight to the hospital. The criminal world had a special term for a guy like this: Propeller.

We talked, my fear and me. And my fear explained to me that this was the path that a man who'd been falsely accused of rape had to walk: First came the fear sparked by the complaint, and then came the fear of being raped yourself. I tried to reassure my fear. Told him that everything would be okay, that the police would watch over me, and that they would be publicly shamed and subjected to major criticism if something happened to me while in custody. My fear told me that I was right, but that we had to prepare ourselves for the possibility of violence. We came to a firm decision: I was simply going to lose it completely with the first guy who tried to touch me. I was going to go batshit crazy. I was going to explode and go at him with everything I had and beat the living daylights out of him. No mercy. That was what we decided, my fear and me. My first move would be to go on the attack. To go for the head of the first person who tried to touch me. Or the neck. I didn't give a crap if I hurt him; I needed to neutralize him. I wanted him on the floor within three or four seconds. A fist to the throat, an elbow to the temple, a knee to the balls. Hopefully, that would do the trick. If I got it right, he'd be down after the first blow, two or three at most, and as soon as he was on the floor, he'd get the tip of my shoe in his face. And then a few more kicks to emphasize my point. The beating would stop only when he stopped moving, or when the guards overpowered me.

I tried to calm down and told my fear that my anger, together with some of the skills I'd held onto from childhood martial arts classes, would help me do what needed to be done. In response, my fear said that, unfortunately, it would not necessarily suffice.

With my Custody Kit in hand, I followed Thug and Leather Jacket, who'd been assigned to transfer me to the detention facility on the other side of town. I asked them the question that had been weighing on me. "Are there photographers outside?"

"Yes," Leather Jacket said. "I'm sorry to tell you but your friends from the media are waiting."

"Fuck! Really?"

"Just keep your head down, we'll give you cover; they won't be able to see you."

"They'll know it's me, and that's what'll turn up on the news: a picture of me trying to disguise myself. That's worse than the alternative."

"So what do you want to do?" Thug asked.

"I have just one request – no handcuffs."

"Has anyone cuffed you today, Cayden?"

I shook my head.

"So you won't be cuffed now either."

"Okay, and one more really small thing: When we head out in the patrol car, I want to be able to rest my arm against the window, so that if they take pictures of me, they'll clearly show that I'm not in handcuffs. Okay?" I had thought of everything, or tried to.

The patrol car began creeping towards the barrier of the police parking garage. A second later, Thug glanced left to make sure there was no oncoming traffic and then burst onto the road at breakneck speed. I had never driven like that. In fact, I had never been in any kind of car with a driver quite as crazy as Thug. I tried to look out, but the wild ride made it difficult. Thug and Leather Jacket hadn't lied: there were photographers out there. But they missed us! The patrol car raced on.

We pulled into the detention facility, and with the cops' permission, I got out of the car, put my Custody Kit on my back, and lit a cigarette. That was it; I was ready. I awaited instructions. They looked at me but said nothing. And then Thug looked down at the ground, and Leather Jacket avoided eye contact as well. What was going on here?

"Are we going in?"

"Sorry Cayden," Thug said, "but at this point, we actually will need to cuff you. It's not our call. That's the protocol here. They don't accept detainees who aren't restrained."

"So." I let out a deep sigh. "The moment has arrived."

Indeed, it had. They cuffed my hands and shackled my legs. It was a cold and rainy night after a few days of sunshine, and I walked slowly; you can't walk quickly when your ankles are bound. Thug and Leather Jacket didn't try to hustle me. They walked in silence, one behind me and one in front.

Back straight and head held high. Back straight and head held high. Back straight and head held high. I knew there could be photographers on the other side of the station's perimeter fence, and that I could be bombarded with flashes at any second. We made our way around the bend, and I let out a sigh of relief: no press, thank God. At least one of my fears had not been realized.

We reached the steps, and suddenly I got a lesson in just how hard it was to climb steps when your legs were shackled. The maximum range of movement between your legs was very small, almost nonsensical. I ascended extremely slowly, taking extra care not to fall forward. If that were to happen, it would be impossible to avoid slamming my face into the edge of a step, with my hands cuffed no less.

We went inside. For a moment, the scene there reminded me of a large stockroom: a counter, a window, and behind it, two people in black uniforms. Thug and Leather Jacket greeted them, exchanged a few niceties, and handed them my detention papers. The events over the next few minutes were perfectly suited to the stockroom image in my head – endless forms, bureaucracy, and signatures. Other policemen showed up, bringing in detainees, escorting out detainees, everything moving along in perfect order: *How many have you brought me? What have you come to collect? Sign here, and sign there too.*

"Well," Leather Jacket said, about 15 minutes later, after they had completed the paperwork. "That's pretty much it for us; we're out of here. Good night."

"Wha – ?" I started to say to them, then caught myself. I had to at least act blasé, even if I didn't feel that way. And indeed this was the toughest part of the detention process. I had become attached to them, to the cops who had arrested me. I knew their job was basically to put me behind bars, but as long as I had been with them, they had been responsible for my well-being. But they were leaving now, and I was alone.

The loud noise of a heavy metal door being slammed shut and locked invaded my thoughts. A sharp electronic beep, like an intercom but much louder and more crazy-making, and then the immediate slamming of heavy steel gates. Those were the sounds of detention.

CHAPTER EIGHTEEN

"**C**ome with me."

"Should I bring my bag?"

"Leave it here."

"Here? On the floor at the entrance?"

"Are you trying to piss me off?" The guard leaned in and snarled.

I followed him to a tiny cell. He asked me to sit on the chair there, where he unshackled my legs. He left the handcuffs on, though. I stretched my legs a little but didn't get up.

"On your feet now," he said. "Pants off."

"What? Why?"

"Protocol," he said, with a bored tone. "Move it. Show me your hands first, let me re-cuff you first, and then drop them, your pants."

"What is this shit?" I took off my pants.

"Now lift your shirt."

"Really?"

"Come on; lift it so I can see."

"Are you serious?"

"As I said – it's protocol. Let's go. Get a move on."

I lifted my shirt.

"Now, squat down until your ass is almost touching the floor, like you're taking a shit outdoors."

I swear to God, they were picking me apart, piece by piece. I was on my knees now, pretty much waiting for him to put a collar and leash around my neck and lead me to my cage on all fours. And I would follow and wag my tail, because "it's protocol." My fate was in the hands of a stranger in a black uniform. At that moment, he was the master of my fate.

"Okay," he said. "You can stand up and get dressed, and then I need to handcuff you again. Wait here."

The guard left the cell, closing and locking the door behind him. I sat there alone and waited for something to happen. And then, something did. My own personal fairy godmother appeared out of the ether. He sat in front of me, lifted the receiver on his side, and signaled for me to do the same on mine. *Marcel! Dear, blessed Marcel!* I pressed the receiver to my left ear. My right hand remained hanging in the air next to my head, still cuffed to my left.

"How are you doing there, my boy?"

"Hello?"

"Can you hear me, Cayden?"

"I can hear you. Who is this, please?"

Marcel laughed. I needed him to see that I still had a

sense of humor, that I was still myself, and that I was exactly the way I'd promised him I would be: hard as nails.

Following a discussion of the next morning's court appearance, I gave him my mother's phone number. There was no getting around it; she needed to be informed that I'd be spending the night in police custody.

"Promise me you'll tell her that everything's okay, Marcel. That I'm strong, that I'm in a good way, and that she has nothing to worry about. Okay? It's really important, and it's true. Look at me! I'm fine, I'm tough. Got it?"

"Of course, my boy."

"Oh, and another thing – don't spend more than a minute or two talking to her. Fill her in, reassure her, pass on my message, and that's all. Okay?"

"I promise."

"And one last thing: Tell her not to show up in court tomorrow. Make sure she knows I'm really serious about this; they absolutely can't be there – not my mom, not my brother, not my stepdad, no one."

"You're sure about this, Cayden?"

"Positive. It won't do any good. Seeing them would only upset and weaken me. I'm sure the media will be there tomorrow, and if my family turns up, they'll be all over them. I know what I'm talking about. Just tell my mom that if they want to help me, they can't be there. Tell them I said this is critical, okay?"

"Will do. Now tell me, what about your cats?"

"Oh, hold on, just a moment," I said. "I believe there's another call coming through. Hello?"

"What?"

"Oh, is that you still, Marcel? Oh well, they must have hung up. Never mind, they'll call back."

Marcel laughed. "Well, if nothing else, it's good to see that you're still capable of making lame jokes. By the way, did they let you present the material you prepared?"

"Yes, but we didn't get to the end of it."

"What do you mean you didn't get to the end of it?"

"We only got to page nine out of 14."

"What? You spent all those hours being questioned and you didn't get through the entire transcript?"

"They said that we'd continue – "

"Bastards. What bastards! Just wait and see what I'm going to do to them in court tomorrow. Don't worry; I'm going to rip them to shreds."

"Sounds good to me."

"Anyway, you didn't answer me: What about the cats?"

"Ask Eddie to feed them. He has the key."

"Okay, I'll talk to him," he said standing up.

"But wait, listen, Marcel, before you go. Why did you tell me last night that there was no chance the police would show up this morning?"

"My dear. Did you have a good sleep at last?"

"One of the best; one of the all-time greats actually. Something like 10 or 11 hours."

"And did that do you some good today during the interrogation: the fact that you had a good night's sleep after a week of hardly any at all?"

"Well, yeah, I suppose so . . ."

"That's the main thing, my boy; that's all that counts."

"Wait a minute: did you know they would come today?

Did you have inside information? Did you lie to me on purpose so that I'd get a good night's sleep?"

"Maybe. Maybe not."

Marcel blew me a kiss from the other side of the glass and left. I grinned, but then I was alone again. That was it. The most alone I had been since this whole story had blown up in my face.

CHAPTER NINETEEN

"Let's go," a guard said, opening the door.

He led me to the cell at the end of the corridor: the one farthest from the guard station. I wondered if he'd hear me if I called out for help. He took me inside, removed the handcuffs from my wrists, gathered up my Custody Kit, and headed to the door.

"Hey wait, why are you taking my bag?"

"No bags allowed in the cell."

"But this is the bag I was told to prepare for jail."

"No bags. Call me if you need something from it."

"I need something from it," I said, and he let me reach into it for the bed sheet, my newspaper, and two packs of cigarettes.

"Cayden, you can take the cigarettes, but you can't take the lighter. It's protocol. Call me if you need to light one."

Then he left. I looked around and tried to estimate the

size of the cell. Around five or six square meters, it seemed to me. Small. Or around 60 square feet. That sounded bigger, but still - small. It contained just four pieces of "furniture," all made of concrete and affixed to the floor or wall: a shelf, a table-type thing, a bench, and a bunk bed. There was an opening at the back end of the cell that led to the shower and toilet: another small space, the size of a public restroom stall. The toilet was on the left. No bowl, just a hole in the floor and filth all around it. In the middle of the space stood a basin and, on the right, a shower – a pipe coming out of the wall with two taps underneath. The soap, of course, was indeed on the floor, caked in filth. Alongside it, in the same puddle, was a single roll of toilet paper. I backed out and took my rightful place inside the cell. I wondered if anyone had been raped in here before, in this specific cell. I assumed someone had.

The physical conditions weren't the thing that made the whole situation so unbearable. The greater issue was recognizing the fact that you were locked up. You couldn't get out even if you wanted to; you could leave only when someone else said you could. A realization that shook you to the core. I found myself using the medical situations that I had covered in news stories to explain to myself what I was feeling now. When a blood clot reaches the brain and blocks the blood vessels, you suffer a stroke. When there was a blockage in one of the arteries that fed the heart muscles, you suffered a heart attack. Well, it seemed to me that locking someone up in detention delivered the same kind of blow. But in this case, it was your mind that took the hit.

I took out a cigarette and approached the iron door.

"Guard!" I called. "Can I get a light?"

A few minutes went by before I heard him walking towards my cell. He stood in front of me on the right side of the bars. I put a cigarette between my lips, and moved my head close to the bars so that the end of the cigarette could meet the flame: the flame, which existed over there, on freedom's side. So close and yet so far.

"Tell me something," he said, looking at me quizzically, "where do I know you from?"

"Channel 3," I said, just like that. What was the point of being coy? It was too late for that.

"Really?"

"Yeah. I'm a news correspondent there."

"Ah, right! That's where I've seen you!"

"Yep."

"So just a sec, what are you doing here?"

"I had sex with someone, a one-night stand, and she flipped on me, claimed that I raped her because I didn't want to see her again."

"Fuck! Poor guy! Your name is Cayden Stone, right?

"*Chase*," I said. "Cayden Chase."

"Whatever. It doesn't matter who you are, doesn't matter what you are: well-known, unknown. If you're a man, this is your worst nightmare. Poor guy! Can I get you anything?"

"Well, if you're asking: Do you have anything to eat around here? And also," I continued, "is there any way I could be in this cell by myself? Like, is it possible not to put anyone else in here with me?"

"We actually had a rape suspect here, maybe two or three years ago, who killed himself," the guard said. "I mean, not when he was here, but later on."

"I see," I said. "So, what do you say about my requests?"

"And he was just like you. I mean, he was a normal guy, not someone who gets arrested from time to time, like most of them around here."

This guard wasn't exactly a master of small talk, that's for sure. "Listen," I said, "I *am* a normal guy, but I'm tougher than I look, I can tell you that," I answered him, trying to convince myself more than him, and hoping that he would miss the embarrassing contradiction between my being a tough guy, and my asking him not to put anyone else in the cell with me.

"Anyway," I continued, focusing on my efforts to get what Marcel had instructed me to ask for. "What do you say about some food for me, and about my being alone in the cell tonight?"

"No problem with the first. As for the second, I'll see what I can do."

Damn, how I wished it could have been the reverse. He left me alone with my thoughts, a bit hungry, very anxious, and, all of a sudden, pretty mad. I mean, why was I in this position anyway? Why me? After all, I wasn't a criminal. My biological father had been a violent man who abused and smacked his wife around for years, and he had never been arrested. My mom killed him when I was a little boy, and she had never been punished for it. Why was I the one now locked in a detention cell?

A short while later, the guard brought me a meal. I sat down at the table and uncovered the tray to find the same food as I'd had at the police station – roast turkey in sauce, with pasta and beans. I ate it all, quickly. I didn't have a cup and didn't want to keep bothering the guard, so from time to time I went into the filthy washroom to drink straight from the tap.

When I was done eating, I stood in the middle of the cell and just looked around. I took out a cigarette and, of course, had to call the guard again. He came right away, lit it through the bars, and went back to his post. I smoked one after the other, lighting each one with the last. After making sure the third was well and truly extinguished, I looked around some more, not that there was anything new to see. I tried to guess the time. Eleven at night perhaps? Midnight maybe? One in the morning? Two?

Thoughts drifted through my mind. I had been on top of the world just six months before, a distinguished guest at the temple of news broadcasting, selected from among many candidates and sent off to enjoy one of the most prestigious learning experiences a television journalist could dream of: a three-week professional enrichment program called the CNN Journalism Fellowship. It was exactly six months ago to the day that I had posed, all dressed up and excited, for that photo of me shaking Ted Turner's hand in those magnificent offices of his in Atlanta, Georgia. And now look at me: imprisoned in a filthy detention cell and hoping to leave in the morning still a virgin.

I folded the sheet I had brought from home lengthwise, laid it over the thin mattress on the bottom bunk, and covered it with the stinking blanket they had given me. I then slipped in between the two layers of the sheet so that no part of me was touching anything but the sheet itself. I tried to fall asleep but gave up. The stench was killing me. I got up, stood in the middle of the cell, and looked at the bars of the metal door trapping me inside. What now? A shower perhaps? After the day I had gone through, I felt like showering. But I came to the conclusion that it wasn't a good idea. What if I was in the shower and just then they decided to put someone else in here with me?

So, what now? No phone, no books, no television, no freedom. How the hell was I going to pass the time?

I sat down at the table again, rested my head on the surface, and closed my eyes. But soon enough I was headed back to bed, inserting myself between the two layers of sheet, and trying to go to sleep. Pointless. The lights in the detention cells stayed on 24/7, and they were fluorescent: white and strong. They penetrated the sheet as if it were transparent. I pulled the blanket over my head. The thick wool did a much better job of blocking out the light, but the smell was unbearable. What was that smell? Mostly urine. But other bodily fluids as well. Vomit, sweat, maybe more. I threw it off, leaving myself exposed to the bright light again.

After looking at the walls for a few more minutes, I suddenly remembered something important: I had a newspaper in the cell. I read it. Every single word of it. And then I tried to fall asleep again. I crept back into the so-called sterile space I had made with the sheet and closed my eyes. And once again I found myself battling too much light, an unbearable stench, and the fucking metallic slamming of doors. I got out of bed and read the paper again. All of it. The ads, the death notices, the whole enchilada. And then I realized I hadn't had a cigarette in a while.

"Guard!"

He came quickly, bleary-eyed and surprised.

"Why aren't you sleeping, Cayden?"

"I can't. I've been trying all this time but I just can't. Can you light my cigarette, please? What time is it anyway?"

"Three a.m.," he said, as he held the lighter to the bars.

"Wow, shit, it's late."

"Yes, you need to sleep. You need to be strong tomorrow. I hope for your sake that this nightmare will be over soon."

"Amen."

"Good night, Cayden."

"You're a good guy," I said. "Thanks."

I smoked four cigarettes in a row so that I wouldn't have to wake him again. When I was done, I went to the basin and drank straight from the tap again, and then I got back in bed and decided I wasn't getting up again until morning, no matter what. If I didn't manage to fall asleep, I'd at least lie there and get some rest. I tried to imagine I was elsewhere, somewhere nicer. I didn't go crazy and picture an exotic vacation on a Caribbean island or anything like that. My imagination took me to the sweet moments of routine, and I ended up fantasizing about nothing more than a coffee shop on the weekend, at noon, in the sun, with a newspaper, a book, or a group of friends.

A few minutes later – or was it an hour? Or was it more? – the door of the cell opened. I heard the guard's voice and a second, unfamiliar, one. They were standing right there, in the room. I pretended to be asleep and listened. I quickly realized that another detainee was moving in with me. The guy was demanding a sheet, and the guard was saying there weren't any; he'd have to get by without one. The detainee continued arguing. He spoke like a criminal. I tried to imagine what he looked like. Small? Huge? One thing I knew for sure: it wasn't his first arrest. He was familiar with being locked up, and he wasn't afraid of the guards. I heard the slamming of the metal door and the guards' footsteps withdrawing. That was it, we were alone: the new inmate and me. I made a point of breathing steadily. I didn't move. My eyes were closed, but I was focused and primed for action like a wild jungle cat seconds before it pounced on its prey. I clenched my fingers into fists and waited. I was ready – in mind and body.

CHAPTER TWENTY

"**H**ey. Your blanket fell on the floor."

That was it. There was going to be a fight. I had been waiting for this for a week already. Under the blanket, I clenched my fists even tighter now. So tight it felt that a small bone in one of my fingers might break. It hurt, but it was good. A good fist had to be tightly clenched. If it wasn't, it would open from the force of the blow to the target's skull.

I didn't respond. I was sure I looked asleep, but I felt like a boxer in a ring waiting for the gong to signal the beginning of the fight. And then it came. My new cellmate grabbed the edge of my blanket, which had indeed slipped to the floor, leaving my feet uncovered. I tensed up, ready to pounce. Then he picked up the blanket edge, placed it gently over my exposed feet, climbed onto the top bunk, and went to sleep.

My cellmate, as it turned out, was just tired. And well-mannered. Yes, he climbed onto the top bunk and went to sleep, unaware of the violent plan I'd been hatching against him in the bed below. After I heard him begin to snore, I unclenched my fists and tried again to fall asleep, but soon enough I heard that terrible slamming metal door noise. The noise this time was particularly loud because it was the door to my cell.

"Up and at 'em, Cayden. They've come to get you. Let's go. Move it!"

It was the guard, accompanied by Thug and Leather Jacket. I didn't know whether I'd slept for a minute, an hour, or not at all, but now I jumped to my feet.

"Can I brush my teeth?"

"Yes, but make it fast."

"The brush and toothpaste are in the bag outside the door. Can I get them?"

"What the fuck? I just told you that you could! Hurry, we don't have all day."

The guard wasn't being nice, the way he'd been the night before. Why? New day, new questions. Maybe he was tired. Maybe he didn't want the cops to know he'd been nice to me. It was difficult to find any rhyme or reason around here; frankly, I just wanted to find the toothpaste in my bag. It took me too much time, because my hands were shaking.

I quickly brushed my teeth and exited the cell. Thug and Leather Jacket led me outside.

"Are you going to put me in cuffs again?"

"Do you have any plans to make a run for it?" Leather Jacket said.

"No; do I look crazy to you?"

"Then there's no reason for us to cuff you."

"So, tell me," Leather Jacket said. "How was the night? You okay? Did you survive it? Do you need anything?"

"I'm fine."

"Are you sure? Do you need anything?"

"I'm fine."

"Okay. Listen, I'm not trying to interrogate you. I was being sincere."

"Where are we going?"

"To the court, for your remand hearing. The police want to keep you in custody for longer."

We got into the patrol car and headed off. We'd been on the road for about a minute when Thug took *his* turn to ask how I was doing. I didn't respond.

"What's up, Cayden?" he said. "You seem angry."

"No," I said, though of course I was. I was mad at each and every one of them. How come they didn't believe me? And if they did believe me, why the fuck did they want to keep me in custody for longer? And how much longer anyway?

CHAPTER
TWENTY-ONE

We drove into the court compound through the back entrance. A Corrections Services officer was there to meet us; he asked Thug and Leather Jacket if they wanted "to leave him with me" so that "my people can take him."

"No, he's with us," Thug said. "Our escort; a police escort."

They took me to the detainees' below-ground entrance. There was an entire underground city down there, below the courthouse – an intricate and complex system of tunnels, passageways, steel gates, cells, cubicles, tiny offices, and elevators. I had always known that detainees were brought up to the court from somewhere, but I had no idea that the area was so large and full of life. With weapons in their belts and two-way radios on their chests, the "residents" of that underground city all wore the uniforms of the various units they belonged to, and some were there to escort detainees in handcuffs and leg irons.

We made our way through the passageways until we finally reached the stairs leading up to the court itself. Thug instructed me to wait, and then asked Leather Jacket to go upstairs to see if there were any photographers around.

"It's filled with photographers," he said, upon his return. "They're waiting there for Cayden."

Thug turned to me again.

"Stay a few steps behind us and keep away from the door; that way, they won't be able to photograph you. We're watching out for you, Cayden."

I nodded gratefully, but I was skeptical. I was nothing if not a quick learner, and what I had learned so far was that nobody was watching out for anyone.

Marcel appeared suddenly, in keeping with his wonderful knack of emerging at just the right moment. He had some bad news for me.

"We've landed ourselves a very tough judge. A woman. And it's a particularly busy day for remand hearings. That's not a good thing for us."

"How much does it matter that the judge is a woman? Is that gonna make things worse for me?"

"I really don't think it matters."

If it didn't matter, then why had he bothered to mention it?

"In any event," he continued, "we may be transferred to a different judge. I'd say there's a reasonable chance of that happening because they have a shitload of detainees to process today."

"And if it doesn't happen?"

"Then we'll have to take up our fight," he said. And then in a whisper, he added, "The two cops escorting you are not your friends. They're police. Just remember that."

Marcel left, and I remained with the two cops who were not my friends – Thug and Leather Jacket. We stayed where we were, halfway up the stairs that linked the underground city with the courtroom. The photographers were waiting on the other side of the door. I could hear them trying to find out when I'd be brought in. Every time the door above us opened, my two non-friend cops nudged me a little further down the stairs, keeping me hidden. They didn't let the photographers take even a single shot of me. I didn't know why they were doing this, or for whose benefit, but I didn't care; I was just glad they did.

We waited there for two hours. The wretched of the large underground city streamed past us. Prostitutes, pimps, foreign laborers in trouble with the law, junkies. They all made their way up the stairs slowly, handcuffed and in leg irons, on their way to a hearing. Most looked defeated, deflated, miserable, and hopeless. Like me, they had spent the night in detention. But unlike me, they did not have the best of the best representing them; they had public defenders. Once or twice, out of guilt, I looked away, avoiding eye contact.

Almost all of them made the same journey back an hour or so later. They shuffled cautiously down the stairs, escorted by armed prison guards, trying not to stumble despite their shackled ankles. They were being taken back to where they came from because, unsurprisingly, the judge had decided not to release them. Marcel reappeared while I was watching them. He had good news for me. He'd managed to get my hearing moved to a different courtroom. We'd be appearing before a different judge – a man.

CHAPTER
TWENTY-TWO

*T*hug and Leather Jacket led me down the stairs, back to the frenetic underground city, looking for a way to get me to the newly assigned courtroom while evading the photographers. I knew Marcel had told me not to trust these guys, not to think of them as friends, and I didn't. Still, it seemed to me that deep in their hearts they must have believed me and felt sorry for me. They would never have said as much, of course. After all, I was the suspect and they were the cops. But earlier, when we'd waited for hours in the underground city and they'd been telling me about their personal lives, they'd both mumbled something about "someone they knew who'd gone through that false complaint nightmare."

And so we made our way through the underground city again. From time to time, Thug consulted with another cop, trying to ascertain the best and least conspicuous way to get to our destination. After wandering through the passageways for a while, we stepped into an elevator, rode up a few floors, and entered a small room, as small as the detention cell where I'd spent the night. Inside the room was a shabby wooden bench, and each of the side walls boasted a heavy wooden door: one on the right and one on the left, each leading to a different courtroom.

My hearing would take place through the door on the right. The photographers were there already. They knew that my hearing had been moved to a different courtroom, they knew I was on the other side of the door, and their lenses were aimed in my direction, waiting for the door to open. Thug and Leather Jacket warned me about them, and every time someone came through, they shoved me into a far corner.

"Be a man, Cayden!" I heard one of the photographers call from the other side. "Come on out!"

I knew him. He was a tall bearded guy called Kimi. In my former life, I had liked him, and even now I wasn't angry with him; I knew he was just doing his job.

I peered into the courtroom. Marcel was sitting on the front bench, browsing through his papers, and behind him were many familiar faces. Friends, both male and female, and my brother. I guess my firm and authoritative prohibition against him coming, delivered via Marcel, hadn't been very effective. But I wasn't mad. Clearly, he felt he had to be there for me. Fortunately, there was no sign of my mother or stepfather.

I sat down on the bench and turned to Thug.

"What are we going to do when the hearing begins?"

127

I said. "The photographers will be all over me."

"They're not allowed to take pictures then," Thug said. "The minute the judge enters, they have to leave."

"But when the judge comes in, I'm supposed to be inside already. That means they'll have a few seconds to get some shots of me."

"I'll see what we can do."

I watched Thug cross the courtroom, ignoring the gaggle of photographers who followed, repeatedly asking him to bring me in and to let them get some shots of me. He went over to a few sturdy guards and ushered them aside for a chat. While they were engaged in conversation, in a far corner of the courtroom, my friend Anna stood up and walked over to them. I was pretty sure I knew what she wanted, and I wondered if she would succeed. After all – she wasn't one of them. Indeed, a few seconds later, they allowed her to join their chat.

The hearing was set to begin, and Marcel embraced me, promising everything would be okay, and then he went back into the courtroom. A few seconds later, Thug turned to me again.

"Hey, listen up," he said, "no matter what happens, you're not to enter until I tell you to. Okay? Even if you look in and see that the judge is already inside. Got it?"

More flashes and more yelling as Thug returned to the courtroom. I stayed where I was behind the door and continued looking in. The judge had already stepped inside. Thug, with the help of three of the court guards, herded the photographers out. The judge was seated on the raised podium by then, observing the commotion in the court. I was supposed to be inside already. I was hoping the judge hadn't noticed my absence.

Then Thug opened the door and looked at me.

"Follow me in now, quickly, and sit on the bench next to me," he said.

I followed him in and sat on the defendant's bench, below the raised podium of the judge and court stenographer. I stared at the title of the remand hearing protocol, printed on official court paper:

The State

vs.

Cayden Chase

My State versus Me.

And the hearing began. Marcel tried to convince the new master of my fate, the judge, that the police didn't really see me as a threat to public safety, that if they had, they wouldn't have waited six days before arresting me. And the same held true for the police's claim that I was a flight risk: If I had wanted to flee the country, I would have done so already. Marcel then wondered out loud with regard to Jade's bedroom habits. He presented the photographs of her in a black leather suit with a whip in her hand. Marcel argued that the pictures proved she enjoyed S&M. They didn't prove that she wasn't raped, he said, but what would have motivated her to erase them, which in fact she had done, a few days after her police complaint? Why would a woman who was truly raped make an effort to conceal evidence?

"She explained it in her statement." Much to my surprise, this answer came from Heavy Metal, who was sitting on the bench in front of Thug and me, closer to the judge than we were. Somehow, I hadn't seen him here until now. And much to my even bigger surprise, Marcel didn't even try arguing the point. I whispered to Thug.

"What the fuck? Why doesn't my lawyer – "

"It's confidential," Thug replied. "Only if you were indicted and there was a real trial would the police reveal the evidence. But this is only a remand hearing."

Surprise after surprise. While Marcel tried to make things difficult for Heavy Metal with questions, Heavy Metal approached the judge and presented him with a document marked "Confidential Report," for his eyes only. The judge's eyes, that is.

The trading of blows continued. Marcel was now trying to badger Heavy Metal with quotes from my recorded conversation with Jade, in an effort to convince the judge that Jade's story was false. Heavy Metal offered short, evasive replies, and occasionally refused to answer. And sometimes, instead of responding out loud, he asked to approach the bench and present the judge with some other confidential document, again for the eyes of the judge only. What was in those papers? Did they contain the "additional evidence" that Heavy Metal had told me about the day before, when he had tried to intimidate and shake me up during the interrogation? Fuck them. Fuck them – them and their confidential documents. They didn't have a thing. I couldn't allow myself to panic.

And then Heavy Metal turned to the judge.

"Your honor, the police ask that the court extend the remand for one week."

Marcel ignored this and pressed on with his assault.

"Is it true," Marcel said, "that my client answered all the questions he was asked?"

"Yes," Heavy Metal said.

"Is it true that there wasn't even a single question that he refused to answer?"

"Correct."

"Is it true that my client gave you permission to sift through his phone and computer to your heart's content, and was even willing to sign a consent form?"

"Correct."

"Is it true that from the very beginning, he asked to undergo a polygraph test?"

"Yes."

"Is it true that he told you that as far as he was concerned, you could ask him any questions you wanted during the polygraph test?"

"Yes."

"Is it true that despite all of this, you did not subject him to a polygraph test?"

"Look," Heavy Metal said, "as part of the investigation procedures, the police..."

"Excuse me," Marcel said. "I asked a simple question: Did you or did you not subject him to a polygraph test?"

"We haven't subjected him to a polygraph test yet, but..."

"You haven't!" Marcel proclaimed. "Is it true that my client asked you to allow him to present the evidence in his possession – evidence he claims proves that he did not rape the complainant?"

"He asked, and we let him present the –"

"Just a moment," Marcel said, "we'll get there in a moment. Tell me, please, is it true that you seized from my client a recording of a phone call that took place the day after the encounter?"

"Yes, but we gave him…"

"We'll get to what you gave him and didn't give him soon enough, but first I want to ask you something else: Is it true that this recording constitutes significant evidence in the framework of the investigation?"

"The investigation is still ongoing," Heavy Metal said. "It's too early to determine."

"Okay, let me put it another way," Marcel said. "Is it true that recordings of this kind, recordings of conversations that take place the day after the alleged incident, could be of crucial significance in an investigation of a rape complaint?"

"Yes."

"Tell me, please, how many pages are in the transcript of the recording?"

"Fourteen, I think."

"Yes, fourteen," Marcel confirmed. "And is it true that during the interrogation, you allowed my client to present the transcript and explain his version of the events, but only up until page 9?"

"The investigation is still ongoing, we – "

"Excuse me, but I asked a simple question, and I'll go back to it in a moment. But before that, another question: Is it true that my client was questioned yesterday for almost 10 hours straight?"

"Yes."

"And now I'll go back to my previous question: Is it true that although you questioned him for almost 10 hours straight, you only got to page 9 of the 14-page transcript?"

"That's true, but the investigation is still – "

"Thank you!" Marcel said. "Is it true," he continued, "that in the days following the encounter between my client and the complainant – when she, at least according to her story, was still traumatized and physically wounded by the rape – posted crude jokes on Facebook?"

"The investigation is still ongoing," Heavy Metal said.

"No problem," Marcel said. "Let me help you out. I'd like to read you a joke that the complainant shared on her Facebook wall page a few days after the encounter with my client: A man – "

"Attorney Beto," the judge said. "Really, with all due respect, spare us the details."

"Your honor," Marcel countered, "and if the honorable court would forgive me, allow me to offer just one small example regarding the frame of mind of the complainant, and this – according to her – at a time when she was sitting at home, traumatized and shattered after being raped. It's a joke that she shared: A man is drilling a hole in the wall of his apartment when he hears a scream from the apartment next door. He realizes all of a sudden that he has drilled right through the wall, against which his neighbor happened to have been leaning at the time. The drill went straight into his behind and out the other side, and drilled into his wife's teeth. Get it? That's how the driller finds out that his wife has been cheating on him. Now how's that for a joke from a young woman who has just been raped? And I have more examples. She also writes about – "

"Attorney Beto," the judge said, "There really is no need for more examples. You've made your point. The court is in recess now for half an hour."

The hearing resumed 30 minutes later. Meanwhile, we got back to the small room that we'd hid in before, and I sat back down on the shabby wooden bench. *In 1,800 seconds, I'll know if I'm going back to the detention cell for another week, or going back home for house arrest,* I thought. I was supposed to be terrified and miserable at that point, I guess, but I wasn't ready to play that role. It pissed me off. I had seen the looks on my friends' faces. They pitied me. I didn't want any mercy, fuck that! I am strong! I have to keep it cool! I looked at Thug and said: "Do you wanna hear the second joke she posted, the one that the judge didn't let my lawyer tell?"

When I went back into the courtroom, the judge was seated, and the photographers had already been ushered out. The judge looked at the parties in attendance and uttered a single word:

"Decision."

CHAPTER
TWENTY-THREE

*T*he judge looked at me. For the first time since the start of the hearing, our eyes met. He appeared to be about ten years older than me, no more. I wondered how it felt to make such enormous decisions about another person's fate. What a way to make a living.

I tried to find a smidgen of empathy in his eyes. Understanding, pity, something. But if there was anything, it escaped me. He looked at me for another few seconds, and then turned toward the court stenographer.

"I have before me," he said, "an application to extend the detention of the suspect, who is alleged to have committed the offense of rape and sodomy, by another seven days. First, the issue of reasonable suspicion should be addressed. As is known, reasonable suspicion, during the arrest stage, does not have to be suspicion of significant intensity. Sometimes, intelligence information is sufficient to establish that suspicion. The very existence of a complaint of rape, together with the existence of certain bruises that were discovered on the body of the complainant, fulfill the requirement regarding reasonable suspicion."

My heart sank. Despite knowing that he was "not my friend," I leaned towards Thug as if he *were* a friend and whispered to him, "I'm done for. He's going to throw me back into detention."

"Wait, he hasn't finished yet."

And indeed, the judge hadn't finished. Apparently, he was just thirsty. He took a sip from the glass in front of him and continued.

"Nonetheless," he said, "I believe that in this case, it is necessary to review the situation in all of its complexity. There is no dispute regarding the meeting that took place between the suspect and the complainant in said apartment, nor is it disputed that they had sexual relations. The bruises that were observed on the complainant's body could also be consistent with the suspect's version regarding aggressive sexual relations. The situation is far from being one-sided nor is it such that it can only be interpreted in one way. It is important to clarify that by saying this I am not criticizing the complainant or her conduct in the situation. It is a woman's right to say no to any offer of sexual relations; however, the question in this case is whether the intensity of the suspicion is sufficient reason to keep the suspect in detention. The investigation has progressed, various materials have been collected, and it seems that at the current stage – and primarily in regard to the complexity of the incident and to my above comments—the investigation can be continued with the suspect being released on conditions that will guarantee, on the one hand, the safety of the complainant and the proper continuation of the investigation, and on the other hand, the suspect's freedom not being affected beyond what is necessary. It goes without saying that we are dealing with a suspect who lacks prior convictions and has been detained for the first time. In light of this, I order that the suspect be released to full house arrest."

"Yes!" I shouted to myself, in my head, and then let out an enormous breath; I hadn't even realized how long I'd been holding it in. I'd been utterly convinced the judge was going to extend my remand. But I'd been wrong; he was letting me go home. My relief was beyond intense.

The judge went on to say that Anna and Megan would vouch for the conditions of my house arrest. They would post guarantees of a lot of money – around three months' salary each – to ensure that I didn't violate the court's terms. If I did violate them – if I left the house or tried to contact Jade to persuade her to drop her complaint – Anna and Megan would be required to forfeit the money, and I, of course, would be thrown straight back into detention. Marcel, apparently, had made the necessary arrangements with my two friends beforehand.

I looked at the crowd in the courtroom. I saw a lot of smiles, and I smiled back. But suddenly, without any warning, Thug, who was still sitting on the bench next to me, stood up.

"Your honor," he said to the judge, "the police wish to appeal."

I turned my head sharply to the side to take a look at

this traitor. *What?*

Marcel stood up and looked at the judge.

"I object!" he said.

The judge's ruling came quickly, sharply, and painfully.

"I am allowing the application and staying the execution of my decision," he declared, "as requested by the police."

CHAPTER
TWENTY-FOUR

I was escorted out the minute the judge rose from his chair. The photographers who streamed inside within seconds found an empty courtroom. Thug ushered me back into the small room, and Leather Jacket – who was already waiting there – slammed the door closed behind us and locked it. I looked at them as if seeing them for the first time.

"What the fuck? Why don't you guys make up your mind already?" I said, too pissed to care how they'd handle my tone. "Do you want to kill me, or save my ass?"

"This appeal wasn't my decision, Cayden. We're just doing our job," Thug said.

"And by the way," Leather Jacket added. "Keeping you away from the photographers is definitely *not* part of our job. Just saying."

A few minutes later, Marcel walked in.

"The hearing will start within the next hour, and the judge is a woman."

Here we went again with the whole woman judge thing. Marcel looked at me as if he could read my mind, the way Heavy Metal had during my investigation, and smiled.

"Don't worry about it, Cayden. I've been a criminal lawyer for many years, and I can tell you that, just as with male judges, I despise one or two of them, am quite fond of one or two, and actually admire a few too, but *none* of them will be tougher on you just because she's a woman. It's simply not a factor here."

"So which of these women is *our* judge? One you despise? One you like? One you admire?"

"Actually she's new here. I don't know her."

"But won't she worry about being criticized precisely because she *is* a woman if she denies the appeal and approves my house arrest?"

"No," Marcel said. "See, that's what I like so much about the court of law, as opposed to the court of social media: What counts here is the evidence, not the number of likes. Listen. Remember my words. One woman got you locked up, another will set you free."

I held my head in my hands. I didn't know how much more I could take. My non-friend cops were trying to throw me back into the detention cell, and the new judge – when all was said and done, and even with all of Marcel's assurances in mind – was a woman. *And* it was only eleven in the morning.

After Marcel left, Thug informed me that we would need to start making our way to the District Court on the other side of the building, and the transition to the northern wing of the building would end up exposing me to the photographers. Again. Naturally. What had I been thinking? Why had I put so much effort into trying to avoid them? I knew that battles like this one were a lost cause from the start. Well, at least I hadn't made it easy for them.

We got into the elevator. I looked at myself in the mirror, straightened my shirt, and adjusted my collar. They were the same clothes I'd been wearing the morning before, when the police had come to get me. A white shirt, long sleeves – pressed – with a collar and buttons. When I was done fixing myself up, I took a deep breath and stepped out after Thug. The photographers rushed towards us.

A photograph was astain. Case files were closed, indictments were shelved, but the pictures always remained, and were fucking everywhere – on Google, Facebook, Instagram, WhatsApp, Twitter, Telegram, TikTok, and who the hell knew where else in the years to come. Some people fought to delete every trace of a stain from their past, and I was doing the same – but from my future.

I ignored the photographers. I didn't look into the camera lenses. I didn't smile or say a word. There were more photographers waiting for me at the entrance to the courtroom. They had formed a human barrier to delay my entrance so they could get shots of me from every possible angle. I made sure to walk upright and forced my way into the courtroom, pushing through them.

Marcel and my friends were already inside. I sat down in the dock. The photographers now stood in front of me and took pictures. They didn't stop clicking or filming for a second. The entire courtroom was lit up with hundreds of camera flashes. It seemed the photographers were making up for everything that had been denied them the past few hours.

The hearing began. Heavy Metal explained to the judge, the new master (or should I say mistress?) of my fate, that the police investigation involved steps that wouldn't be possible if I were only under house arrest, and therefore a seven-day remand was necessary. He said that if I were under house arrest, I could speak on the phone at will, and thereby hinder the investigation. He promised the judge that if they were to complete their investigation in less than a week, they would "favorably consider" releasing me to house arrest.

The stress was unbearable. What was the judge going to decide? Was it bad that she was a woman, despite all that Marcel had said? Maybe he was just trying to cheer me up, or himself, or both of us.

When Heavy Metal was done with his presentation of the police's arguments, Marcel stood up and began his address to the court. He fired off quotes from the recorded conversation and the correspondence between me and Jade, quotes that refuted her version of the events. He explained to the judge that Jade had become obsessed with me; he read out more excerpts from the jokes she had posted on her Facebook page; he asked Heavy Metal if such behavior were typical of a woman who claimed to be traumatized following a rape. Then Marcel answered his own question, stating adamantly that of course, it wasn't.

"The suspect in question is someone who has no criminal record," Marcel continued. "He's a Channel 3

News reporter who has been caused unfathomable harm. The court shouldn't be intimidated by the use of the term 'rape,' as if it were a magic word that requires incarceration."

I thought about the words "unfathomable harm" and cowered in my seat. I could actually feel myself shrinking.

Marcel concluded his presentation, and Heavy Metal was given the chance to rebut. This time, he offered the court Jade's explanations concerning some of the things she'd said during the conversation I recorded.

"With regard to the transcript of the phone call, we asked the complainant about her statements, and she said she was trying to ascertain what had happened, that in light of the bruises on her body, she was still unsure about what had happened, even at the end of their conversation."

"Your honor," Marcel said, turning to the judge. "Please let me remind the court here that the judge from the previous hearing already said – and I quote: '*The bruises could also be consistent with the suspect's version regarding aggressive sexual relations.*'" And then he turned to Heavy Metal.

"Tell me please, how is it possible that in the week following their meeting, Jade tried to see Cayden again? Why would she want to meet the man who raped her?"

"She was confused," Heavy Metal said. "She had a lot of questions about what had gone on between them that night, and she wanted to clear things up. When Cayden refused, she turned to a close friend, who insisted she call the National Women's Organization for Sexual Assault Victims. She did so, and asked if she could send them photos with the bruises. They said no, it would be useless, that she needed to go to the police. That's when she explained that it wasn't so simple, because the man who assaulted her was a well-known news reporter. The women from the organization said that they would make a special effort for her; they met with her a few times, promising that they would support her throughout."

Marcel smiled at Heavy Metal. "Of course they did," he said, and then turned to the judge and added, "I'm sure these individuals also provide that kind of support for the other victims who contact them." I could practically taste Marcel's sarcasm in my mouth.

"Regarding Attorney Beto's last remark," Heavy Metal said, to the judge, "I have to say that we specifically asked the complainant this question, about whether she felt pressured to file a police complaint, and she said no: No one had persuaded her to do so. She said that the individuals at this organization simply helped her realize that maybe the suspect had slipped something suspicious into her drink."

"Your honor," Marcel said angrily, "even the complainant herself uses the word 'maybe!' And yet the law enforcement authorities want to hold my client in detention for an entire week! This is outrageous!"

At this point in the hearing, Heavy Metal put forward a new request.

"Your honor, the police will make do with even one day's remand, just a single day, your honor. Solely for the purpose of completing a number of crucial investigative procedures, and then the suspect can be placed under house arrest with restrictive conditions."

The judge appeared to be leaning towards granting Heavy Metal's request.

"Attorney Beto," she said, turning to Marcel. "The police are happy to make do with extending your client's remand by just one day. Why would you be opposed to such a move for the good of the investigation?"

I was nervous, but Marcel remained calm.

"Has your honor seen the pictures that the complainant posted on her Facebook page?" he said to the judge.

"Which pictures are you referring to, Attorney Beto?"

"Here we go, your honor. Let me show you."

Marcel approached the judge and showed her the pictures of Jade posing for the camera, dressed in a black leather suit and clutching a whip. He told her that she erased them a few days after her police complaint, and wondered again - why would a woman who was raped try to conceal evidence?

The judge leaned forward and looked closely at the pictures. After a few seconds of that, she looked at Marcel, and then she looked at Heavy Metal, and only then – for the first time – she looked at me. And then back to the pictures. It was a defining moment. After several long moments, during which she browsed through the pictures and occasionally paused to home in on one of them, she leaned back and sighed, as if the weight of the world had just fallen on her, and her alone.

CHAPTER
TWENTY-FIVE

"**I** have reviewed the investigative material," the judge began, dictating to the court stenographer, "and the exhibits presented by the defense, including correspondence between the complainant and the suspect on Facebook, the transcript of a recorded phone conversation, and the pictures of the complainant that were presented to me. I believe that at this stage, house arrest under restrictive conditions will suffice. To those conditions, I would also add a ban on any contact on the part of the suspect with outside parties – via the telephone or via the internet, via his own personal devices or via the devices of others. Subject to the aforesaid, I hereby reject the appeal."

—

Before leaving the courtroom, the judge looked at me with what seemed to me an angry gaze. Maybe she had read my mind, just as Marcel had, and just as Heavy Metal had, and she was angry with me because she knew: she knew I had questioned her integrity because of her gender. She'd been able to feel it. Or maybe she hadn't, and she was looking at me now for no particular reason. In any event, I put my right hand on the left side of my chest and, holding her gaze, nodded my head gently toward her. If she couldn't read my mind, then she probably thought I was just thanking her. But if somehow she could, then she knew I was asking for her forgiveness. Not all heroes wear capes. This one wore a robe.

The judge left the courtroom and the photographers rushed in, but I was no longer bothered by their presence. I approached Marcel.

"Marcel!" I embraced him. "My brother, my hero, you're a star!"

"You know what this means, right?" he said.

"That I'm going home instead of being thrown into a small disgusting cell!"

"Yes, but not only that. There's something else as well: They can't take you into custody again. Even if they decide in the end to indict you. And I don't believe that's going to happen; I believe they'll close the case against you. But even if they do indict you, God forbid, they can't hold you in detention. You will stand trial as a free man or under house arrest, but not as someone in custody."

Not being one to take yes for an answer, I said, "Shit, do you think they're going to indict me?"

"No," he said. "Didn't I just say the opposite? I'm saying that if they do, you'll be able to wage your war in court as a free man, and not while you're in detention. It's good news,

Cayden, good news!"

"Fuck that, Marcel. Even the good news here feels bad."

I looked around and noticed that the photographers had stopped taking pictures of me. They had found something else: something new and more interesting. They were photographing Jade's pictures, which were lying next to Marcel's briefcase, scattered on the table. It was the first time I'd examined them myself properly. Only then I realized that it wasn't really a leather suit, it was some kind of a black leather dress corset with deep cleavage. It was pretty provocative but it wasn't something I hadn't seen before. I mean, girls wear things like that sometimes, at costume parties for example, or maybe even for a regular party, I guess. What do I know? I'm not a fashion designer, and it's just a black dress for me. In some of the pictures she sat on a chair and held the whip in her hand, and in two of them she was lying down on a couch, on her side with her head resting on her hand.

"I wanted to give the press some additional visual material," Marcel whispered. "The photographers already have their pictures of you. And now they also have pictures of her too. Maybe she'll give an interview at some point, to tell her side of the story. But if she does, she certainly won't be doing so wearing that, or in that position." He pointed to a picture of Jade lying on the couch. "So it will do everyone good to have these images made public, in case they try to present a different side of her character."

I still didn't get what the big deal was with her outfit. Am I stupid?

"Marcel, I must say that I haven't figured out what's

the ..."

"Cayden, *I must say* that you're really stupid sometimes."

We left the courtroom and stood together in the lobby. Within seconds, we were surrounded by more cameras, and now microphones too. I froze. Marcel squeezed my right arm and whispered that he was going to tell the police to fuck off twice, once for each court, and then he looked straight into the cameras. "Two honorable courts, both the Magistrate's Court and the District Court, have decided not to hold my client in detention for even a single day. We view this as resounding proof that my client fell victim to a malicious fabrication, due to his insistence on cutting all ties with the complainant. Thank you."

"My client" – that was me, of course. I was no longer Cayden Chase, a news correspondent for Channel 3. Now, I was a client. I was a suspect. I was tired.

CHAPTER TWENTY-SIX

I couldn't believe I was going home. Real detention would have been a crushing blow. Someone could come along at any moment and stomp all over me. Detention would also have been bad from an image perspective: *Look, they've extended his remand, he's definitely guilty!* Even friends might have thought so. House arrest also came with a logistical advantage, because a battle like the one I was facing was best fought on familiar territory.

My house arrest came with stringent conditions. I wasn't allowed to receive visitors, except for close family members and Marcel. I wasn't allowed to speak to anyone on the phone. And I was banned from all internet communication – Facebook, WhatsApp, Instagram, email. But as far as I was concerned, these were not restrictions; they were blessings in disguise. After all, I had been avoiding almost everyone who had tried to contact me for the past week anyway, and

I had been talking primarily to Marcel. So now I had a great excuse. I wasn't allowed to.

We headed over to the front desk in the lobby of the court: a convoy headed by two policemen, followed by the client's lawyer, the client himself, the brother of the client, the client's friends, and a few photographers who were still on the client's tail. The members of the convoy were in relatively high spirits; even the policemen, who despite insisting the court to throw me to the dogs for an entire week until a few minutes before, appeared relieved to see me placed under house arrest instead. But who knew? Maybe I was wrong.

When we arrived at the lobby's front desk, Anna and Megan signed the personal guarantees. Both of them held what had recently become the ominous fixture of the mass anti-government women protests: small figures of women in crimson robes and white caps. These protests are an amazing sight of dozens, hundreds and sometimes even thousands of women, walking heads bowed and hands clasped, dressed as characters from Margaret Atwood's dystopian novel, "The Handmaid's Tale," and the eponymous TV series. They protest against the government's plan to overhaul the judiciary, because they're afraid to end up like those miserable women in the TV series, if the start-up nation becomes an autocracy.

I asked Thug if I could talk to Anna and Magen. Not just yet, he said. We needed to go to the police station first, "to complete a few procedures related to your release."

I bid my friends farewell and slid into the back seat of the unmarked police car. Next to me was a large blue light, the one that would be put on the car's roof if they needed to race through the streets in an emergency.

"Hey, can you turn on the siren and the light?" I said to Thug, and then added, "It can be your way of compensating me for that attempted betrayal a few hours ago."

Thug turned to look at me, with a half-smile, and said, "I told you, man; that wasn't my call."

Whatever. I wasn't even that mad anymore. I just wanted the full treatment and, perhaps due to his guilty conscience, Thug obliged. Bright blue flashing lights filled the vehicle, which sped off with a screech of tires. The siren wailed loudly; the noise inside was deafening. My body reacted with an adrenaline rush. I grinned like a kid as I turned around to look at my friends on the street behind us receding further and further into the distance, before disappearing from view. It was a sweet but not entirely unambiguous moment. I felt that while, yes, I had won this particular battle in court, it had only been one battle, and I knew very well that I could still lose the war.

We drove to the police station in the northeast of the city, the same place I'd been questioned the day before. When we arrived, we went up to the fifth floor, to the Interrogation Division. The TV in the lobby area was on, and one of the cops was going back and forth, switching from CNN to the BBC and back again:

"For months, hundreds of thousands of citizens have been taking to the streets across the country, to protest far-reaching changes to the legal system. The protesters argue that some of the changes might threaten the country's democratic foundations, politicize the judiciary, and could lead to an authoritarian government. The reforms aim to give the elected government decisive influence over the choice of judges, and limit the ability of the Supreme Court to rule against the executive or strike down legislation. The government argues that the changes are essential to rein in the Supreme Court, which they see as insular, elitist, and no longer representative of the people, and that the reforms are designed to stop the courts overreaching their powers."

I wished I hadn't seen it. Channel 3 had criticized the police a lot recently, for being needlessly brutal with protesters. And now I was still in their hands. I reminded myself that Thug had been nice to me today, but that hadn't stopped him from appealing the court's decision to place me under house arrest.

I felt tired and drained. My feet ached. I asked the cops if I could sit down. One of the officers was quick to bring me a chair. Another cop brought me a glass of cold water. A third offered an espresso from their new machine. Someone else handed me a box of cookies. I ate three or four. I was hungry. Another policeman, who noticed as much, handed me a sandwich wrapped in aluminum foil that he had brought from home. I quickly removed the silver paper and devoured it. I felt like I was at a homecoming party of sorts. The police, who had been so insistent on extending my remand, were now celebrating their failed plot with me. It was bizarre, but I wasn't complaining.

I tried to find out what lay ahead. I thought that, given the sympathetic and pleasant atmosphere, I'd be able to glean some details about the confidential investigation material that had been presented to the judges.

"Hey," I said to Fingerless. "Are you going to question

me about the pictures of the bruises on Jade's body?"

Fingerless suddenly seemed less friendly. "How do you know we have pictures, Cayden?"

"They said it came up in court? That you submitted pictures of Jade. I was hoping you could show them to me because honestly? Jade shouldn't have had any marks on her body that… "

"Cayden, the investigation material gathered by the police is confidential. You'll see everything after you've been indicted. The State Prosecutor will pass everything on to your attorney."

After you've been indicted. As if closing the case against me and giving me my life back weren't even options. Boom; a headbutt to the face. Just like that, in the middle of my "homecoming party." A wake-up call. Yes, I was suspected of rape and sodomy, and the court's decision to release me was no guarantee that the case against me would be closed.

I was Citizen Joseph K. I was doomed. I was dazed and confused. I had been thrown into the cogs of a system in which I had once believed, and I couldn't even figure out the direction they were spinning. One way or the other, they were turning on me, and the metal teeth were ripping into my flesh. I was strong, but my flesh was tearing.

CHAPTER TWENTY-SEVEN

I sat on the chair and drank a glass of water, resting, gathering strength for the next stage. A few minutes later, Leather Jacket turned to me.

"Come on. Time for the polygraph test."

So that was what they meant by "a few procedures" related to my release. Good. I'd been begging for this test from the start.

I stood up, gulped down the remaining water in the glass from my "homecoming party," and followed him. We took the elevator down to the polygraph lab, where we were met by the new master of my fate. Leather Jacket shook his hand.

"This is Cayden Chase. He's yours now."

My newest master took me into a large room with a huge chair in the center that would have looked like a place to sit comfortably watching TV were it not for the maze of cables and wires hanging from it.

"Should I sit there?"

"Not yet. The main part of the polygraph is just the two of us having a conversation. The test itself only happens at the very end. Have a seat here first, across from me." He spoke in a Russian accent, which, on top of the rest of the scene, made me feel as though I were in a movie.

I guessed it must have been around seven or eight in the evening, although who the hell really knew at this point? What an insanely long and harrowing day this had been, and it wasn't over yet. The two of us sat facing one another, the desk between us. The polygraph guy's eyes were fixed on me.

"You're a VIP here, Cayden."

"Oh yeah?" I said, not knowing whether this was good or bad.

"I'm the officer who oversees all the polygraphs in this district, and I received orders to personally conduct this test with you, so instead of going home, I've been sitting here waiting for you."

Okay, well, I was pleased to be facing a senior officer. I'd learned that polygraphs had an accuracy rate of about 90 percent, meaning that there was a 10 percent chance I could come out a liar, even without actually lying. It was like Russian roulette with a revolver that had 10 chambers in the cylinder, and only one of them loaded with a live round. I had a 10 percent chance of having my brains blown out. So it was good to have the test conducted by this guy. Perhaps that would lower the brain-blowing chance to only 5 percent. On the other hand, was he in a bad mood and mad at me because if not for me he could have been home by now, in front of the TV with a beer? Would he, even unconsciously, take his anger out on me? And if he did, what would happen to the polygraph's accuracy rate? It would go down from 90 to 80 percent, meaning that the chance of having my brain blown out would go up from 10 to 20 percent.

I watched him enter my information into the laptop. It was a good opportunity to study him in detail without staring. He was almost elegant, with a very neat appearance, his black hair meticulously styled. He looked like a businessman, not a cop. I wondered how old he was, and if he had served in the KGB before leaving Russia. He was nice, courteous, and intimidating. I will, of course, from this point forward, be referring to him as KGB.

KGB leaned back in his chair and looked at me before asking if this were my first polygraph. I said it was. Then he said that he was going to explain it to me and added that if there was something I didn't understand, I could ask him to clarify. Not just that I could, actually, but had to. He told me it was crucial that I understand everything, which added to my overall anxiety: *What if there were things that I didn't understand that I didn't understand?*

"So this is how it works," he said. "A polygraph is based on a simple mechanism – a measurement of the discrepancy between what you say and what you feel. When a person is asked a question, he makes a choice about the answer he wants to give. He can choose to tell the truth, and he can choose to lie. His brain sends an instruction, and his mouth verbalizes it. We are in control of what comes out of our mouths. All clear so far?"

"Yes," I said, as calmly as I was able.

157

"Okay, so unlike the words that come out of our mouths, there are physical processes that occur in our bodies that are not under our control. Like pulse rate, blood pressure, and tiny movements in different areas of the body. These processes can be measured, and the results provide an indication of what the subject knows about the answers he's given. When someone gives an answer that he knows is the truth, these bodily processes will respond in one way, and when he knows he's lying, they will respond in another way."

"Got it," I said. "Is that why in the movies the examiner sometimes asks the guy to lie on purpose?"

"Exactly. That's the initial stage of the test. What we do is we calibrate the machine to the subject's base measurements." He went into some more detail then, about pulse rates and blood pressure and almost imperceptible movements in one's fingertips, all of which only made me more nervous. Finally, he said, "So then let's move on to the next stage – formulating the questionnaire for the polygraph test."

"What do you mean?" I said. "I'm the one who decides what questions will be asked?"

"We decide together. I won't ask any questions that you haven't signed off on beforehand."

"Really?"

"Yes, that's how it goes."

"Okay, so I want you to ask me if I raped Jade."

"I can't ask that question."

"What? Why can't you? That's the reason I asked for a polygraph in the first place – so that you could ask me that question!"

"Let me explain, Cayden. Here's a question for you. What is rape?"

"What is rape?" I almost laughed. "Rape is forced sex; when a man forces himself on a woman against her will."

"Okay, now define force," KGB said. "And while you're at it, define *against her will*. In other words, where do you draw the line? What do you mean by *against her will*? When she resists? Screams? Cries? Begs? Looks at you sadly? Freezes? Do you know that some women who are raped are unable to ask the rapist to stop? And what's forced sex? Forced by means of bodily strength? Just a threat perhaps? Or is it enough for you just to ignore the signs indicating she's not interested?"

"I always thought that no was no and that was it."

"That may be true, but not for a polygraph. A polygraph can't include questions whose answers are a function of your subjective perception of reality. You may sincerely believe that you are not a rapist, and you may well still be a rapist."

"Then can you give me an example of a question whose answer wouldn't be a function of my subjective perception of reality?"

"Sure. *Did you spike Jade's drink with a date-rape drug?* That's an example of a question that offers no room for your interpretation of reality. Either you slipped a date rape drug into her drink or you didn't."

"Got it. So I want you to ask me that question."

"Okay, Cayden, here's what we're going to do: We're going to have a chat now and come up with a list of agreed-upon questions, like the one I just gave you. I witnessed a lot of your interrogation yesterday; you obviously know that every little detail in this investigation is important. So if there's a question that could trip you up, tell me. Don't be ashamed to. I'll ask you to explain why you think it's not a good question, and we can try to reformulate it or come up with a different one that will give me what I need. Got it?"

I nodded, but despite my total confidence in my innocence, I was sweating profusely.

I thought about the fact that KGB had observed my interrogation, and I tried to imagine how many other investigators had been there too—maybe it was more people than I'd thought.

It took us about an hour to formulate the questionnaire. It was a minefield, and you needed to be careful where you stepped. When it came to a polygraph, if you had even the slightest doubt about your response, you could find yourself in trouble even if you weren't lying. It was scary as shit.

When we were done putting together the questionnaire, I signed a document that included the following questions:

1. *Is it true that there is a desk in this room?*
2. *Did you spike Jade's drink with a date-rape drug?*
3. *3. Is your name Cayden?*
4. *Are you the kind of person who tends to shirk responsibility and place it on others?*
5. *Did you slap Jade?*

KGB then instructed me to sit on the polygraph chair, before connecting me to eight sensors: three clips attached to three fingers on my right hand, two straps around my chest, a blood pressure gauge, and two pressure bars under my feet. I wondered if there were sensors in the backrest and armrests of the chair.

After hooking me up, KGB sat down at his computer, asked me to focus on a point on the wall, and told me to respond to him with only a yes or a no. He began asking questions, and when he was done, he asked the same ones again – but in a different order. When he repeated the questions a third time, he again changed the order, but this time asked me to respond only with a nod or a shake of my head, and not to use words. The final round of questioning involved verbal responses again.

"So, Cayden," KGB asked when it was over, "how did you feel during the test?"

"I had a problem with one of the questions."

"Interesting you say that," KGB said. "Which one?"

"The one about the slap. During the test, I kept trying to remember whether maybe I actually did slap her back once, like just a small slap. I have this vague memory now of saying to her 'See how annoying that is? Do you understand why I keep asking you to stop?'"

"There was indeed a problem with your answer to that question."

"Crap! Really? The truth is, I wanted to ask you to replace it. I wanted to say: Don't ask me only about a single slap; ask me if I hit her to make her have sex with me, or something like that. Let's do the test again – just that question."

"Cayden, you can't –"

"Fuck. I should have said something during the test."

"Yes, you should have. But don't get stressed out. You have a piece of paper and a pen here. I want you to write and sign a statement outlining everything you've just said to me about the slap question and your answer to it."

"I don't want to make a statement. Let's do the test again! I've got nothing to hide! Please!"

"We can't, Cayden. But don't worry, you're not the first to go through something like this. Write the statement. Got it?"

Yes, I had it, but that didn't mean I could relax. KGB disconnected me from the cables, and I went to sit down at the desk again, in front of him. He handed me a pen and a blank sheet of paper bearing the police logo. I wrote out my statement and added that I wished to retake the test, then signed my name and handed the paper back to him. He read it, signed it, added a police stamp, and placed the sheet of paper on top of a pile of documents. He had basically been okay to me, KGB, hadn't *seemed* mad at me for keeping him at work overtime, but then again, who knew? Who knew anything?

He escorted me to the fifth floor again. On our way there, while walking down the corridor, I saw Jade. I tensed up. I could feel the adrenaline coursing through my blood again.

I was ready for the fight.

CHAPTER
TWENTY-EIGHT

When we got to the Interrogations Division, KGB approached Leather Jacket.

"He's yours. I'm going home."

For them it was just another day at the office; they obviously met a lot of people like me, people whose worlds had been turned upside down. But for me, it was incomprehensible that when all was said and done, I was just routine.

I asked Leather Jacket if I could smoke. I needed a cigarette after the polygraph and before the next challenge – perhaps the biggest challenge yet. He took me back to the interrogation room where I'd been questioned the day before. I hadn't missed this room.

I lit a cigarette and puffed on it vigorously, inhaling deeply, filling my lungs and insides. And then the door swung open. Heavy Metal was there. I hadn't missed him either.

"Is he ready?" he said to Leather Jacket.

Leather Jacket responded in the affirmative, which was apparently Heavy Metal's cue to leave. Leather Jacket approached.

"No matter what happens, Cayden," he whispered, "don't lose your cool. Capiche? No shouting, no cursing. Remain calm. Understand? Keep it together."

A few minutes later, Heavy Metal opened the door again.

"Let's go," he said. "Now."

—

During my training for this moment with Marcel, he explained to me that the confrontation between an accuser and a rape suspect was a new police interrogation tool in the start-up capital. It was a tough option created to help accusers like Jade base their allegations. It was common especially in cases with little formal evidence, more of a man's word against a woman's word. Only the accuser's consent was required for this procedure. They could simply seat me in front of her whenever and wherever they wanted, and then let the play begin. If I refused and argued my right to remain silent, it could be used against me. Anyway, I had no intention to be silent. I was waiting for this moment. The real battle was just about to begin, and I had never been so impassioned to fight in my whole life.

I followed Heavy Metal into one of the small interrogation rooms, in the middle of which stood a regular work desk. Behind the desk sat Supercop, and Heavy Metal took the chair beside her. Jade was sitting on a chair on the other side of the desk, in front of them, and next to her was an empty chair. That was mine. She wore jeans, white sneakers, and a white t-shirt, her hair was up in a ponytail, and she looked straight into my eyes from the moment I entered the room. She was going to give me a fight, and she definitely prepared for that moment.

"Jade, Cayden," Heavy Metal said. "Now begins the confrontation, but this isn't meant to be a free-for-all. My colleague, Chief Inspector Lara, and I will be overseeing things. You can ask each other questions, but when we ask you to stop, stop. Understand?"

"I understand," Jade said. "And I'll do whatever it takes to put this dangerous and depraved individual behind bars."

"I also understand," I said. "And I'll do whatever it takes to prove that this evil person is lying, so that she's the one who goes to jail, not me. But I'm realistic, so I'll settle for the first goal."

Heavy Metal ignored our dramatic statements. He turned to Jade kindly and said, "Before we begin, Jade – how are you doing so far? I'm sure this isn't easy for you. Would you like Chief Inspector Lara to get you a glass of water, before we start?"

"I guess I'm okay," Jade said. "But, yes, actually a glass of water would be helpful."

Supercop rose to her feet, flashed Jade an empathic smile, and left the room. She didn't even deign to look at me. *Oh, don't worry about me, Supercop, I'm good, I'm not thirsty, thanks so much for asking!*

While waiting for Supercop to return, I took the time to look at Jade. I didn't stare, just stole a few glances. That was all I needed. Unfortunately, she only looked scared, appropriately scared, not crazy. Things would have been so much easier to explain – to myself, to others – if she had just looked, talked, and behaved like a crazy person. Everyone's seen the movie *Fatal Attraction*. But Jade was no Glenn Close; it was going to be hard for me to prove she was lying.

Supercop returned and handed Jade a small bottle of mineral water. A few seconds later, Heavy Metal said: "Okay then, you can get started."

I decided to go on the attack. Jade had filed a false complaint against me; she wanted to put me in prison for a long time; I was fighting for my life. If I could shake her, perhaps she would break and admit to having accused me falsely. It could happen.

The first thing I did was lean back in my chair and take a super relaxed position. I lifted my left knee towards my chest, wrapped my arms around it, and rested my foot on the edge of the chair, with my right leg stretched out straight towards Jade. Then I gave her a big, broad smile.

"He's messing with me," she cried out. "He raped me, and now he's messing with me! Do you see what's happening? He's mocking me!"

"I'm not messing with you, I'm smiling. Smiling's not a crime."

Heavy Metal glared at me.

"Sit up like a civilized human being, Cayden," he said.

I put my left foot on the floor, sat up straight in the chair, and addressed Jade.

"Do you know why I'm smiling?" I said to her, "I'll tell you; maybe they haven't told you yet. I'm smiling because the court decided to send me home. That's it – no more detention for me."

Heavy Metal cut me off.

"Cayden," he said. "House arrest is still an arrest."

I ignored him and continued speaking only to Jade.

"The police brought me before a court this morning and the judge decided that there was no reason to keep me in police custody. Because the judges obviously understand that you're lying and that you want to punish me for rejecting you."

"I'm not lying. You behaved as if things were normal and ordinary. They weren't normal and ordinary, and I'm not lying."

"No, of course not, you're a very kind-hearted and trustworthy person. Anyway, the truth is starting to come out, Jade. It took some time, but everyone's beginning to realize— the judges, the police."

Heavy Metal cut me off again.

"I'll say it again, Cayden," he said. "The judges have only decided that there's no cause at present to hold you; that's all. With the emphasis on 'at present.' Besides, you have no idea what the police are beginning to understand or not. So, do me a favor and don't speak on our behalf, okay?"

I ignored him again. He didn't need to bullshit me. Marcel had prepared me for moments like this. I knew that in most cases, rape suspects weren't released after just one night in custody. When a court didn't extend a rape suspect's remand, it was a good sign.

"This whole nightmare will be behind me very soon, Jade."

"You raped me, Cayden. You know very well that you raped me."

"Listen, sometimes when a person repeats a lie often enough, they start to think it's the truth. But you know you're lying, and now your lie has been exposed. The fact is, the court released me and sent me home."

I looked at Heavy Metal.

"Sorry," I said. "I meant to say that the court decided to release me to house arrest, which is just like regular detention, except for one 'small' difference. I'll be at my own house, sleeping in my own bed, eating whatever I like, doing whatever I want, reading books, newspapers, watching TV."

"You raped me, Cayden. I was drunk out of my mind, I was totally out of it, I tried to resist you but I couldn't. And you just ignored me when I kept crying: No!"

"Yes, yes, I've already heard that ridiculous story of yours. Thank God you're not very smart, just evil."

"Fuck you, Cayden. Do you know what you are? You're a monster."

"I'm a good person, Jade, and you said it yourself, the day after our encounter. Actually, come to think of it, you used the word 'monster' to describe yourself. By the way, do you know how I remember that conversation so well?"

I turned to face Heavy Metal and motioned for him to come closer. I had something to say for his ears only. He leaned in towards me. I hid my mouth with my hand so that no one could read my lips.

"Am I allowed to tell her that I recorded the conversation?" I whispered to him.

"Yes, you are."

I had grown accustomed over the last two days to asking permission for everything: to sit, to stand, to walk, to pee, to get into a patrol car, to get out of a patrol car, everything. Being arrested wasn't just a matter of being shut in by four walls with no chance of escape.

"Lara," Heavy Metal said to Supercop. "Make a note, please, of the fact that the suspect asked for permission to tell the complainant that he recorded the conversation between them the day after their encounter."

Jade wasted no time eloquently expressing herself.

"I knew you were recording me, you son of a bitch!" she shouted. "What did you think? That I didn't know?"

"You don't say!" I said. "Jade the detective! No one can touch you; you're the female Poirot with lip filler! How on earth did you discover I was recording you? You're a genius!"

"Fuck you Cayden!"

Jade burst into tears.

"Seriously, Jade," I said. "It sounds strange to hear you say that you knew I was recording you, because you spoke very openly for 19 minutes. I don't know, it's odd. Most people, if they suspect someone's recording them on the phone, they hang up."

"Get fucked, you piece of shit! You, that's the way you work – you get a woman to come over, ply her with alcohol, foist God-only-knows-what on her, and rape her. Fuck you, monster."

"Now that I'm free to go home, maybe I will get fucked. But this time, I'll find someone beautiful, not someone ugly and evil like you."

Jade wasn't ugly at all, of course. She'd been pretty the

night I met her and she was pretty now. Even as she lost it, crying and screaming, I couldn't help but admire her delicate features and silky hair. She bombarded me with profanities and kept accusing me of raping her and – in my humble opinion – undermining her credibility. Happy that she was doing my work for me, I looked at her in silence and smiled. It only drove her crazier, and that was exactly what I wanted. No holds barred when you were fighting for your life. If I had to get dirty, I'd get dirty. I felt in control; I felt that the confrontation was moving along exactly in the direction I wanted it to.

"Hey, Jade, just out of curiosity," I said. "Do you have any mental illnesses? Do you take psychiatric medications on a regular basis? Were you on anything the night we met?"

"Hey!" Heavy Metal said before Jade could say anything. "She's not under interrogation here and you're not a police investigator, Cayden. You're a suspect who's facing charges of rape and sodomy. Got it? This is a confrontation, not an interrogation. You can ask her questions about what happened between the two of you, and that's it. That's what we're concerned with here."

"Fine, fine," I said asking a new question – a "legitimate" one. But then Jade, looking pretty furious, turned to Heavy Metal.

"I'll answer the douchebag's infuriating questions, even though I don't have to. The answer is no. No to everything. No mental illness, no psychiatric drugs, not that night, not ever." And then she looked at me. "And since you brought it up, let me just remind you that of the two of us, on that night, the one who was actually on drugs was you, not me.

You smoked a joint. You offered me some but I refused because I don't do drugs. And let me save us all some time here, and stop you from asking another stupid question: No, I haven't filed complaints against other men in the past. Much to your dismay, I'm not a serial complainer."

I brushed off her answers and tried not to let them distract me. I had to stay focused. "So, Jade," I said, "when I raped you, was that before I lay on my back and you rode me and I massaged your clit? Or maybe it was after you said: 'Fuck me harder?'"

"I didn't ride you and I didn't tell you to fuck me harder."

"Are you sure about that? Because that's not what you said in the conversation I recorded."

"You're so manipulative, Cayden. You know how to mess with people, to play with their heads, and you almost managed to do that with me. But I was on to you, I knew what you were trying to do to me during that phone call; you're a bad person. You raped me."

"Yes, of course, I'm actually a kind of magician. I hypnotize people and plant thoughts in their heads. Tell me, you idiot, do you understand that I have a recording where you clearly admit that you told me to fuck you hard? Would you still have gone to the police if you'd known about the recording? Be honest now, don't you feel a little foolish? If I were in your shoes, I'd be embarrassed."

"You knew what to say to make me say things that would work in your favor. I was in a horrible psychological state, and you led me straight into a trap. You're a piece of shit, Cayden Chase. You raped me. You fucking raped me."

"Yes. And after I 'raped' you, I tucked you in, kissed you

goodnight, brought you a glass of water, and asked if you needed anything else. And then, after we had another round of sex – pardon me, another round of 'rape' – we spooned."

At this, she became truly hysterical. "Fuck you, you bastard! I didn't come to you for sex! I didn't want it at all!"

"Yes, yes, I know your version: You didn't want it, you're not a nympho who wants to ruin my life, you never have sex on the first date, you're actually some kind of nun, a nun with a whip. You moron; I knew you'd erase those pictures, so I printed them."

"Listen to me good you piece of trash," Jade said, "I'm just a public school second-grade teacher, and you're a celeb – "

"Celeb?" I said. "Jade, what does me being a celebrity have to do with any of this?"

"I'm just saying, he's got connections and status. I earn 50,000 a year, and he makes 300,000."

"First of all," I said to Supercop, interrupting Jade. "I earn 150,000, not 300,000. And second of all, what does my salary have to do with anything?"

"It's a good question," she said. "Tell me, Jade, what does Cayden's salary have to do with anything?"

"I'm just saying that he's someone with connections and status, you know what I mean."

"Let me tell you what my salary has to do with it," I said, turning to Supercop. "She was convinced she'd won the lottery, that she'd nabbed a semi-celebrity who earns 300,000 a year. She's 32 years old and single, and she wants to meet someone and get married. We hook up, have sex on our first date, and speak on the phone the day after because she wants to make sure I didn't leave our 'get-together' thinking she was cheap. She asks if we can meet again, I promise that we will, and she tells me I'm a great guy. So everything's fantastic, she ends the conversation feeling terrific! She's in a romantic movie and the previous encounter is actually our first date, and the second and third, and fourth dates will surely follow. But then she tries to make arrangements with me, and they don't materialize. And a few days later, she speaks to me on the phone and realizes that I didn't really mean what I said in our previous conversation, and that I have no intention of meeting her, ever again. In other words – no second date and no 300,000 a year. She feels like someone who won the lottery but lost her ticket. She's mad. She realizes I lied to her when I said we'd meet again. And then she decides that if she can't have me, no one can."

Jade let out a ridiculous-sounding laugh. "Seriously?" she said. "If I can't have you, no one can? And you say that I'm the one in a movie here? Please, give me a break. You're a rapist, and you're gonna go to jail for a long time." Then, as if becoming newly convinced of her lies, she added, "How can you say that you didn't force yourself on me? You sodomized me!"

"Listen, you can invoke that fucking legal term till you're blue in the face, but we both know what went on. It was anal sex, as per your request, and you loved every minute of it."

She started heaping another barrage of profanities on me, only to be cut off again, but not by me.

"Jade," Supercop said. "I don't get the significance of Cayden's being a person with connections and celebrity status. Can you explain what you meant?"

She shrugged. "He's on television, and he knows a lot of important and connected people, and that's why they released him from custody. Everyone's on his side. Isn't it obvious?"

I saw an opportunity to land a real blow, assuming that the powers-that-be would be patient, indulge me, and allow me to build my case step by step.

"What exactly do you mean?" I said to her, "Are you saying that if I weren't a television personality, I'd be in detention now? That they wouldn't have put me under house arrest?"

Jade looked at Heavy Metal.

"Excuse me," she said angrily to him. "I don't get it. Who's in charge of this confrontation? You? Or him?"

"He's allowed to ask you this kind of question, Jade, just as you're allowed to ask him. You agreed to this."

"Fine," she said, but she didn't like the fact that someone was actually taking my side for a change.

"So?" I said to her. "What's your answer? If I weren't on television, and I didn't know all kinds of important people, I'd still be in police detention?"

"Well, yes!" she said. "Of course."

"In other words, everyone involved here – the police investigators, the State Prosecution, the two judges – they're all on my side, and that's why they let me go?"

"Yes, Cayden Chase, don't try to act all innocent and naïve. I knew it could happen, and that's why I wasn't sure if I should file the complaint in the first place. I was warned that everyone would take your side, but I realized I had to go forward. If not for my sake, then for the other women you may have raped, or the ones you'll rape in the future."

"Oh my God, spare me," I said. "You're the anti-feminist here; your bullshit story will just make it that much harder for real victims."

"You're the bullshitter, Cayden. Yes, you managed to fool me during that phone call, to manipulate me. You're good, but you won't be able to fool the police."

"Yeah, right, of course, whatever." I refused to allow her gaslighting to distract me from my goal. "Do you really believe that if it weren't for my connections and status, I'd be in detention now?"

She rolled her eyes. "Yes of course. How many times do I have to say it?"

"You know that's a very serious allegation, right? You're accusing the police, the State Prosecution, and two judges of corruption."

"I'm not accusing anyone of anything! Don't try putting words in my mouth again, like you did when you were recording me. The fact is, Cayden, they released you, even though you raped me. Fact."

I leaned back and smiled at her. She didn't like that.

"There he goes again. He's making fun of me. He raped me and now he's making fun of me. And you, the police, aren't doing a thing about it."

"I'm not making fun of you, Jade. I'm smiling because I've just realized how pathetic your complaint actually is. Your claims are so full of holes and contradictions that sitting here right now with you makes me realize that everything will be okay, that soon enough everyone will see that you're a liar, and the whole story will be over."

Of course, I didn't really feel her complaint was pathetic, or that everything was going to be okay. I didn't know shit. How could I possibly know? Mostly, during this confrontation, I felt the opposite. It seemed that she had reasonable answers for everything: even to the blow I dealt her when I told her I'd recorded our conversation, and reminded her of the things she'd said. But I was trying to scare her, to drive her crazy, to do whatever it took to make her admit that she was lying. Because if she won, I was done for.

"Jade, don't you want to just get it done with and tell the cops the truth before they find out for themselves?"

"You raped me, Cayden. Your creepy and manipulative recorded call won't save you from jail."

"I'm not going to jail."

"Yes, you are. You raped me." And then she lowered the ax. "You made me bleed."

"What?" I said. Dear God, she'd stop at nothing! "I made you bleed? I didn't see even a drop of blood. Where were you bleeding from? When were you bleeding? When we had sex in the living room? When we had sex again afterward in my bedroom? Where exactly is this blood of yours?"

"I was bleeding. I can't believe you're denying this."

"Where? Why don't you answer me? Don't start playing for time so you can make something up, tell me now. Where in my apartment did you bleed?"

"I was bleeding. You made me bleed, you fucking son of a bitch."

"So why don't you say where? Where in my apartment

did it happen? Don't avoid the question! If you say you were bleeding, I want a police forensics team at my apartment right now. Let them find bloodstains and match them to your DNA. If you bled, they're sure to find something there. Where did you bleed, Jade?"

"In the bathroom. You saw that I was bleeding there."

"In the bathroom? And I saw?"

"Yes, you saw. You helped me in the bathroom because I was so drunk and out of it."

"I did *what*? Are you being serious?"

"Yes, I remember it clearly. I remember you had some kind of anti-hair-loss cream there."

"Oh my God, I can't believe this. "

Heavy Metal intervened.

"Cayden, did you not help her in the bathroom?"

"Of course not! Why would I have done that?"

"Because she was drunk. She says she couldn't stand on her own two feet."

"What a load of crap! She stood on her own two feet very well. She went in, closed the door, did what she needed to do, and then, after a brief nap, was all over me for more sex."

"Cayden, did you not take her to the bathroom?"

"I showed her the way," I said. "She was my guest, after all. I showed her the way to the bathroom, I turned on the light for her, I opened the door, and went back to the living room."

"She says you brought her a towel. Is that true?"

"Of course, I gave her a towel. What do you think? She was going to dry herself with toilet paper? I gave her a clean towel from the closet in my room. You searched my apartment; you saw that I keep my towels in the bedroom closet."

The bathroom thing caught me by surprise. I didn't know she'd made up all that crap during her questioning. It was simply unbelievable. She was allowed to come up with whatever she liked, tell it to the police, and have her lies filed under the title: The Complainant's Version. And then a damn court could rule that "the very existence of a complaint of rape," was enough to fulfill the requirement regarding reasonable suspicion and justify an arrest.

But then I caught a nagging voice in the back of my head —*what if she did bleed?* I mean, sometimes women bled a little from sex. That didn't turn the sex into rape, of course, but I'd insisted that she hadn't bled, and I'd even asked the police to send a forensics team to my apartment. So what if they went ahead and found bloodstains? *Did she bleed?* Fuck! I had a problem with the polygraph; now I'd created even more trouble for myself. Fucking Jade.

"Let me tell you something, Jade," I said. "If there is a God, then he's really putting me to the test now. But apparently, he's also got a score to settle with you. Know what I mean? If there is a God, you're in deep shit!"

She burst into tears again. I smiled at her. I was glad she was crying. I wanted her to break, to admit her lies in front of Supercop and Heavy Metal, and before the hidden cameras. I didn't know why she burst into tears at that particular point, but I guess I'd made her nervous. She believed in God; she'd told me so the night we were together.

Jade turned to Heavy Metal, wiping her tears with a

tissue from her purse.

"I don't get it," she said. "He raped me, and now he's torturing me. Why are you letting him do this?"

"Again, he's allowed to ask you questions, Jade," Supercop said. "And you can ask him questions too. That's the way a confrontation works. You agreed to this, remember? This is getting out of hand, though. Listen, you can each ask each other one more question and then we're done here. You first, Jade."

Jade turned to me and said, "Why did you record me? I'll tell you why: You recorded me because you raped me, and you thought the conversation would be your savior. You knew you were guilty and that's why you recorded me. Soon, the court will understand it too, and then they'll throw you into jail, where you belong."

"Making that recording was the best decision of my life. Meeting you, by the way, was the worst. And you know what drives me crazier than anything else? That for fuck's sake, not only did I not rape you, but I was nice, I was a fucking gentleman! I invited you to spend the night. I could have behaved like your typical douchebag, the kind who sends you home the minute the sex is over, but I didn't."

"Yeah, well, Gentleman Cayden, all that *doesn't* mean that you *didn't* rape me. Thank God none of your so-called gentlemanly behavior matters, for my sake and for all the other rape victims out there. The cops here know it, the State Prosecutor knows it, actually, I think most people nowadays know it. Only you, the dumb fuck, don't get it. But hey man, now we have a new nickname for you, Gentleman Cayden. And you'll actually need one soon, in jail of course. And I hope for you that the other prisoners don't take it the wrong way. I bet they like the gentle guys there, in jail." And she actually *winked*.

Damn, she was mean. And good. Her words literally made me tremble. Heavy Metal turned to me and said it was my turn now: my last question for Jade. There it was – my last chance to win this battle. I attacked the one and only thing I recognized as being a potentially vulnerable point.

"Tell me, Jade, aren't you scared? You told me the night we met that you believe in God. You could go to hell for this, you know. Why don't you just get it over with now, and admit you lied? They usually don't prosecute women who file false rape complaints. That's the law. You're safe. So if you admit you lied, you won't pay any price, in this world or the next. Sounds like a good deal to me. If I were you, I'd take it."

"Fuck off. Of the two of us, you're the one who's going to burn in hell. After years of being jailed, I should add. And they'll rape you there, Gentleman Cayden. Just like you raped me."

"Okay Jade, got it," I said. And then I turned to Heavy Metal. "I'm done," I said. "Can I return to the other investigators?"

He nodded, so I stood up and smiled one last time at Jade.

"The night we met, you told me you hadn't had a real relationship in three years, and you really wanted one. Jade, this is not going to happen for you. You'll never get married and you'll never have children. Understand? Never."

Jade seemed stunned, she didn't say a word. Supercop

and Heavy Metal remained silent too. When I left, I closed the door behind me and heard her burst into tears from outside. I lit a cigarette and headed towards the interrogation room, to smoke it. I knew her sobbing wasn't genuine, but it was music to my ears, like the singing of a choir of angels. Fuck her. Fuck her and her Gentleman Cayden bullshit.

Truthfully, I felt as if I'd placed a curse on her there, a spell. It was the first time I'd wished something bad on her. Until that moment, I'd been so preoccupied with my own survival that I hadn't given Jade's fate much thought. But now, when she was sitting right there in front of me, my anger catapulted to the surface. I tried to understand how she could possibly be capable of doing such a thing to another person, but I couldn't. So, I cast a spell on her instead.

CHAPTER TWENTY-NINE

*F*ingerless was waiting for me outside the room.

"Okay, Cayden," he said, "we're done with you for the day. You can go now. Your friend Anna will take you home. She's here, being interrogated herself; standard procedure. We'll wait for her downstairs in the lobby. Take your bag and come with me."

I was so excited by this turn of events that I immediately picked up the pace. By too much, apparently.

"Hey, Cayden, are you trying to run away?" he said. "You know, even with only four fingers on my right hand, I can still shoot."

Having been reminded of my status, I slowed down and followed Fingerless. As we passed by the interrogation rooms on the way to the elevator, he stopped and knocked on one of the doors.

"Hold on a minute," he said.

The door opened and Anna emerged. She rushed over and hugged me tight. Over her shoulder, I could see Supercop, who'd been questioning her. Anna placed her hands on my cheeks.

"How are you, Cayden?" she said. "You okay?"

She had tears in her eyes. How long had she been here being interrogated? How many of my other friends were also going through this because of me? I was sure she was not the only one. I felt like shit.

Fingerless took me down to the lobby, where Anna arrived a few minutes later. "Let's go," she said to me with a tired smile. "I'll take you home, to your place."

"Ah, so you're up first?" I said with a laugh – an ironic little laugh. "Lucky you."

"Yes, I'm taking the first shift."

I was greeted outside by my friend Eddie and, of course, by Megan, Babysitter #2, and I actually felt – amazingly enough – pretty good. It was the first time in two days that I was in the company of friends only, without any cops or prison guards around.

"Get in the car, Cayden," Eddie said. "You're going home."

He started the engine. Anna was in the passenger seat next to him, and I sat in the back next to Megan. My armpits reeked; the stench filled the car. Mortifying.

Eddie and Megan dropped Anna and me outside my apartment building, and the two of us went up. My apartment was dirty. Very dirty. The search had uncovered a ton of dust and dirt. And two women were moving in with me. Not nice.

Seeing the condition she was in, I told Anna to go ahead and take a shower. In the meantime, I launched a cleaning assault on my bedroom, quickly sweeping and mopping the floor and changing the linens. I looked around when I was finished; good enough, for now. I then retrieved another set of linens and a blanket from the closet and took them out to the living room, for me. I also took the laundry basket and added the stuff from the Custody Kit: the change of clothing that I hadn't used, and the sheet that I had used. Yes, I should have thrown that shitty sheet right into the trash, I know. But I couldn't let it go. After all, the court had freed me, so maybe this shitty sheet was actually my lucky sheet? I left the basket outside the bathroom and waited for Anna to come out.

When she emerged, she glanced at the laundry basket and gave me a look.

"What the hell?" she said. "What's that terrible smell?"

"That's the sheet I slept on in the cell," I said. "That, my friend, is the stench of detention. I know I should burn it, but I can't. I'm holding onto it in the hope that someday soon it'll just be a souvenir from a tough period in my life, one that's already behind me."

I put my clothes and the sheet into the washing machine, sat down at the bar, opened a cold bottle of beer, and lit a cigarette. I was wiped, but a few minutes later I refilled the bucket with water and detergent and swept the entire place, scrubbed the toilet and sink with bleach, dusted, tidied the balcony, and cleared away some old junk that was just taking up space. I also scrubbed the kitchen counters and cupboards and then gave the floor a good mopping. It was four-thirty in the morning by the time I was done. I looked around. I felt good. Given the circumstances.

I went back to the bathroom, put the now-clean clothes into the basket, and carried it to the balcony. I opened the drying rack and hung up the wet items. I was worried that the horrible detention stench would be too strong for the laundry detergent, but the sheet was clean and fragrant. And then, at last, I stepped into the shower myself, to surrender my body to the steaming hot water. My God; I couldn't believe how good it felt. A simple shower. I could feel the adrenaline dying down, replaced by weariness.

I placed the sheet on the living room sofa, lay down, and covered myself with the blanket. Ian and Amy fixed me with that indifferent stare cats manage so well – their usual look, in other words, but with a slight touch of surprise too. I could understand them. I was sleeping on the couch in the living room, and someone else was sleeping in my bed. What were they to do now? It must have been a pretty confusing situation for them. I mean, I knew the cats liked me, but they also liked Anna, and the bed was much more comfortable than the couch. Cats were practical animals, so I made a deal with them: they could sleep with Anna, but only after we had some stare-down fights.

Ian was first until he gave in. He turned away, meowing in frustration at his defeat and heading off to seek comfort in his food bowl. I was tired, but I wanted to maintain my operational proficiency so that if and when the time came, I could deal with the eyes of Heavy Metal. I continued my practice with Amy, who stared at me unblinkingly. I responded with a piercing and intimidating stare of my own, and she too gave in and slinked away. It was then that I opened the bedroom door for them both; a deal was a deal, after all.

CHAPTER
THIRTY

*D*ay two of my house arrest, and I woke up at eight a.m., after only three hours of sleep. Obviously, I needed more than that, but the adrenaline had yet to dissipate and my sense of time was out of whack. What day was it? What was the date? Tomorrow will be exactly one month since my encounter with Jade. The notion made me think of the start of a new relationship when you celebrated your one-week, one-month, year-long anniversary. I had forgotten all my ex-girlfriend's "anniversary" dates, but the day I met Jade? I'd never forget that one.

About an hour later Anna woke up and turned to her own work – emails, phone calls, and other tasks she could do from the apartment. I asked her if I could use her phone. Not to contact anyone, God forbid. Doing that would have landed me back in detention, not to mention that it would have obliged Anna and Megan to pay the court a lot of money. She handed me her iPhone. I took it, opened the Facebook application, and went into Jade's profile. I was forbidden from contacting her, of course, but I was allowed to browse through her pictures and posts. And so I did. I had already done it several times before, when I'd been waiting for the cops to come to arrest me. But back then I'd always been short on time. Now, under house arrest, I had all the time in the world, and at this particular moment, nothing better to do. So I took my time and dove into Jade's Facebook profile and Instagram account.

After about 20 minutes, I received a jolt. I hadn't seen it coming. I knew Jade loved animals because I'd seen how much she enjoyed petting my cats. But I hadn't been prepared for the picture I saw now. It was pretty old, dated more than three years ago, which is probably why I hadn't seen it until now. It had been posted by an animal aid organization, and in it, Jade was receiving a certificate of appreciation. I read the text below the picture:

Jade, In the name of all the unwanted, abused, and abandoned animals you have helped to rescue, in the name of all the homeless dogs for whom you have found new homes, we have two words for you: THANK YOU! And three more words, because we just have to say it: WE LOVE YOU!!!

I then read the comments underneath and learned that Jade was an active and much-loved volunteer in the organization: She was always available to join urgent rescue missions, even high-risk ones. A few months before the picture's publication, as I learned from the comments, she'd gone after an illegal dog-fighting group. She'd told them that if they didn't hand over their dog while it was still alive, she would call the police. She was attacked by the owner and dog alike, but eventually succeeded in rescuing it, and then finding it a new home.

Jade hadn't posted this stuff herself. In fact, I wouldn't have even seen this picture unless she'd been tagged in it. And she didn't comment on it either. If it had been me, I would have made it my profile picture. But not Jade. Apparently, not only was she kind and brave, she was also cool and modest. I was beyond baffled. How could someone so bad be so good?

The picture freaked me out. I saved it in Anna's iPhone through a screenshot, handed the phone back to her, and asked her to print it out for me sometime. Then I went to the balcony, lit a cigarette, and tried to stop thinking about it.

CHAPTER THIRTY-ONE

*A*nna took a break from her work and joined me on the balcony, my favorite part of the house and the reason I rented it from the start. It overlooks a bunch of coffee places and restaurants, so it could be pretty noisy, but I installed double-glazing windows all over, and a big bar with few stools, so it's amazing sitting there any time - with air conditioning in the summer and heating in winter.

We had a lot to talk about, but we didn't know what was allowed. I was the suspect, and she had been questioned the day before. If she were to tell me what she'd been asked, would that be a disruption of the investigative process? I had no idea. How could I know? But it would probably be okay, right? After all, the court had appointed her to supervise me. Presumably, we were permitted to talk about anything. But logic had left the building; it had moved out, and paranoia had taken its place.

I told Anna what was worrying me. She assured me I'd only be seen as trying to obstruct justice if I did something active, like contacting a friend who might be questioned. She said that she herself didn't count because she'd already been interrogated. It was hard for me to relax though.

"If I asked you what you were questioned about," I said warily, "wouldn't that be considered obstructing justice? Obviously, I'd be trying to figure out where they were going with the investigation. I might be questioned again, so in a way I'd be preparing for my own interrogation via your information."

"I still don't think that would be seen as you trying to obstruct."

"Maybe they're testing me? Maybe it's a trap? Maybe they planted listening devices here while I was in detention. Who knows?"

"Cayden, I don't think so."

Anna understood the police a lot better than I did. For three years, up until a few months ago, she'd been a crime reporter for Channel 4, and it seemed to me she was the one and only person in the start-up capital who had moved from tech to journalism, rather than the other way around. In 2020, she left Unit 8200, the national cyber agency where she had been seen as an incredibly talented and promising officer. Legend has it that the head of this prestigious intelligence unit, in an attempt to convince her to stay, told her that in a few years, she would *probably* become the first woman to head it, and Anna answered him that it *probably* shouldn't be a consideration for her, and that she wanted to move on with her life.

The timing of Anna's retirement was not, in my opinion, a coincidence, because legend also had it that she was the one who'd gotten the golden nugget of intel that launched the assassination - by air force strike - of Qasem Soleimani, the commander of the Quds Force, the special operations division in the Islamic Revolutionary Guard Corps in Iran. It had all gone down in Baghdad in January 2020, and I understood her wish for a career change, pronto. After all, how could anyone top that, and at the age of only 30?

So she decided she wanted to become a news correspondent, and Channel 4 offered her a job as a crime reporter specializing in cybercrime, even though she'd had no experience in journalism. It made sense though, because no other journalist had – or has – connections like the ones she had, to so many intelligence organizations. Priceless connections. And indeed, she was a good crime reporter despite her lack of experience. But then, after three years she grew restless, and when Google offered her a position as Communication & Public Affairs Manager a few months ago, she didn't hesitate, and now she earns twice as much as I do, and three times what she herself earned at Channel 4. Hi-tech workers sure do seem to have a better present and a safer future. It's not only the big money they make; it's also the fact that they can always find a new job, a job that will likely be better than the one they already have, as opposed to journalism, a profession I'm not sure will even exist ten years from now.

So now, because of the circumstances of my own present and unclear future, instead of working from her fancy office on the thirty-something floor of Ampa Tower, Anna was working from my two-room rented apartment, in a building with no elevator, on the fourth floor.

To try to deal with my developing paranoia, she suggested some music. We put on my all-time favorite DJ Jenia Tarsol's techno set, turned up the volume, just in case the police were listening, and chatted on the balcony. And that became standard procedure.

At four in the afternoon, the doorbell rang, and I jumped. Could it be the cops again? Arriving to take me in for more questioning? Anna looked through the peephole and opened the door. It was Megan. I relaxed. The changing of the guard.

And that too became standard procedure – updates, a hug, a kiss, a quick switch; one friend would go back to her regular life, and the other would remain stuck with me for the next 24 hours. On occasion, they'd shut themselves up in my bedroom, asking to be left alone for a bit, and whisper to each other. I knew they were talking about me. They had met each other through Marcel only a few days before the house arrest. They weren't friends; what else would they have been talking about?

—

I was allowed to receive visits from first-degree relatives, and so at eight o'clock that night, my mother and brother arrived. This was the first time I'd spoken to my mother since telling her about the complaint, and the reason I had worked so hard to avoid seeing her was that I was worried she'd fall apart. In legal terms, strictly speaking, she was actually a cold-blooded murderer who'd never gotten caught.

But all of that was a long time ago, and in practical terms, she was just a 60-year-old woman who was waiting for me, her oldest son, to get married and make her a grandmother.

I acted as if everything was fine, as if everything was under control, and I was in good spirits. I even tried to make them laugh by telling them what I'd been through. And I explained that the judge's decision not to extend my remand meant the beginning of the end of this whole thing. I wasn't so sure myself, yet I felt I'd put on a convincing performance. After 30 minutes or so, I got tired of the act and made up an excuse to send them home.

—

Day four of my house arrest. At six a.m., I'd finally managed to fall asleep, with the help of a few shots of whiskey, and then at nine, Anna woke me. Marcel was on the line. I quickly jumped off the sofa, snatched the phone from her hand, and went out onto the balcony. Meanwhile, Anna cranked up the volume on the stereo system.

"Listen, we have to deal with the gag order," Marcel said.

I felt my stomach plunge. I knew what this meant. "Okay," I said, trying to keep my shit together. "What do we do?"

"As of now, it's still in place, but the police could ask the court to lift it at any time. Make no mistake, they didn't request it to protect you in the first place; they did it for themselves. Now that you've been arrested, they don't need it anymore. They might ask the court to lift it."

"Yes, I know," I said, my stomach tying itself up into more knots. "They want the media to be able to report the story, right? To see if anyone else comes forward? Shit. They talked about that during my interrogation. So now anyone who's ever had a grudge against me, about anything, can come forward and make up some bullshit story. Marcel, if this thing goes public now, I'm a dead man. I mean, truly, they'll have killed me."

"I know, kid," Marcel said. "Let me see what I can do."

—

Day five of my house arrest, and we'd fallen into a routine. Anna and Megan replaced each other every afternoon, arriving on my doorstep with their laptops for 24-hour shifts. They worked from my apartment, and I took care of the rest – prepared food, changed the bedding, and cleaned frequently. Everything. They worked, and I was the househusband.

So, it was like this: one really bad woman had upended my life, and then one decent woman released me from detention, and now two great women were managing the fallout. The only way for people to ask about me or send messages was through them; their phones were an endless nuisance. People they didn't know had gotten ahold of their phone numbers; they'd call, explain their connection to me, ask how I was doing, and pass on words of encouragement. Every now and then, someone would just show up. In that case, my protectors would open the door, explain that I was okay, and turn the concerned visitor away. No discussion. Now. Please. Leave. Goodbye.

—

It was day six of my house arrest, and nightmares were plaguing my sleep; I couldn't get more than one or two straight uninterrupted hours. I would wake up in the middle of some god-awful nightmare, guzzle some water, smoke, and try to go back to sleep. But as soon as I drifted off again, I'd be back in the nightmare, at the exact same place where I'd left off, like an image from a TV movie you've paused while going to pop yourself some popcorn. Eventually, I gave up. Some of these dreams were the nighttime remnants of daytime thoughts, so I guess it was the only way for my mind to contemplate them. Because in my dreams, I had no control.

—

At 11:30 p.m. on day seven of my house arrest, the landline rang. I heard Megan say, "Yes, he's here. He's okay. No, he really is fine. Just a minute, I'll ask him."

"It's someone named Catherine," she said, turning to me. "She's calling from Australia. She says she hasn't been able to reach you for two weeks now and she's concerned; she's insisting on hearing your voice. What should I tell her? She sounds anxious."

I had met Catherine at the CNN training program in Atlanta six months earlier and we'd stayed in touch ever since. Then, when all hell broke loose, I left her a Facebook message saying something had happened and she wouldn't be able to reach me for a while. And then I disappeared. I would have been worried about me too. But I couldn't update her because I wasn't allowed to speak on the phone. I asked Megan to come closer.

"Hey Catherine," I said, loud enough so she could hear. "Listen, I can't talk to you right now, and I'm not allowed to hear you either, so don't answer. Just listen. I'm fine. Honestly. I promise to contact you within the next two or three weeks. Please, don't worry."

I signaled to Megan that I was done.

"That's it, Catherine," Megan said into the phone. "That's pretty much all there is for now. Yes. Good night to you too, or good morning, if I'm not mistaken. Yes. Goodbye."

—

On the afternoon of day eight of my house arrest, Heather showed up. At the time, I was sitting alone in the living room, and Megan was napping in my bed, so I went to the door and peered through the peephole. Heather and I had met about two months earlier, and we'd only gone out once. I liked her; she'd been so passionate about her studies. The title of her master's dissertation was *"What about the children?"* and during our dinner out she'd gotten really worked up about it.

"There are many kinds of abuse," she'd said. "You don't hear about the kids who are weaponized by their parents; these creeps will do anything to get back at their exes. They'll use their own kids for their twisted goals. It's sick. In my opinion, it's a form of psychological abuse, and I'm working to make sure others see it that way too."

I'd been impressed by how strongly she'd felt about the subject, and had wondered whether she herself had been one of those weaponized kids. But I'd never had a chance to find out because, idiot that I am, I'd never called her again. Now, seeing her standing there on my doorstep, I was filled with regret. Why hadn't I called? Why had I, instead, gotten involved with Jade? Why did I have to be such a typical bachelor?

I looked through the peephole again, assuming that the reason Heather was standing there was because she'd heard about what happened, tried to reach me, and couldn't. But was it odd for someone who – let's be honest – hardly knew me, to be concerned enough to actually come by?

Maybe it wasn't a concern at all; maybe it was something else. Maybe it was something bad. Maybe she had also come to accuse me of raping her. I had no way of knowing. I just kept looking at her standing there, shifting from foot to foot. I wasn't even allowed to speak to her through the closed door. I could have woken Megan and asked her to go out and explain. But what for? What was the point? I realized there was nothing for me to do other than stare at her through the tiny hole in the door - trying to figure out if she was here to accuse or support me - until she gave up and left.

—

On day ten of my house arrest, I woke up, did some push-ups on the balcony, and took a shower. When I was done, I looked for a new can of deodorant to replace my empty one and found it in a small straw basket on the bathroom counter by the basin. Next to it was a small bottle of Rogaine. The war against baldness. Lots of men used it.

I looked at the Rogaine lying there in the basket, with various other things: sunscreen, toothpaste, and aftershave.

There was nothing special about the Rogaine; it was in its usual place. Nevertheless, a penny dropped. And then I got angry. Really angry. Fucking Jade. She'd gone through my stuff. Which meant . . . *Damn!*

The fact that I hadn't known about this in time, during the confrontation itself, agitated me. I could have proven right then and there, in front of Supercop and Heavy Metal, and for the hidden cameras, that Jade had been lying: about everything. This wasn't good. Marcel had said that every ounce of evidence was crucial, so I called him.

"Phone the police right now," he said, with an unusual sort of urgency. "Time is of the essence."

I did as I was told, but alas, to no effect. In a somewhat panicked frame of mind, I called Marcel again and told him I was getting no answer, no one was picking up the phone in the Interrogation Division, and what was I supposed to do now. That was when he suggested calling Supercop on her mobile.

"Her mobile? Chief Inspector Lara? Are you sure? Isn't that a little out of line?"

"No, it's an important statement in an important investigation."

"Well, I don't have her number," I said, feeling more and more hopeless.

"Anna has it. And Megan too. It's part of the house arrest."

Megan did indeed have Supercop's cell phone number, but Supercop said she couldn't talk now; whatever it was would have to wait. Megan was to call back the following morning, and hopefully, I wouldn't have died by then, of cardiac arrest brought on by code-red levels of frustration and panic.

—

I was still in boxers and a t-shirt the next morning, day eleven of my house arrest, when I was on the line with Supercop. I hadn't been able to sleep all night; I'd just been sitting on the couch waiting till the clock struck eight, the earliest hour at which it was reasonable to call. Upon hearing my story, and before I could even suggest it, Supercop asked if I wanted to come in and make a statement. Indeed I did! She asked when I could get there. *Would yesterday be too soon?*

When I hung up, I realized I had more questions, like, well, how was I supposed to get there? Just hop on my motorbike and ride over? And what about my house arrest? I wasn't allowed to be alone, after all. Was I supposed to ask Megan to come with me? Should I call Supercop again and ask? Maybe I should ask Marcel? It felt strange to be leaving the house without asking permission from someone, and yet that seemed to be the plan.

I went into the bathroom and took a picture of the bottle of Rogaine to prove my point to the police. I used Megan's phone and asked her to send the picture to Anna so that she could print it for me. Now. Normally, I would simply have used my own phone, but of course, the police had taken it and the judges had told me I couldn't use any phones at all, and damn it all to hell anyway, who was I kidding? Nothing was normal anymore.

I showered, dressed, grabbed the bottle of Rogaine, and went down to my motorbike. It was my first time outside the apartment since my house arrest, and though I had given a great deal of thought to this moment, for 11 straight days now, I felt nothing when it came.

About half an hour later, after I had collected the printed picture from Anna's fancy office, I pulled up outside the police station and crossed the street, my eyes focused on the gray and intimidating building, the only color coming from the large flags boasting the police emblem. I stared at them for a few moments. And still felt nothing.

I went up to the fifth floor and pressed the intercom. And soon enough, there I was, walking into the Interrogation Division once again. I was warmly welcomed back by my three non-friend cops – Leather Jacket, Thug, and Fingerless. They shook my hand, like friends they weren't. I suppressed a laugh when I noticed Leather Jacket wasn't wearing a leather jacket, Thug wore fingerless gloves, and Fingerless himself was now wearing a leather jacket.

Supercop approached us and asked me to follow her.

"Okay, Cayden," she said when we arrived at my latest interrogation room. "I'm going to type up everything you say, and when we're done, I'll let you read it to make sure I haven't missed anything. And then you can sign it. That's the procedure when it comes to making a statement. Okay?"

"Yes," I said, wishing her tone sounded a bit friendlier, but settling for the one she offered.

"So go ahead," she said, "you can begin."

I took a deep breath and began. "During the confrontation with Jade, she claimed she was so out of it after I raped her that she couldn't even stand up. She said I'd helped her in the bathroom. She also said she remembered seeing an anti-hair loss product there. Now it's true that I do have one, but if she was so out of it that she couldn't even walk, how in the world could she have noticed it? Just take a look at this picture."

I produced the picture and placed it on the desk in front of Supercop. I watched her absorb the implications, and then I continued with my statement.

"The bottle of Rogaine is in the small basket next to the door, as you can see. Do you get what I'm saying? I mean, honestly, we're dealing with a bottle the size of a pack of cigarettes."

I retrieved the bottle from my bag and showed it to Supercop.

"The size of the lettering, where it says *Regrow's hair. Preventing further hair loss* is very small," I said to her, trying not to be mortified. Why did I have to show a female cop what I used on my head in order to grow hair? Ugh. But I couldn't let such concerns divert me from my goal.

I held up the bottle in front of Supercop's face, pointed at the writing, and continued. "The bottle is in a basket along with a bunch of other things, like aftershave and toothpaste and stuff like that. If Jade was totally out of it, how could she have seen such a small bottle, hidden among other things, and located so far away from where she says I showered her?" I stopped momentarily, before launching into my dramatic summation. "I'll tell you how. Because she wasn't raped, and she wasn't knocked out. She was having a grand old time sifting through my personal belongings. That's how."

"Okay, Cayden," Supercop said, the tone of her voice giving no indication of whether she'd found my argument as convincing as she should have. "I'll print it out now, and you can read through it. If you find any inaccuracies or wish to add something, tell me and I'll make the changes."

No inaccuracies. No additions. I signed the document and asked if I could have a copy. Supercop said she couldn't give me one. Regulations.

I considered asking her whether her actress friend, Alina, succeeded in her audition and got the role of a TikTok star who discovers one day that she can make all the magic from her TikTok clips come true in real life. But then I remembered that when I had overheard Supercop talking with Alina on the phone, while keeping her eye on me at the police station 13 days ago, and asked her to wish her friend good luck at the audition, she had told me to shut up. I wasn't about to forget that. So I didn't say a word. Experience.

—

Megan opened the door for me when I got back; Marcel was looking for me, she said. He had some news. She used the word "news." I opened a bottle of beer, lit a cigarette, and went out to the balcony to call him.

"The State Attorney will not be asking for an extension of your house arrest, my boy," he said. "What do you say? I think you can now allow yourself a smile."

A smile? I was certainly happy with "the news," but a smile was a big thing for me. A huge thing. I was suspicious, and anyway, I was pretty sure I'd forgotten how to smile. I'd consider trying, but not before I asked a few questions.

"What exactly does this mean, Marcel?"

"It's a good sign! In general, when the State Prosecutor's Office plans to file an indictment, they ask the court to extend the house arrest."

"Hold on," I said. "Does this mean they're going to close the case?"

"No, but it means that they probably will close it in the end."

"But not for sure, right? They *can* still decide to indict me, right?"

"Yes, Cayden, but it's unlikely. Look," Marcel said, "complacency is a criminal defense lawyer's worst enemy, so I want to remain cautious. Anything's possible. But so far everything indicates that the case is going to be closed. I'm telling you; you can smile now." He paused, then said, "Hey, Cayden, I can't hear a smile on your face."

"But what are the chances, Marcel? What are the actual chances that the case will be closed?"

He paused for a second, then said, "I'm guessing about 80 percent."

Smile my ass. Statistics were haunting me: A 10 percent chance of appearing to have lied during the polygraph test, despite having told the truth. And now, a 20 percent chance of being indicted for rape, despite having told the truth. Statistically speaking, things were only getting worse.

"Cayden, this also means that starting tomorrow night at midnight, you're a free man. The house arrest is over. You can do whatever you like; you can meet and talk to anyone you want."

At first, I didn't say anything. I wondered whether I could possibly dare let myself feel good. But as far as I was concerned, this was only one, single, positive development, after which there could still be many negative ones. I was a free man for now, yes, but I could easily become a dead man walking. Finally, I said to Marcel, "Well, good; it's about time."

"Just don't make any contact with Jade, of course."

"Are you kidding? I've had enough of her to last me a lifetime, and then some."

—

It was seven p.m. on day twelve: my house arrest would come to an end in just five hours. Friends had been calling Anna to tell her they'd be at my door at midnight, promptly. They didn't ask, they told.

I thought about it and then told her she should tell my closest friends to come at ten-thirty. I decided to take a chance and bring forward the end of my house arrest by an hour and a half, without asking anyone's permission. Ten-thirty, final. That was it, the house arrest was over. I was regaining control of my life.

They came. Six, ten, twelve, maybe two dozen friends showed up. There was a lot of laughter, a lot of hugs, and rejoicing, and I did my best to act as if I were truly free, though the niggling doubt was there. Was it over? Or was it just the beginning? I couldn't tell. So far nothing has really worked out for me as planned. I'd fucked it up with one of the polygraph questions. And in the confrontation with Jade, she'd had reasonable answers for all my super-smart questions, and she'd blamed me for putting words in her mouth during the recorded phone call. So basically, I knew nothing. I didn't even know what I would do with myself when all my friends left this so-called party, and I would finally be alone.

By two in the morning, the apartment had emptied out, and for the first time in weeks, I was completely alone. No cops, no handcuffs, no prison guards, no cellmate, and no friends watching over me 24/7. I was still a rape suspect, but my status had been upgraded. From a legal point of view, I was a free man.

I turned on the laptop, to continue the writing I'd been doing throughout my house arrest: the writing of this book. When my eyes started to close, I got ready for bed, reminding myself that I should be enjoying every single second of this precious new freedom of mine. With Anna and Megan no longer on duty, my bedroom was available as well, but I slept in the living room, as if I were still under house arrest.

CHAPTER
THIRTY-TWO

*A*t noon the next day, the free man that I was, I got on my motorbike and drove over to the pet shop. I wanted to buy cat toys for Ian and Amy. Yes, that was the first thing I did when I was no longer under house arrest. What can I say? I really love cats. I know, most people prefer dogs, but I think cats are underappreciated. Cats fascinate me. They're the perfect combination of wild and domestic animals, like having mini-tigers in your house. But for some reason, there are people who find the whole man-loving-cat thing a bit weird. A few weeks ago, someone published a Facebook post on a popular cats fan group, in which she said:

"I'm sorry, but a single straight guy who has cats, not dogs? It's too awkward, it doesn't work for me."

And she got 300 likes for that crap! I couldn't restrain myself, so I added a comment below:

"Hi, I'm Cayden, 33, single, straight, loves cats, and loves women. I can't decide whether your post is more homophobic, or more stupid. Meow."

I got 500 likes for that comment. I remember the number.

So, I planned to buy a few toys, motion-activated sound chip toys, toys that sound like real mice. Ian and Amy love this kind of toy; it seems to satisfy their natural hunting instincts. The store was a well-known family business and I had been a regular there for many years. I greeted the owner, a kind woman who always had good tips for cat lovers.

Now, turning to the little girl standing next to her, she said, "Go with Cayden and show him the best cat toys we have." Then she whispered an apology to me, explained that she had no other help at the moment, and that she hoped I wouldn't mind being entrusted to her granddaughter while she tended to another customer. "She's a wonderful salesgirl, and she's already ten years old!"

"Ten years old, my goodness! You're practically a grown-up!" I said. "I'd be honored."

The little girl, taking her job very seriously, said to me, "Do you want a toy that looks like a real mouse? And makes sounds like one too?"

"I sure would!" I said. "In fact, that's exactly what I'm looking for!"

And then we were alone in the showroom, just the two of us, and it hit me. I couldn't be there. I was a rape suspect, and I was alone in a room with a little girl. I had to get out of there. Immediately. And then, just as I started walking out, the girl's mother came in. I knew her because she worked in the business as well. She had also always given me good advice, the way her mother did, and I'd always felt she liked me. She'd even told me once that I was one of her favorite customers.

Well, no longer. She walked briskly over to her daughter, picked her up, made an excuse for why she had to rush, and hurried out again. She knew. She definitely knew. She knew, and she panicked when she saw her daughter alone with me in an unattended room. She knew. Or, on the other hand, maybe she didn't know, and she really *was* in a hurry. But what difference did it make? After all, even if she didn't know, that was exactly how she would have behaved if she did. That was how everyone would have behaved. Me too. Who would leave their daughter in a room alone with a man suspected of rape? Who wouldn't panic, knowing that their child was already in there, alone, with him?

That was it; I was tainted. Welcome, stain. *Welcome?* No. Damn you, stain. I knew you'd be coming. But I didn't think you'd show up quite this fast, already on my first day out.

Maybe I was better off this way. Maybe it was good that the stain had reared its ugly head now, before I'd had a chance to think I could escape this fate. But I wanted my stain to know that he and I would never be friends. I would never come to terms with his existence. I knew that he would be with me forever, even if the case against me was closed and I didn't get indicted. Closed or not closed would make no difference. Rape was rape, and someone's daughter wasn't going anywhere near a person who'd been accused of it.

I paid for the toys and left – or fled, rather – as fast

as I could on my bike. I was trying to flee my stain, but I couldn't. No matter how fast I went, it remained stuck to my clothes, my skin, my receding hair. I picked up speed nevertheless. Perhaps the wind would strip me of it. No, it didn't work, so I slowed down. If I were to get pulled over by the traffic police now, I'd be in big trouble.

I lowered my helmet's visor. If I couldn't shake the stain, perhaps I could at least try to hide my physical self from the world. I had been planning to make a few more stops; I had lots of catching up to do with errands that had been neglected over the last several weeks. But I didn't feel like doing anything else. I made my way home, and didn't leave the apartment again that day, or the next one either.

CHAPTER
THIRTY-THREE

*O*n day three of my freedom, I woke to the sound of my ringing landline. It was Marcel. The police had completed their investigation and the case had been passed on to the State Attorney's Office, presumably without any recommendations – neither to indict nor to close the file. Marcel said this was a strange state of affairs, and when I asked him nervously *why?* he said he'd make some calls to try to find out.

The new masters of my fate were now the State Prosecution authorities. They would be the ones to decide whether to indict me or close the case and give me back my life.

—

I had become a ghost. It was day five of my freedom, and while people most likely knew that I existed, I had basically become invisible, and getting ahold of me had become a near-impossible task: I didn't have a mobile, my Facebook profile and Instagram account were frozen, and I hadn't checked my email for more than three weeks. I was living life totally offline. I communicated with my close friends and family via my landline, and since it seemed that most people no longer called each other to actually communicate, a technological downgrade to what had been acceptable a few decades ago was now enough to enable your actual disappearance.

Aside from necessary errands, I left the house only to go to my regular café, where I sat during the day at the bar inside, as isolated as possible, and worked on this book. Sometimes I was tempted to sit outside, in the sun, but I realized I wasn't ready. The café was situated on a busy pedestrian walkway: my old stomping grounds. Up until the year before, back when my career had been on the rise and I had started earning enough money to upgrade apartments, I had lived in this area. But if I'd sat outside now, people would have seen and approached me, and I knew I wasn't up to that yet. Two of the café waitresses noticed that something was up with me, because I had started smoking again, and I had also lost weight. They tried asking me what was wrong but, gauging my response, dropped the subject quickly.

—

On day six of my freedom, I had an appointment with a dermatologist. There was a large beauty spot on my arm that had doubled in size, and a doctor I'd interviewed not long before had warned me that it would be ironic if the

Channel 3 News health correspondent died of skin cancer because he'd been too lazy to check it out.

The dermatologist assured me that everything was fine and that it was still too early to draw up a will. She also scolded me for not using enough sunscreen.

"I use it when I go to the beach," I told her, a comment that didn't seem to impress her much.

"We're exposed to the sun everywhere," she said. "Not just at the beach."

"True," I said. "I promise to be more diligent." And I meant it. The phrase *It can't happen to me* had been erased from my lexicon.

When she was done with her examination, she asked if there were anything else she could do for me. At first, I said no and got up to leave, but then I remembered something.

"Actually, yes," I said. "You know this new drug that's supposed to stimulate hair growth? I have a good friend who's been using it, and it's really worked for him. Maybe you could write me a prescription?"

"It's actually not that new," she said. "Propecia."

"And does it really work?"

"Yes, but not on everyone."

"So why don't all balding men try it?"

"Listen," she said, "it's a drug you need to take religiously, every day, and it takes a good few months before you see any results. And it isn't cheap."

"Is it true that it can also have some bad side effects? I mean, really bad?"

"Impotence, a decreased libido, and a low sperm count."

"Wow. And you're not even guaranteed hair."

"Well, we're talking about side effects that show up in less than two percent of users, and as soon as you stop the medication, the side effects disappear. There's no irreversible damage."

"Well in that case . . ." I said. "Could you give me a prescription?"

What can I say? I'm not a particularly vain person, but I do have an issue with my hair. Well, actually, I have two issues: my height and my hair. The way I see it, I got screwed twice on the physical appearance front. I've always been a bit short, but then, when I turned thirty, I also started going bald. Since the height is a lost battle, I've focused my efforts on the war against baldness. If I'm never going to be tall, at least I might get my hair back.

I was eager to try this medication, but the impotence thing did worry me a little. If that were to happen to me during a sexual encounter, how would I know if it was the drug or just an understandable side effect of the ordeal I'd been through? I went to the pharmacy and bought two packages, but decided not to start taking it yet.

On my way out of the building, I was approached by a woman my mother's age, 60-ish. She wasn't someone I knew, but I recognized her from the doctor's waiting room; I'd noticed how she'd been stealing glances at me. She moved towards me now, but didn't smile. My heart pounded. Maybe she'd heard about me. Yeah, she probably had. Maybe she wanted to say that she hoped I'd rot in jail for the rest of my life.

"You're from Channel 3, right? A news correspondent?"

"Yes," I said, and then I took two steps back, just in

case she tried to slap me.

"Remind me of your name. You cover health issues, right?"

"Yes, health issues. I'm Cayden. Cayden Chase."

"I really like your reports," she said. "Health issues interest me."

"Thanks so much!" I said. In the old, pre-Jade days, I took such compliments in stride. Now I was just grateful when my fears of being spat at and called a rapist weren't realized. Fucking Jade.

—

On the morning of day seven of my freedom, my brother called and managed to persuade me to borrow an old iPhone of his. He said I could use it until I got my own back from the police. The truth is, I really didn't want it, but I could see he wasn't going to give up, so I finally agreed and he brought it over. But, honestly, it suited me well to be without one.

About an hour after my brother took off, on my way to the café to continue writing, I stopped at a kiosk that sold lottery tickets. I knew that buying lottery tickets was a foolish thing to do, and that was why I'd hardly ever done it. But now, in my new life, a lot of surprising things were happening, so I decided to see if there were any pleasant surprises in store for me, and I purchased two scratch cards. I looked skyward and said to the man up there that if he truly existed, he should make himself known by generously compensating me for the hell I'd been through. I scratched the two cards. I got nothing from the first one, and although the second one yielded earnings, they were barely enough for a pack of cigarettes. I looked to the heavens again and mumbled that I didn't want to sound greedy, God forbid, but that I thought I deserved more.

—

On day nine of my freedom, I was screening my calls like never before. I didn't have the patience to listen to the same words of encouragement, support, pity. Only now did I realize what a great favor I'd been doing when the judge hadn't allowed visits or phone calls?

My days at this point were mostly made up of running errands: the things I couldn't sort out over the phone or via a friend. On this day, I walked over to the shopping center at the port. I lived nearby, but generally, I didn't hang out there the way many of my single friends who lived in the start-up capital did, because the seaside promenade was mostly a favorite site for tourists and families. However, there were a few well-known nightclubs there, and I passed by one of them on my way to the sporting goods store: Shalvata. Just next to the farmers' market. The sign in the entrance read:

This Friday night, doors open at 23:59, DJ Jenia Tarsol
B2B Dj Magit Cacoon. No further questions.

Damn, what a great line-up! Indeed, no further questions. I would definitely be going . . . if I wasn't a rape suspect.

Anyway, back to the sporting goods store: I needed new sneakers. I was eager to get back to the gym already, and the sneakers in my closet were past their expiration date, to put it mildly. The salesman offered me a choice: an expensive pair of New Balance trainers or a cheap pair of Adidas. He asked if I was a runner, and when I said yes, he said I absolutely had to go with the New Balance. I was usually very easy to persuade, an easy target, but this time I left with the Adidas. My boss, graciously, had still been paying my salary, but a rape charge didn't come cheap. Even after the very nice discount Marcel had given me, I'd had to take out a bank loan.

I went to the café, took my usual seat at the bar inside, and continued writing. The writing was my savior. It helped me not to lose my mind and made me feel productive. I was writing in real-time, and it felt as if I were in some crazy reality show, but with a keyboard instead of a camera.

It was during my fifth smoking break outside that reality intruded on the life I had been quietly creating for myself. I tried to hide behind a potted plant at the café's entrance, but it was too late: I'd been spotted. It was Janina, someone I knew from my old life. For half a second, I thought maybe I could still get away with slinking back inside the café. Nope.

"Cayden!" Janina said, embracing me. "Oh, Cayden!"

"Hey, Jennie," I said back, and embraced her too, though I didn't want to. "Nice to see you."

"My God, it's so good to see you," she said, still holding tight.

"Thanks."

Then she put her mouth close to my ear and whispered, "No one believes you did it."

"Good to know, good to know," I said. But I wanted to crawl out of my skin. Desperate to change the subject, I said, "How are you?" I had no reason to think she didn't mean what she'd said, but on the other hand, there was every possibility in the world that she meant just the opposite. Or maybe I was just being paranoid? After all, she was still hugging me.

She took her leave, and after another couple hours of writing, on another cigarette break, I blew a column of smoke skyward and watched it dissipate. When I looked back down, I saw that it was about to happen again: someone I knew was walking towards me. The same pit in the stomach, the same wish to flee.

"What's up, Cayden?" he said, holding out his hand to shake mine.

"All okay, Steve," I said, trying to convince him, with a solid handshake, that this was in fact true.

"Truth is, I've heard about what you've been going through," he said. "How are you doing?"

I shrugged. "Surviving, you know. I hope it'll be over soon."

"I hope so for you too, bro. Hope you get your life back soon."

"Thanks. How are you? What's new? Where's Carla?"

"She's right here actually. There, on the bench along the avenue."

An awkward silence. Steve's wife Carla usually greeted me warmly, with a hug and kiss on the cheek.

"She . . . listen, Cayden, she . . ."

"Oh," I said. "So, she's heard too, right?"

"Yes, she . . . she . . ."

"Gotcha."

"I told her there was no way you could have done such

a thing, but, well, you know."

"Forget it, you don't have to explain. It's not your fault. It's okay."

But nothing was okay. When we parted ways, I went back inside the café to pay my bill and pack up my stuff, and then I left for home. A few days before, in the pet shop, I had told myself that maybe I was just being paranoid and that this whole thing was only in my mind. But this time, there was no denying it: It was real. And I felt as if my self-confidence had taken a huge hit. The hugest ever. I had never, ever, felt this shitty about myself.

CHAPTER
THIRTY-FOUR

*M*y friend Nicole had been trying to see me for two weeks already, ever since my house arrest had come to an end, and now she was insisting. She said she wouldn't hear of me spending Friday night at home alone while everyone else was out having fun. I told her it was okay, that I was using my time to write a book about what I'd been through, and anyway, it made no difference to me what night of the week it was; they were all the same to me.

"You're writing a book?" she said. "Really? Can I read it? I promise to be totally discreet and not reveal anything to anyone; I swear!"

I hesitated for a second, but then figured what the heck? "Sure," I said. "I guess so. Why don't I send it to you by email? I could do it right now."

"No, no, no," she said. "I need to see you in the flesh

and don't argue with me. I'm coming over."

Nicole was one of those people who looked like what she did: She was in advertising, and she looked like an advertisement. She was a very pretty woman. Suffice it to say, anyone would want to buy whatever she was selling—especially men.

We'd actually had sex once when we first met, about five years before. After that, I wanted to meet again, but after two or three declines on her part, I let it go. Nicole liked cats, and her big dream was to write a book. Clearly, we had a lot in common, and since she didn't want me as a boyfriend or, as a friend with benefits, we became simply friends.

A few hours later, after she'd arrived at my place and given me a lengthy embrace, Nicole looked at me and said, "Now Cayden, don't tell me anything. I want to read it in your book and I don't want any spoilers. I brought my iPad."

"Right now?" I said. "Like, right now while you're sitting here next to me?"

"Yeah, why not?" she said. "But let's drink something first. No alcohol for me, of course," she said pointing to her breasts.

I brought Nicole an apple juice and a bottle of beer for myself, and a few minutes later, we were sitting side by side at the bar doing our own thing: Nicole reading on her iPad, me writing on my laptop.

She was a fast reader. And then, after about an hour, I noticed that she was crying.

She kept shaking her head; then she wiped her eyes with a tissue and looked up at me from the text. "I cannot believe what this woman has put you through," she said. She had just read the scene where I'd told my mother. Nicole stood up and hugged me, but then quickly returned to her reading. It was hard for me to sit there next to her, wondering what she was thinking now, and now, and now, and I couldn't concentrate on my own work. So I got up and busied myself around the house, moving ashtrays from here to there, and then I initiated a few stare-down fights with Ian and Amy.

Finally, when she was done, Nicole came over to me and put her arms around me again.

"It's okay," I said, rubbing her back, as if she were the one in need of comfort. "I'm doing okay. Really. I'm hanging in."

"I know you're hanging in," she said, but at the same time she continued whispering in my ear: "You poor thing." Her embrace had also turned tighter and closer. I could feel her big breasts pushing against me, flooding me with confusing and contradictory feelings. What was she up to? "You poor thing," she cooed again into my ear. The "you poor thing" comments were becoming annoying, but on the other hand, her touch felt good. I could feel her nipples against my chest. Couldn't she feel it as well? Was she doing this on purpose?

Her nipples seemed to me to be unusually large, perhaps because she was breastfeeding. Like several other thirty-something women in my social circle, she had decided to have a baby on her own. She could have gotten any man she wanted in the start-up capital, but she never wanted them. She'd always said her dream was to become a mother and an author, not a wife.

So, as mentioned, she'd never gone for another hook-up with me, after our first and only one. So why now? I leaned back against the bar and closed my eyes. I felt Nicole's lips on my left cheek and opened my eyes. Hugs or kisses on the cheek could certainly be considered platonic, but now her lips had started fluttering all over my face and coming closer to mine. She had definitely gone beyond "friendly" here. I hadn't been touched like this in over a month, and the last time had been with Jade. I felt like someone with lung cancer being offered a cigarette.

I tried to respond to her. It wasn't coming naturally. I closed my eyes again and placed my hands on her hips. She moved and kissed me, trailing her lips gently over my closed mouth for several seconds. I pulled away and went to get another beer.

Drink in hand, I sipped from my glass to moisten my crazily dry, crazily stressed-out lips. When I was done, Nicole came back, and with a purposeful look in her eyes, stood stock-still in front of me. She grabbed me by the shirt and pulled me towards her, her hands slipping under my shirt, lightly caressing my stomach and chest, and inching down to my waist. She hooked her fingers into the belt loops on the sides of my jeans, gripping them and pulling me even tighter against her. We were as close as we could be: Chest pressed to chest, the zipper of my jeans brushing against the buttons of her pants.

Nicole slowly unzipped my jeans and started stroking me. My head began spinning. I reached for my beer, took a sip, and closed my eyes. I had hoped the alcohol would give me the boost I needed to continue, but it didn't help at all.

I moved her hand aside, zipped up my jeans, went over to the kitchen sink, and washed my face.

"Too soon, Nicole."

"I can see."

"You realize that I've been waiting for this moment for an eternity, don't you? To be honest, I never thought it would happen again with you. But this isn't the right moment."

"It's okay, Cayden." I was surprised by how quickly and good-naturedly she was willing to give up on the whole thing. I mean, I've never raped anyone, but in my previous life, if it had been *me* trying to get sex, I would likely have given it another shot or two. But now, our roles had shifted, and I was appreciating her for not doing what I would have done myself. Things like that make you think.

"Cayden, you're going to meet with a psychologist, right?" Nicole said.

Her question stopped my train of thought immediately. There I'd been, actually trying for the first time to understand what I was perhaps doing wrong with women, and the woman before me was telling me I needed mental help.

"Hadn't planned on it," I shrugged.

"But you must. What are you saying? That's it? No more sex for you?"

"I'm not saying that at all," I said. "I'm just taking a break, and I'm not worried, because I know that the moment the case is closed, everything will work out fine, including in this area of my life." Well, maybe I was a *little* worried, but I preferred to keep that to myself.

"Are you sure you don't need to do something about it?" Nicole said, "Take care of yourself?"

"I'm fine just the way things are for now, Nicole. I've realized that life is a lot simpler if you take sex out of the equation. Maybe sex is overrated. Anyway, it sure frees up a lot of time."

"You really are traumatized, aren't you?" Nicole said.

"No, I am not. As a matter of fact, I found out that writing *about* sex is much more enjoyable for me than actually *having* sex."

"Shut up, you can have them both," Nicol said. "You know, by the way, that it wasn't a pity fuck I was offering, right?"

"Actually – I didn't think it was, but now that you mention it ... "

"Cayden, no!" she protested. "Damn it, if only you knew how horny I am right now. Fuck! I don't know; maybe it's all that reading I just did. I think you should ask Johnny Depp to read the book in the audio version."

CHAPTER
THIRTY-FIVE

*T*he next day was a holiday, Memorial Day, but I had already decided not to go to the traditional family gathering. I wasn't up for a whole bunch of relatives right now. With dread, I called and explained to my mother that I knew it sounded radical, but I had no choice. I just needed to be alone these days; I desperately needed to be alone.

Much to my surprise, the conversation went smoothly. No drama at all. My mother said she understood and hoped that this whole thing would be behind us soon, and then we could have a big family meal to celebrate. And that was it. Actually, I guess I shouldn't have been so surprised. After all, it was my mother. She knew a thing or two about radical solutions.

Feeling relieved, I lit a cigarette, assuming the hardest part was now behind me and I could relax. But it wasn't over. The phone didn't stop. Friends kept calling to say how upset they were that I'd be spending the holiday alone: No family? No friends? Like a dog, alone? At a certain point, when I decided that the attention and concern had gotten to be too much, I muted my phone and turned the other way when I saw it light up. But then I saw Megan's number appear on the screen. I couldn't ignore her or Anna after everything they'd done for me.

"But that's so sad!" she said to me when I told her my plan of nothingness. "How can you?"

"It'll be fine, Megan," I said. "Really. Hopefully, this whole story will end soon. But in the meantime, I'm happier this way. On my own."

"But everyone's celebrating tomorrow," she said. "I can't bear the thought of you being alone."

My patience was running out. I tried to end the call, but Megan wouldn't let up.

"I'm just worried about you, Cayden."

"I know. But everyone's pushing me, and it's enough. It's hard for me to explain, but I really feel like I'm fighting for my life, and this is how I have to do it."

"Okay," she said, "I understand. I do. But we're having a barbecue the day after tomorrow, at Chris and Mia's place, and you're coming!"

"I don't think so."

She was undeterred. "You're coming, Cayden!" she said. "All your closest friends will be there, everyone who's been supporting and helping you."

I thought of the expression *when you're dead, lie down* and realized that in this situation, I was definitely dead.

"Okay, okay," I finally said.

No sooner had I hung up than the phone rang again; it was my brother.

"Tell me," he said. "Why aren't you coming for dinner tomorrow?"

"I don't feel like it," I sighed. "I'm just not up to it. I told you."

"What are you gonna do instead?"

"I'll write my book."

"What can I say?" he said. "It just doesn't seem right for you to be all alone on a day when everyone else is together, celebrating. It doesn't feel good to me. And mom is also unhappy about it. She's here with me. She wants to talk to you."

What was going on with them? And hadn't my mother seemed fine about this whole thing just a little while ago? What had changed? A second later, the picture became clear. Crystal clear. They were worried I would off myself. I could hear my mother crying before she'd even gotten on the line.

"Mom," I said, hoping that the sound of my voice would calm her. "Mom. Listen, I'm just going to say it since nothing else seems to work: We're not *there*, God forbid. Not even close. Don't worry; I am not going to kill myself."

It did the job. She stopped crying and we ended the conversation. If she'd have been a mind-reader, she'd have known the full sentence was, *Don't worry, I'm not going to kill myself – yet . . .*

Yes, in the back of my mind, and not even so far in the back, I still had my plan. What could I say? This plan brought me immense relief. Paradoxically, the thought that

I could end my life, if necessary, was a lifesaver.

—

At four in the afternoon the day after the holiday, I showed up at Chris and Mia's place for their post-holiday barbeque with a bottle of wine in hand, and other friends joined soon after. The first part of the get-together was devoted to my situation: analyses, assessments, words of encouragement, and comfort. But then the talk shifted to other matters, and though I tried to get involved in the new topics of conversation, I couldn't; I felt lost and out of place. I watched as my friends hung out easily, and happily, and thought about how I – until a month prior – had been just like them. But I wasn't like them anymore, and I wondered whether I would ever be again, or whether this experience had irrevocably changed me, had changed everything. I was tired of talking about me and my situation, but on the other hand, I couldn't seem to talk about anything else either; didn't know how.

I said my goodbyes and decided there would be no more socializing of this nature for me: at least not until the day arrived when a decision about my fate was finally handed down. I knew my friends wouldn't be pleased with me for leaving so soon, but this was the new me: the non-people-pleaser. So I went back to my new best friends, who were waiting at home for me – Johnnie Walker, Jack Daniel's, and Jameson.

CHAPTER
THIRTY-SIX

I got home, opened a fresh one, lit another cigarette, and went out onto the balcony. And then I heard a blood-curdling howl coming from the direction of the living room. Shit, it could only mean one thing: Ian was lying in a puddle of his own urine, twitching as if plugged into an electrical outlet, spittle and foam dripping from his mouth onto the floor. He was having such violent convulsions that every time his small bones hit the floor it sounded like the beating of a drum. Amy was standing over him, her teeth embedded in his neck. It wasn't playing. She was genuinely trying to kill him. I tried chasing her off, but then she came at me too. A cat was a small animal, domesticated and friendly, but it could sometimes show a wild and savage side. I grabbed a large towel, quickly turned it into a whip, and flicked it hard at Amy's head. I had no choice; she would have killed him. The little monster released her bite from the neck of her victim, her soulmate for the most part, and fled to the balcony. I sat down on the floor next to Ian, put him on my lap, and whispered comforting words. As expected, the convulsions subsided, and a minute later his legs had stopped shaking against my thighs. He just lay there on me, panting, giving me a puzzled look. I stroked him until he got off me and stood up.

It was an epileptic fit. Yes, it happens to cats too, and Ian was an epileptic cat. He had a seizure every two or three months, and this was exactly what it looked like. The vet said there was nothing to be done – neither with the seizures nor with Amy's reaction. He said there was no point in treating Ian with medication; not yet. He instructed me to do exactly what I had done – to separate them, comfort him, make sure he drank a lot of water afterward, and put him on medication only if the seizures became more frequent. So far, thank God, for the past four years things had remained the same, and I was hoping they would stay that way.

I cleaned Ian up and when I was done, I took him over to his bowl to drink. Amy snarled as we walked past her, and I knew I wouldn't be able to leave them unsupervised for a while. That was just how it went. She was always aggressive towards Ian for a few days post-seizure, and it could end badly. When I'd leave the house, I'd have to close them off in separate rooms with water, food, and a litter box. An absolute division of forces. That's what I would do in normal times, but now I decided to just stay at home. There was nothing out there for me anyway.

Eight in the evening, and the TV was on. All of a sudden, I could hear the theme music signaling the start of the Channel 3 newscast. I ran to turn the bloody thing off. I had been trying to steer clear of the news; it was a too-painful reminder of the life I used to have.

Just then I got a text message from Heather, or rather "the one who got away," as I'd begun thinking of her: no doubt romanticizing her, seeing her as the perfect foil to Jade, seeing her as the one who might have saved me from this fate if only I'd called her again after our one date. As it turned out, she'd been questioned by the police, and she thought it would be nice to know what the hell was going on. Crap. Here she'd been subjected to police questioning, and then I'd gone and barred her from entering my apartment. I immediately apologized via text and explained that I hadn't been allowed to open the door for her that day. I promised to make it up to her, to explain everything, and we agreed she'd come over the following evening. Would I get a second chance?

I looked at Ian dozing on the sofa in the living room, exhausted from his seizure. Amy was asleep on the floor opposite him, at a safe distance. I could feel that she wasn't quite done with him yet. She knew I wouldn't let her get near him now, and she was waiting for the perfect moment – the moment I looked away – to launch an attack.

CHAPTER
THIRTY-SEVEN

*H*eather knocked on my door shortly after nine, and this time of course I let her in. We hugged, but her embrace felt hesitant. Understandably. She and I had met just once before, and she had paid for it with a grilling from the police.

We sat at the bar.

"Okay, Cayden. I'm all ears."

"First of all, I have to tell you, I'm really sorry for everything. I owe you an explanation."

"Seems like it."

So I told her everything, about the whole damn thing, and when I was done, I said it was her turn. I wanted to hear exactly what she had been through.

"Initially I was contacted by a female cop," she said. "At first, I thought it was a joke. I mean, why would the police be calling me in for questioning? And then she asked if I

233

knew why they were calling. I told her I didn't even know if she was really a cop, how would I know why she was calling? She said I should get to the police station as soon as possible. I asked her why but she wouldn't tell me. I asked her a few times, and got the same answer: 'You'll find out when you get here.'"

"And you had no idea it was all because of me?"

"Only on the bus, on my way to the police station; that's when I started thinking about how you'd disappeared not only on me, but from the TV as well. I remember talking on the phone with my friend Natalie and her saying to me, 'It sounds like he's screening your calls and ignoring your messages; sounds to me like he's blowing you off.'"

"You can't imagine how far from the truth that is."

She shrugged. "I'm just telling you what she said. Anyway, I told Natalie I had the feeling something really bad was happening with you. I told her I was worried, and she said: 'Why worry about him? Look what an idiot he is. You were together once, and already he's gotten you in trouble.'"

"Well, she wasn't wrong," I said.

"Nah," she said, brushing it off, kindly, graciously, and then continued on with her story. "So when I got to the police station, they kept me waiting for about 40 minutes. I was just standing there outside the interrogation room in the corridor: no chair, no bench, and most importantly, no explanation for why I was there. And then a female officer came out and asked me to come with her. She looked vaguely familiar to me; I had the feeling I'd seen her on the news or something. "

Okay, so she'd been questioned by Supercop.

"Will you tell me what she said to you?" I asked. "And what you said to her? And do you mind if I write everything down? I'm writing a book about all the shit that went down with this thing, in real time. It helps me not to freak out."

"Wait a minute," Heather said. "So I'm a character in your book?"

I nodded, slowly, trying to gauge her response. This was something I hadn't given much thought about what if the people I was writing about didn't want to be written about? But before I had a chance to ask for permission to do what I was already doing, she said, "Cool! That's so cool! And by the way, could I be called Heather in your book? I've always loved the name Heather."

"Heather it is!"

As it turned out, Heather had done something unbelievable: She'd made a recording of her Supercop investigation on her iPhone.

I was slain. How amazing was this? The one who got away had balls!

"I was actually pretty shocked and dumbfounded that she didn't ask me to hand over my phone," Heather said. "I'd just been sitting there waiting for her to finish her own phone call, reading the usual shit on Facebook and Instagram, and then, when I had the feeling her call was ending, I just hit 'record' and put the phone in my bag, without zipping it closed. I wasn't really thinking, I just did it. And I got it all."

"Damn, you're amazing, Heather!"

"Yes, I am." She laughed. "And besides, I was pissed at her. Do you know how long she'd kept me waiting? She'd given me a lot of time to think, so screw her."

I couldn't stop shaking my head, smiling, laughing, in awe of her gutsiness.

She laughed too. "It seemed like a good idea at the time." She said that once, years ago, she had worked as a secretary at a big law firm and had been sexually harassed by one of the senior partners. "Of course, he was about twice my age. And very married," she added. So she decided to record him. The result? The firm paid her a lot of money to settle the matter out of court. Ever since then, she'd had "a kind of fetish for recordings," something I could certainly relate to, post-Jade.

"So," she said, tantalizingly. "Do you want to listen?"

"Uh, yeah?" I said, since "want" was pretty mild for how I felt right then. I turned on my laptop, lit a cigarette, and typed:

Supercop: Do you know a guy by the name of Cayden Chase?

Heather: Cayden Chase? Uh, yeah. Why? What's going on? Is he okay?

Supercop: How do you know one another?

Heather: We met through a mutual acquaintance one night when we were out at Habustan, it's a nightclub. Two months ago, maybe a little more. What's going on here? Why am I here?

Supercop: We'll get to that. Are you, or have the two of you ever been, involved with one another?

Heather: Umm, yes.

Supercop: Did he come on to you?

Heather: Actually, to be honest, I'm the one who came on to him. He seemed like a nice guy, so the day after we met, I sent him a message on Instagram. After that, we spoke a few times, and then I suggested we move to WhatsApp. We spoke a few more times, and then I suggested that we meet. And we did.

Supercop: Where did you meet?

Heather: We went out, and then we went back to his place.

Supercop: Who suggested going back to his place, you or Cayden?

Heather: I would never have suggested it; I mean, I'm not that forward. Cayden's the one who suggested it. But only after I asked him why he wasn't suggesting it. But hang on a second. What's going on here? I still don't know what this is all about.

Supercop: You'll get the picture in a minute, Heather, I promise. So, what happened when you went back to his place?

Heather: We hung out, chatted; it was nice.

Supercop: Did he offer you a drink?

Heather: Yes. I suppose you want to know what kind of drink? I had a vodka Red Bull.

Supercop: Did he pour it for you?

Heather: I think so; at least as far as I remember.

Supercop: Did he pour it in front of you? Did you see him pouring?

Heather: Umm . . . I'm not sure. How am I supposed to remember? This all happened about two months ago, and I didn't know I'd be questioned by the police about it.

Supercop: Two months, Heather, not a year; it's not such a long time. So let me just confirm: You're saying that you can't discount the possibility that he might have poured your drink in a place or in a way that you did not see him doing so?

Heather: How can I answer that kind of question? Who remembers those kinds of details? He certainly didn't force me to drink, and he certainly didn't force me to have sex with him, if that's what you're implying.

Supercop: Did he use a condom?

Heather: Yes.

Supercop: Did he try to have unprotected sex with you?

Heather: No.

Supercop: Did he try to have anal sex?

Heather: No. And even if he had – I would never have done anal on a first date.

Supercop: Okay, now during the sex, was he aggressive? Violent?

Heather: What? I don't really follow –

Supercop: Did he hit you? You know what I mean – slap you or spank you or the like.

Heather: No, not at all.

Supercop: Not even a little slap? No spanking your bottom? Nothing?

Heather: Nothing. Not even close.

Supercop: Did he pull your hair, or put his hands on your neck as if to choke you?

Heather: No!

Supercop: If I were to tell you he's been accused of rape and sodomy, what would you think?

Heather: Fuck, no way! I mean, sorry for the f-word, but no way!

Supercop: Why no way?

Heather: Just a minute here. Are you telling me that someone filed a complaint against Cayden?

Supercop: Yes, that's what I'm telling you.

Heather: It doesn't make sense.

Supercop: You know, the fact that you slept with this guy once doesn't mean you know him. Why would someone file a complaint against him for nothing? You know what they say: Where there's smoke, there's fire. So, please try to remember: Is there any chance that he put a date-rape drug in your drink?

Heather: No way! And I truly don't believe he would do something like that.

Supercop: Listen, I've got to ask you: The two of you met only once, and yet it seems like you're really trying to help him out here. Why? You don't really know him, after all.

Heather: It doesn't matter that I don't "really" know him. I just know that he would never do something like this, so as far as I'm concerned, he's like someone who's been badly injured in a car accident, and he's lying there in the middle of the street, asking for help. And I'm a bystander; okay, so I don't "really" know him, but I know him enough, and of course, I'll help him.

Supercop: I must say: That's an interesting point of view. Tell me, Heather, do you like him? Do you like Cayden Chase?

Heather: We only met once, you know. We've only been on one date.

Supercop: You know what I mean; are you hoping to see him again, if and when he manages to get past this complaint?

Heather: Wow, what a question.

Supercop: It's an important question. As is your answer. So?

Heather: Well….

Supercop: What's the hesitation about?

Heather: Well, you know … he is a little short for my taste. I can't wear heels around him.

Supercop: Funny.

Heather: I thought so. Anyway, the answer is yes. I'm definitely hoping to see Cayden Chase again.

Supercop: Thank you, Heather. We're done. You're free to go.

CHAPTER
THIRTY-EIGHT

I turned off my laptop. What could I say to a woman I barely knew, but really liked, in the wake of her run-in with the police – a run-in for which I was solely responsible? With all that I had been through and was still going through, I felt sorry for her.

"Stop worrying," Heather said to me, taking my hand in hers and patting it, after I apologized for the thousandth time. "It's all good now. I'll admit it was pretty unpleasant at the time, but you're the one going through hell, not me. And one more thing – I hope I didn't make you uncomfortable with what I said to that cop, about how I wanted to see you again."

"Not at all," I said. "I wanted to see you again too."

"Yeah?" she said. "Well, that's nice to hear! But anyway, that isn't why I'm here. I really just wanted to know what this whole thing was about. And also, I met someone. It's only the very beginning, but he's cute."

Ahhh. So she had met someone. So she was, indeed, the one who got away. I felt a slight twinge at the thought of the lost opportunity, but mostly I was okay with it. I was discovering that I didn't really know how to be with a woman anymore. Or at least not yet.

I went over to the refrigerator, retrieved a bottle of Coke Zero, and poured two glasses. I, of course, didn't offer her alcohol. I handed one of the glasses to her and raised my own towards my mouth to take a sip. But then Heather rested her glass on the bar, cupped my cheeks in her hands, and kissed me on the lips.

"Didn't you just say, like a minute ago, that you're seeing someone?"

"I did, yes," she said flirtatiously, "but if you'll recall, I also said that it's super early; we've only gone out twice. I would never cheat on someone, but this wouldn't qualify as cheating because he and I haven't had sex yet. On the other hand, who knows? Maybe *he is the* one, and now *you* will be my last fling."

"Very romantic," I said, nervously, stalling for time. "But listen, I have to tell you, it's been kind of a long time, and –"

I stopped myself. I wasn't going to do this to myself again. No, not again. Enough with the excuses. Enough already.

I lay down on my back and allowed her to do as she pleased. Lying there next to me, she caressed and kissed me. But I didn't dare touch her. After a few minutes, I opened my eyes to see that she was looking at me.

"Are you okay?" she said. "You've just been lying here

with your eyes closed for, like, forever."

"I think it's best that way, don't you?" I said. "It lessens the chances of my getting slapped with a complaint somewhere down the line."

"Oh, come on now," she said. "Don't be crazy."

"Just kidding of course," I said, but I wasn't. Not really. I was lost. Three different women had thrown themselves at me within a matter of weeks, I was living the dream, but the dream had become a fucking nightmare. The first was trying to throw me in jail and the other two I suspected of pity fucks.

"Heather, tell me the truth – is this a pity fuck?"

She laughed. "You tell me – do I look like someone who's offering you a pity fuck?"

She sat up next to me and in one fluid movement removed her shirt. Then she slid her left hand up her back, and with one hand managed to undo her bra so that it easily fell off her shoulders and dropped down to her waist. It always seems so simple when they do it themselves. Heather didn't lose eye contact with me for even a second during the process. Then she reached for me, pulled me up and towards her, easily lifted the tank top I was wearing over my head, and threw it over to the sofa on the other side of the room. When I felt her hands grab the sides of my pants, I raised my hips and pelvis slightly and allowed her to pull them down, as far as my knees, in one tug. Then she peeled them off entirely, one leg after the other until my feet were free too. She also threw my pants onto the sofa, adding them to the growing pile of clothes already there.

By the time she finished undressing me, I was ready for

her. Primed, erect, armed, and loaded. At first, I responded, and felt, gratefully, like a man who had risen to his feet after weeks of a mysterious paralysis, a paralysis that had shown no signs of ending. I felt ready to resume normal service. I kneeled in front of her, mirroring her position facing me. She touched me. Felt me. Caressed me. And then she leaned over and placed a small but noisy kiss on the tip of my cock. But she didn't continue going down that road; she was just teasing a bit. She sat up straight on her knees again, looked at me, and said, "Maybe afterward if you're a good boy."

"Heather, if I were a good boy, you wouldn't be here right now."

She certainly made me want to please her. I thought about how things hadn't worked out with Nicole on this front and was greatly relieved to realize that maybe *she* had been the exception, and *this,* now, here, was the rule. How from now on I'd just be back to normal, good to go, gentlemen start your engines. And then, while she continued stroking my dick, Heather looked at me and said, "Tell me, are you wondering if I have doubts about you? Do you think that maybe I think you really did rape her?"

My God. The effect of her questions could not have been quicker or more embarrassing. Not only did my dick shrink, my whole image of myself as a man shrank as well. Were her questions meant to let me know that, actually, she wasn't sure about me? That she harbored suspicions, despite the whole conversation we'd had – despite her words to Supercop? I wanted her to get off my sofa, put her clothes on, and get the hell out. But she continued to stroke me.

"What's going on?" she said. And then: "Wait a second;

you didn't think I was serious right now, did you? Come on! Do you actually think I'd consider fucking you if I thought there was any chance you're a rapist?"

I didn't answer. Her words made sense, but in a way, they didn't matter, because I wasn't there anymore. My desire had vanished. I no longer needed her to get out, but I didn't want sex either. She hadn't gotten the memo: Her hands were still trying to bring me back to life. Touching, caressing, holding, tugging, grabbing, playing. And all for naught. It wasn't working. How could it, after questions like those?

Heather reached for my face and began caressing my cheeks with one hand. She came closer to me. I thought she wanted to kiss me, but she didn't. She brought her lips close to my ear, not my mouth. And then, with her other hand still wrapped around my cock, a source of shame right then, she whispered, "If I had even the slightest doubt, I wouldn't have looked after you the way I did during the whole police thing. I could have said: 'Listen, he didn't rape *me*, but what do I know? We met only once. I don't really know him.' I could have said that, and I didn't."

I said nothing. In the meantime, she continued performing a miraculous combination of sorts: one hand caressing my cock, which was beginning to demonstrate surprising and wonderful signs of recovery, the other hand caressing my cheek, her mouth uttering soft nothings in my ear. "I fought for you, Cayden. Do you think I would have put up a fight like that if I had doubted you? Let's put it this way: If everyone who was questioned by the police spoke about you the way I did, then you're in excellent shape."

These words also had a quick and powerful effect on

me. It seemed we were back in business. In fact, I was so hard that it almost hurt. Heather could feel my miraculous recovery: She placed her hands on my shoulders, gently pushed me back, leaned forward, and took me in her mouth. Deep. All at once. And then she gagged. Her eyes watered. I panicked, pulled my cock out of her mouth, and put a little distance between us.

"Sorry," I said.

"For what?"

I shrugged. "For making you gag?"

"You're a sweetheart, Cayden. Hold on, let's try again. No gagging this time. Don't move."

She bent over me again and wrapped her lips around my cock, slowly sliding them down the shaft. Bit by bit, I watched as took me in her mouth. I could feel the head of my cock rubbing up against the back of her throat.

I placed my hands on her shoulders, with the intention of pushing her away from me and pulling out before she gagged again. But Heather was one step ahead of me, and did the exact opposite: She placed her hands on my hips, gripped me tight, and pulled me towards her, all at once, quickly, with a force I hadn't been prepared for. She simply swallowed me entirely. I could feel my whole cock thrusting hard into her mouth, pushing down her throat, and sliding deep into a wild fantasy I had never before realized could be a reality. Until then. My cock was actually in her throat. It felt different there than just in her mouth. It was tighter and narrower, and the sensation was different too. It was simply unlike anything I'd ever felt before. A mind-blowing experience the likes of which most men would probably never get to experience.

I looked down at the magnificent spectacle before me. My cock had disappeared inside her. Completely. I could feel her nose brushing against my stomach and her chin pressing against my balls. There was nothing left for me to offer. And I didn't resist. I got the message. She knew what she was doing; this wasn't a first for her. It was amazing, startling, delightful, shocking, incomprehensible, arousing, enticing, weird, wild, and mesmerizing. And, above all, it was almost scarily sexy. I didn't dare move with my cock deep in her throat like that, but I felt that if I didn't pull out now, I would explode in there. So, I pulled out.

"Cayden," Heather said. "Why did you do that?"

"Because I knew I wasn't going to be able to hold on much longer."

"So?" she said. "What's wrong with that? I was all ready for you to – "

"Not yet. But it's good to know I can."

We had sex for the first time since Jade. And then she did her "thing" to me again. Several times actually. As many times as I wanted. I found myself wondering why a woman would do such a thing. Did it actually give her pleasure? It seemed like it did, but was I naïve to think a woman could enjoy it? I wanted to reciprocate – tried to! – but she waved me off. This, apparently, was meant to be all about me.

She had a fixed ritual, which consisted of leaning over me, placing her hands on my ass or hips, wrapping her lips tight around my cock, pulling me towards her and anchoring me deep in her mouth at the same time, stopping, tilting her head back to create a very specific angle between her mouth and throat, and then sliding me in for the second part of that wonderful journey: into her throat. The experience was so powerful in every way that I completely forgot about the question she'd asked me before, the one that had offended me. And that wasn't the only thing I forgot. I forgot I was a rape suspect. I forgot about the fact that I could still end up going to jail. I forgot everything. And in the end, I accepted her invitation to do what I had almost been unable to stop myself from doing till that moment. This time I didn't pull out when I felt I was close. The sensation was so strong when I came that I actually went blind for a second.

"Wow, Heather, I – "

"Yes, I know," she smiled. "You came so deep in my throat that I couldn't even taste your cum."

"Do you always do that?"

"Seriously?" she said. "Do you really think so? I didn't do it last time we had sex. And I also had no intention of doing it this time. I only do it with boyfriends, or in very special cases."

"Special cases?"

"Yes, like in the case of a traumatized man who was badly hurt by a joke he didn't understand."

—

After Heather showered, I told her she could help herself to a pair of sweatpants and a top from my closet, and then I showered too. When I came out, I saw her wearing a tank top bearing the logo of my favorite nightclub – a souvenir from a party marking its fifth anniversary. The logo was an illustration of a dog whose tail was not a tail but rather a cat's head. A half-dog-half-cat. Looking at it, I was reminded of the life I used to have. I flashed back to the dance floor there, where I'd often gone with friends. To hang out. To let go. To dance. To have fun. For a few seconds, the memory was so strong that I could actually hear the music, smell the cigarettes and the cannabis, and taste the drink in my hand.

I went to the refrigerator, retrieved the pack of Propecia pills, and took one. Now that I knew I could function properly in the sex department, I could start taking the medication. If I were to have any impotence issues, I'd know it was from the pills, and not from a woman aversion.

—

Heather stayed the night, and at noon the next day, after coffee on the balcony, she suggested that we take advantage of the beautiful weather and do something nice together – go out to a café, walk around, and be social. But I didn't feel like it. I didn't want to see people.

"You go," I said. "Really; make plans. I'll take you wherever you want to go, on my bike."

Heather arranged to meet a friend; my plan was to go to my usual café and continue working on the book. I unlocked my bike and gave Heather my leather biker jacket.

"Must I?" she complained. "It's so heavy; so uncomfortable. And we're not even going far."

"Fatal accidents can happen on short rides too," I said. I sounded like an old man, but I didn't care. I reminded myself that the phrase *it can't happen to me* had been erased from my vocabulary.

"And what would I say to your mother? *Hi, it's Cayden*

Chase; remember me? Is the guy responsible for the questioning your daughter underwent at the police station? Yes, it's me, again. Listen, I'm here at the hospital now. We were in a motorcycle accident. Heather's in the ICU."

"Okay," she laughed. "Point taken."

On my way to drop off Heather, while driving east, we found that the start-up capital's main road was blocked off. Thousands of protestors were walking there, holding the flags of Hungary and Poland. It was a weird sight, to see the flags of other countries being waved around. I had never seen anything like it. In fact, a stranger might have gotten the wrong impression – as if this were some kind of demonstration in support of Hungary and Poland. But I wasn't a stranger, and this wasn't a demonstration of support. The protestors were trying to issue a warning about how we were in danger of *becoming* like Hungary and Poland, if the parliament were to go ahead and approve the big legal reforms that the government was trying to promote. They argued, among other things, that the influence of the government over the choice of judges would politicize the judiciary.

Were the protestors' fears justified? A politicized judiciary would have been bad news *for me*, that's for sure. I mean, the only reason I wasn't locked up in a small cell right now, as the police had requested in court, was that the judiciary was *not* politicized. The court was the Iron Dome that protected me from the state's brutality. Both of the judges who had been handling my case, Judge Benny from the magistrate's court and Judge Judith from the district court, were super professional. They weren't afraid of possible public criticism for having declined the police's request to arrest me, and they didn't care about anything that wasn't relevant to my case: not my age, not my gender, not my being a well-known TV reporter, not the support that Jade had gotten from the National Women's Organization for Sexual Assault Victims. By the way, although I'm using the words "they didn't care," the real truth is, and forgive my language, it actually seemed to me even more than that: They didn't give a *fuck* about any of this stuff. Not the man Judge Benny, and not the woman Judge Judith. They were above all that. It's not that they were above the law, they *were* the law, and they cared about one thing and one thing only: the evidence.

I turned my head to Heather, and said: "We should turn around and go west."

CHAPTER
THIRTY-NINE

*T*he next morning, I woke up late; I'd been writing until four in the morning, still the best form of therapy for me. I didn't remember putting my phone on silent, but when I opened my eyes and checked, I suddenly saw there were 19 missed calls and dozens of texts. I flew out of bed. Something had happened. No doubt something bad. My stomach clenched.

After reading a few of the messages, I understood that for the previous few hours, I'd been the subject of a public internet shaming, beginning with a blog by an online activist for sexual assault victims. I didn't get it; I didn't know how this could be happening. I called Marcel.

"According to the court's ruling, your case is still under a gag order, and violating it is a criminal offense," he said. "That's why the mainstream media haven't been reporting on it."

"So then shouldn't we file a complaint against her?"

Marcel laughed a kind of bitter laugh. "Forget about it, Cayden," he said. "There's no point; she'll never be punished. You'll just make a hero out of her."

I opened the blog to find that its writer described herself as a "feminist, humanist, professional in the public sphere, who reads, writes, reacts, has an opinion on every issue, coupled with an increasingly thick skin and sharp perception." Earlier that morning, she had posted a text with the title, "The Code: A Gag Order."

It's a story that will never be told, about an individual familiar to many (more so to some than others), a woman familiar to no one, and the unequal interaction between the two, during the course of which one is alleged to have raped the other, so brutally that "vicious" doesn't begin to describe it.

Then her conspiracy theory, regarding gag orders in general:

An excellent way of protecting people in positions of authority, members of the media or judiciary, the wealthy and politically connected, and politicians from the consequences of their actions. And thus, they are able to avoid paying a social price for their wrongdoing, to have their cake and eat it, and to continue with their lives undisturbed. This story will illustrate that.

I assumed that the price, according to her way of thinking, was the embarrassment and shame involved in media exposure, and that I was an excellent example of the *politically connected*, an individual who got away without paying the price, thanks to the unique gag order tool.

I was losing my mind, reading all of this. The law stipulates that *every suspect* has the right to request a gag order, and many do so and are granted one, including those with limited means who are represented free of charge by lawyers from the Public Defender's Office.

I can imagine her voice. So here is what I have to say to you: I wholeheartedly believe the woman who filed the complaint. Her friends describe her as a trustworthy individual, an upstanding woman with values. I hope with all my heart that she will have the wherewithal to file a civil suit and take every penny of your money, even if your money disgusts her. Do you think you've managed to avoid paying the necessary social and professional price? Well, think again.

When I read the words, *I can imagine her voice*, I assumed this person had actually heard Jade's voice. But I soon discovered that, no, she'd never met Jade, had never spoken to her. In a talkback underneath the post, she explained to a reader that the entire blog had been based on things that Jade's friends had said about her, because "Jade's mental condition" had been too severe for an in-person meeting, or even a phone call. *Not even a phone call! What??* A few weeks before I had told myself that logic had left the building, and paranoia had taken its place. And of course, the stain had moved in too. And now there was another new resident in this scary building: absurdity.

I remembered Marcel's words just about an hour ago, when I suggested filing a complaint against her. But I wanted a second opinion, so I called Anna and asked her to help me to get one. She knows many of the best lawyers in the start-up capital, she interviews them for her stories on channel 4. She said she would contact a lawyer named Yaheli Ruth Cohen, apparently "the best one for gag orders in the country".

A few minutes later, Anna texted me. It was the second opinion. She forwarded Yaheli Ruth Cohen's message:

"Amor Fati dear Cayden, love your fate, as Nietzsche said. Or in my words: Don't tease your fate, sit down, be quiet, and pray that the case against you will be closed. Remember this: In the start-up capital, all you need to convict an innocent man and throw him in jail is a determined and convincing accuser, a lazy criminal lawyer, and a cowardly judge."

I read the post that the activist for sexual assault victims had published again. At first, I decided not to read any more comments; then, of course, I read them all.

Accurate and wonderful post – thanks!

Who's the guy? If you tell me, I'll make sure the son of a bitch's name gets out there!

Good luck to the complainant; she has my support and understanding!

This rapist is disgusting!

This particular blog was the main source of my public shaming, but hardly the only one. A little while later, similar posts by others started appearing, and of course were immediately shared on Facebook, Instagram, TikTok, and Twitter.

For the rest of the day, my family and I received dozens of phone calls and messages from friends and acquaintances. My mother solved the problem by switching off her phone and getting into bed. I poured myself a glass of whiskey.

Then another. And then one more. Then it was off to bed for me, where I closed my eyes and tried to remain optimistic. After all, tomorrow was a new day, right?

CHAPTER
FORTY

*J*ust like the bad old days, it was five in the morning by the time I fell asleep. But then, a minute later, it was ten-thirty, and my phone rang. An unlisted number. I didn't answer. It rang again. The police. Fingerless was on the line, asking me how I was doing.

"I've been better," I said. Fingerless chuckled, but I thought I could hear some nervous tension in his laugh.

"I'm calling to let you know that we're going to court this afternoon at three o'clock. To request the lifting of the gag order."

It was like another crushing blow to the head. Although a few bloggers had already violated the gag order, and many people knew about the whole affair, I believed that *most* people still *didn't* know because, as Marcel said, the mainstream media hadn't violated it. Lifting the gag order was a game changer. As a journalist myself, I knew very well what would happen if and when they lifted it. All the footage from the court, all those hundreds of pictures and videos of me sitting there embarrassed on the bench, would burst onto people's TV screens and the front pages of their newspapers. I was so terrified that I couldn't speak.

"Cayden? Are you there?"

"I'm here," I said. "Why are you doing this to me? The investigation is over. So why now? I would have understood earlier when other people might have come forward. But now? Why?"

"Because as far as we're concerned," Fingerless said, "the order is no longer required."

"Okay, I get it, *but why now?* Where's the logic? The media are going to crucify me! Why can't you wait? If I'm indicted, okay then, lift the gag order, go ahead, tear me to shreds. But if the case is closed, then why do this to me?"

"We've got no choice, Cayden. It's not my decision," Fingerless said. "We've been instructed to do this."

When we hung up, I did the only thing I could think to do, even though a part of me just wanted to crawl into bed and stay there forever. I called Marcel. What I mean is that I tried to call, but my hands were shaking so badly that I dropped my brother's loaner: It fell from my fourth-floor balcony all the way down to the ground below. I grabbed my house keys and started running down the steps, hoping that my SIM card had survived. It was only when I got to the second-floor landing that I muttered to myself, *Have you lost your mind?* I ran back up and called Marcel from my landline.

"Motherfuckers!" he yelled when I gave him the news.

257

"They're playing dirty. Let me see what I can do."

This time I made my way all the way down to the ground floor, only to find that the SIM card had not, in fact, survived the fall. I picked up the broken pieces. What a morning. My life was beginning to resemble my ruined phone. I took a deep breath and climbed back up. I needed air. I needed a new SIM card. I needed a new phone. I needed a new life. I needed alcohol.

About an hour later, Marcel called. It turned out there would be a court hearing before Judge Benny, the same judge from the magistrate's court who declined the police's request to extend my remand. Marcel would try to persuade him that lifting the order was pointless, since the investigation had already come to an end. He promised me he'd "take the police to the cleaners in the courtroom."

I returned to my computer and quickly discovered that the online attacks had intensified. Another activist had posted that Jade had been "hospitalized for a full week after the rape." The rape, according to what this woman posted, had been so brutal that Jade would never be able to have children.

"Fucking fake news!" I shouted at the top of my lungs.

Nobody gave a shit about the truth anymore, as long as the story was good. They even created a hashtag for the whole damn thing: #JailCaydenChase. Out of desperation, I tried to see the glass as half full: maybe Jade really *couldn't* have children. Maybe the spell I'd put on her had worked. Ha.

I doubled over in my chair, clutched my stomach. I had recently contemplated going back to the gym, but now I saw that there was no way. No way! I couldn't imagine even stepping outside my door.

I was ill. I hadn't really given it much thought until now – the shame, that is. I had thought about the stain, but not about the shame. The stain referred to what others thought of me, but the shame referred to what I felt about myself. Pure shame, an evil, and poisonous shame, it could eat you up inside if you let it. At first, logic had left the building and paranoia had taken its place. And then another new resident joined: stain. And then absurdity. And now it was a shame. What a horrible building.

I called my mother to prepare her for the possibility that whatever she was reading on the internet was just a hint of things to come, since the police were asking for the gag order to be lifted.

And then I came to a decision: I was going to put myself under house arrest. Yes. The thing that I had been so eager to free myself of, the court-ordered house arrest? Well, now I wanted it back. I wanted it more than anything, in fact. I was simply too ashamed to show my face in public. I tried calling my Australian buddy, Catherine, on FaceTime but she didn't answer. I tried again on WhatsApp. Nothing. Strange. Catherine usually answered pretty quickly.

Then again, perhaps not so strange at all.

—

I woke up to an interesting tidbit. A well-known and respected crime reporter for a major radio station, posted the following on her Facebook page:

Just a heads-up: The storm surrounding the investigation into the Channel 3 news correspondent is nothing more than a tempest in a teapot. The correspondent was questioned and found to be telling the truth, with the investigation culminating in the fact that there had been no rape. The State Prosecution found no cause for an indictment, and the case has been closed. Thanks to the police investigation, the correspondent was spared any injustice. Believe me . . .

This crime reporter didn't say a word about any of this in her formal radio broadcast; she posted it only on her private social media platform. And she was violating the gag order too, just like the online activist who had subjected me to public internet shaming. Two different women who didn't know me and had never even met me committed the same criminal offense, and yet the first did it to hurt me and the second to protect me.

I still wasn't jumping for joy, of course, because as Marcel had said, this whole thing would only come to an end when I received an official document from the State Prosecution. Naturally, the crime reporter's post reassured me, but I still didn't get it: If the case was closed, why hadn't the State Prosecutor's Office published its decision? And why were the police insisting on lifting the gag order now?

I realized something then: I'd had enough. I'd been sitting around too long doing nothing but waiting. I'd become a passive eunuch of a man, and I was tired of it. And so I decided to get active. To make some calls and inquiries. Enough was enough; the investigation had run its course. I began looking into the motives behind the crime reporter's Facebook post and found that, yeah, the State Prosecutor's Office had decided to close the case, but this decision had yet to be published because of "bureaucratic issues." Fuck bureaucracy. I also discovered that the request to lift the gag order had come from the very top. The reason? The online criticism against the police's alleged use of the gag order to protect me. I guess the way they saw it, better for me, the so-called famous news reporter, to suffer than for them to be criticized. Fuck that too.

I tried once more to get ahold of Catherine, but I couldn't. Now I really began to feel suspicious. Maybe she had run my name through a Google search? And after doing some reading, decided to put as much distance as she could between the two of us. *Fuck, my stain was going global!* I sent her a message, asking if she was angry with me.

CHAPTER
FORTY-ONE

"**W**ake up, sleepy head!" Marcel yelled cheerily into the phone the next morning. "I've got good news for you!"

Really? I couldn't take the ups and downs anymore. "They haven't closed the case against me, have they?" I asked.

"No," Marcel said. "But the court – I mean Judge Benny – has upheld our request for the gag order!"

Marcel suggested that we meet for breakfast; he wanted to show me the minutes of the court's ruling. He proposed a café, but I didn't want to be seen in public, so we decided he would come to me. I went to the kitchen to prepare breakfast: I made shakshuka with four eggs, put out some gourmet cheeses, and served an excellent bread on the side that I'd purchased the night before. Then I made a big salad with Tamar cherry tomatoes, cucumbers, bell peppers, carrots, radishes, canned corn, romaine lettuce, and olive oil. It was my favorite combination. It was perfect. In my opinion, they should start putting this salad on cafe menus and call it *"that amazing salad from Cayden's book."*

When Marcel arrived and showed me the official document, I realized that the title, just as before, read, "The State vs. Cayden Chase," but the State itself wasn't really against me this time. It remained on the sidelines, on the fence and uninvolved, as the police laid out in its request to the court:

> *At present, there are no legal grounds for the gag order as the investigation has been completed. The court may or may not decide to grant the gag order request filed by the suspect at its own discretion.*

I read the minutes of the court's decision and realized that Judge Benny had understood the politics behind the police's request. According to his ruling, he gave the police exactly what they'd requested: "The court makes it clear that the gag order now in effect is as a result of the suspect's request."

And that was exactly what the police had wanted: proof that they were not protecting me because of my status as a television reporter. That was it; they were not my protectors. Their hands were clean.

Judge Benny, my own personal Iron Dome against the state's brutality, had made a brave decision. He understood why the police had made their request. Now he was the "guilty" one, and I was sure it was only a matter of time until he became the new online target of cooked-up hate.

My new phone with the new SIM card I'd purchased

didn't stop ringing, but I ignored it. I fussed over Marcel, making him another cup of coffee, trying to fatten him up with cookies and chocolate. He ate my guardian angel and invited me to join him, but I still had no appetite. When he was done with breakfast, we sat together in the living room. He asked me for a cigarette. Apparently, like me, he'd taken up smoking again after many years of being abstinent; it seems I'd spread the wealth.

We ignored our phones and sat there chatting, enjoying the relief of having overcome the last obstacle before the big one. All that was left to do now was quietly wait for the final decision.

We smoked another cigarette, or two, or five. After Marcel left, I turned on my laptop, taking a deep breath before diving into the latest horrors. So, what had they written about me today? I began typing my name, but before I'd even finished, the search engine presented me with the most recent popular search options: "Cayden Chase raped," "Cayden Chase rape," "Cayden Chase under arrest," "Cayden Chase arrested," "Cayden Chase suspect." No punches were pulled; Google was without sentiment. The algorithms slapped me in the face with reality.

It was two in the afternoon now, and I could relax a bit, but I knew that the adrenaline in my veins would make it hard for me to fall asleep. I was quite familiar with this feeling by now. I poured myself a double shot of whiskey to speed up the process, downing it all in one gulp.

The whiskey did the trick. When I woke up, I turned on the computer, saw that there was a message from Catherine, and actually gasped out loud. I was going to get my answer now. I was going to find out what she'd read about me, what she thought about me, whether she hated me or was disgusted by me. I was going to be smacked across the face with the fact that, yes, my stain had indeed gone global. I closed my eyes, clicked on the message, then slowly opened one eye. "Hi, honey," it read. "Angry with you? Why would I be angry with you? What's up?"

CHAPTER FORTY-TWO

I had every reason to expect that any day now I would be hearing from the State Prosecutor's Office, telling me that the case was closed. Maybe today, maybe tomorrow, maybe the day after. Who knew? It was a crazy nerve-wracking time, and fortunately, Anna showed up to help me wait it out. But I could tell from the look on her face that something was up.

"What?" I said.

"No," she said, "nothing."

"Not nothing," I said. "Something. I can tell."

She tried to keep things light and casual, but the words she said made me sick. "There's this rumor out there," she said. "But, actually, even the word rumor is too strong. There's just this one person who seems to think the State Prosecution is going to file an indictment. But Cayden, listen, even he said it might just be talk."

I fell to the couch. I put my head in my hands. How was I going to survive this? Did this mean they believed Jade's version of events? Or that they thought I'd manipulated her into saying what she'd said on the recording? Maybe I failed the polygraph? After all, I knew I'd done poorly with one of the questions! And I remembered there was a 10 percent chance that the polygraph could brand me a liar, even though I'd been telling the truth. This fucking Russian roulette! Was I getting a bullet to the head?

The whiskey bottle was empty, and it was the last one. I went to the freezer to take out the bottle of Grey Goose, my favorite vodka, but it was fucking empty too. I wanted to *blame it on the Goose*, in the immortal words of Jamie Foxx, but no, this one was on me. All on me. On top of everything else, I feared I was becoming an alcoholic.

I needed the alcohol now. Not in ten seconds; not in five. Now. But there was no alcohol in the house, only bad thoughts. Most men who were indicted for rape charges went to jail. That was the simple fact. I was sitting, but it felt as if I were moving. Dead man walking, exactly as I had predicted.

Anna was looking at me with concern, but I shrank down inside myself and didn't care. The stress was killing me. My heart was pounding so violently that I could hear my pulse in my head. Or was I imagining things? Could one feel one's pulse in such a way? I was sinking deeper and deeper into an abyss, plunging, dying to hit bottom already so I'd know I could go no further.

I dialed Marcel with a shaking hand. "Why haven't we heard from the State Prosecutor's Office?" I demanded.

"Why haven't we been told that the case has been closed?"

"I don't know," Marcel said. "Listen, from a legal perspective, my assessment hasn't changed. The signs are good, but – "

"But what?"

"I have a feeling – and I want to emphasize it's just a feeling – that there's a fight going on. In the State Prosecutor's Office."

"You mean between the people who want to indict and the people who don't?"

"Yes, maybe," Marcel said. "But it's just a feeling. Look, again, nothing has changed from a legal perspective. But because of all the online fuss, they may be concerned about being pilloried if they don't indict. In principle, it shouldn't make any difference, but you know how it is."

"Yes. I mean, no. I don't know how it is. Not really. But I guess I have no choice but to know. Listen, Marcel, I'm dying here; what are the chances the case will be closed?"

"Complacency is a criminal defense lawyer's worst enemy," Marcel said, "so I want to remain cautious."

Dear lord, not that line again. I hated that line. The first time he'd used it, regarding the house arrest, he'd said there was an 80% chance that things would work out in my favor. I was afraid to hear the number now.

"The chances are still good, Cayden," he said. "I don't know, let's say around 70 or 75 percent."

No. No. That was not the number I'd been looking for, and now I only felt more desperate. I reached for another cigarette; I lit up. The statistics only went from bad to worse. If the truth played any role at all in this, it was hard to see what. It seemed to be just one mere factor out of many, and not the most significant one.

"In any event," Marcel said, "don't forget that I've asked for a hearing in case they do decide to indict."

When I didn't respond, Marcel continued, "That's where they have to reveal everything – all the confidential material that they gathered during the investigation – and then we get to make our case for why they're mistaken and why they should close the case."

"Do these hearings ever do any good?" I managed to say. "Does the State Prosecutor's Office ever actually change its mind and decide not to indict?"

"Yes," Marcel said. "Of course."

I took a deep breath and decided to chance it. "What about in a rape case?" I said. "Has a decision in a rape case ever been reversed after one of these hearings?"

He paused. "Listen, Cayden, I don't know offhand. I'd need to check."

The bottom never came. There was no bottom.

I wanted to climb out of my body, out of my very self, and run as far as I could. Anna was on the balcony, talking on the phone, which was just as well; I wouldn't have been able to hide how I was feeling. I looked again at the picture of Jade receiving the certificate from the animal aid organization. I had asked Anna to print it out for me when I discovered it online, and now I kept it in my wallet, for God only knew what reason.

I looked at the text below the picture. I focused on the words "Thank you" and "We love you." I freaked out but for a different reason than the first time I'd seen those words.

Back then, I'd been confused by the idea that one person could contain so much good and so much evil; it had been almost impossible for me to reconcile the two. But now it was something different. New. Something stronger, darker, something that till now hadn't even crossed my mind: Was it possible that I actually *had* raped Jade? Maybe I'd lost it that night and just couldn't remember. Maybe I had temporarily become someone else, but blocked it all out for some reason? Or maybe exactly the opposite – maybe I had become *myself* temporarily and not someone else? Maybe I was just like my mother? After all – she had shown herself capable of something pretty damned horrible, and then acted as if nothing had happened. Maybe I was just my mother's son.

For the first time since being thrown into this hell, more than two months earlier, I felt my strength waning. And my awareness of my waning strength only increased my anxiety. In my current condition, if I'd been required to undergo one of Heavy Metal's 10-hour interrogations I would have been in trouble. Huge trouble. In front of the hidden cameras, I could almost see myself admitting to the possibility that I did it – that I raped her. Never before had I been able to understand how someone could confess to a crime he hadn't committed. But now I understood it. I felt it. It was a risk I didn't even know I was taking.

My mother called and immediately realized that something was wrong.

"No, Mom, I'm fine," I said.

"I don't believe you," she said. "I know you, and I know you're not fine," and then she burst into tears.

I tried to reassure her, telling her that really everything

was the same, everything was okay, but at a certain point I just couldn't do it anymore, and I told her I had to go, and that Anna was there with me. I knew she wasn't convinced, but I couldn't stay on the line and wait for her to calm down. I couldn't help anyone right now. I couldn't help myself. I was sinking. I hung up and noticed Anna staring at me.

"You're having a panic attack, Cayden."

"Nah," I said. "This is my life, Anna. This is my new normal."

"No, this is a panic attack," she repeated. "And you need to deal with it."

Some 20 minutes later, Megan showed up, bearing a handful of benzos. When Anna had been out on the balcony talking on the phone, this was the plan she'd been cooking up. I looked at my two saviors standing there now together. Apparently, my house arrest had been the beginning of a beautiful friendship.

"Are you fucking crazy?" Megan said to me. "This is the first time you're medicating yourself? During this whole horrific experience? You're like one of those weird, brave women who gives birth without an epidural."

Looking at the two of them standing over me reminded me of the alternating shifts they'd taken at my apartment a few weeks back. I was having a panic attack: not the best time for flashbacks to my house arrest. I wanted to consult with a doctor before swallowing a pill that would mess with my head, but I was too embarrassed to call any of the psychiatrists I knew through work. Anna took care of this for me too. She used her own connections, putting me in touch with a psychiatrist who told me to take one orange

0.5-milligram tablet.

"Take two," Anna said when I hung up, and she seemed so confident that I did.

An hour later, I was feeling no pain. I didn't feel joy, but at least I was calm. A little drowsy too. But my mind was still sharp, and now that the panic had subsided, I decided to do the obvious thing, the thing I should have done earlier: check out the actual situation. I made a few calls and within the hour I had my answer. The rumor was, in fact, incorrect. At present, the State Prosecutor's Office had decided not to indict me, but they delayed the publication "until the fuss on the internet dies down a little." Fuckers.

Still, the bottom line seemed to be good; I knew it wasn't definite, and that I could only hope that this answer was truer than the rumor had been. But I was shocked by the way I'd let the whole episode paralyze me, the way I hadn't done what I ordinarily would have done in such circumstances: investigated.

"It's not that surprising," Anna said when I said all this to her. "You should know this. You're a health affairs correspondent, for heaven's sake; you're very dumb for a smart person. Panic attacks are real."

"It's just that this was the first time during all of this that I really lost control," I said. "I really just lost it. And I'd been so on top of everything before."

"Well, now you know," Anna said. "It's like after you get your wisdom teeth out. You should never wait till the pain becomes unmanageable, because then it's harder to beat. Same here. Next time, pop a pill before things go south."

I called my mother to tell her about the results of my

inquiries, but I spared her my reasons for conducting them in the first place. My updates were very selective, and I left out the scary details.

CHAPTER FORTY-THREE

"You have to open the link I just sent you on WhatsApp," Anna said. "Read it now."

So I opened it and found myself on a website that I'd never seen before

Free Cayden Chase!

Dear Celebs: We need your help to liberate Cayden Chase! As three women united for a common cause, we ask you to support Cayden, a Channel 3 news correspondent facing a false sexual assault allegation. You've all endured the anguish and humiliation of false accusations:

1. Johnny Depp: In 2018 your ex-wife described herself as a "public figure representing domestic abuse" in an op-ed she wrote for the *Washington Post*. In her testimony during the April-June 2022 defamation trial, she accused you of sexual violence, but you won the case. The jurors found that your ex-wife's accusations were false, and that she had acted

with "actual malice." In your reaction to the verdict, you wrote: "I hope that my quest to have the truth be told will have helped others." So, Johnny, will you help us get justice for Cayden Chase?

2. Justin Bieber: In 2020 you were the victim of a false sexual assault claim in Houston, Texas dating from 2014. A Twitter account from a woman known only as Danielle claimed that after a surprise performance in front of a small crowd at a bar, you invited her and two friends to the Four Seasons Hotel, where the sexual assault happened. You denied the accusation, and tweeted: "This story is factually impossible... As her story said, I did surprise a crowd in Austin at SXSW where I appeared on stage with my then-assistant side stage and sang a few songs. What this person did not know was that I attended that show with my then-gf Selena Gomez." So, Justin, will you assist us in freeing Cayden Chase?

3. Neymar: In 2019 you were accused of rape by a Brazilian model with whom you became acquainted on Instagram, and then met with at a hotel in Paris. In response, you posted on Instagram – "My world has come crashing down and hit the ground" – and claimed that you were the victim of an attempted extortion. You said that it was consensual sex, and after the case was closed and the woman was charged with fraud by the Brazilian police, you said: "I hope it isn't just a new beginning for me but for all those who have suffered from false accusations." So, Neymar, now someone else is suffering from false accusations. Will you help us free Cayden Chase?

4. Cole Sprouse: In 2020 you denied allegations of sexually assaulting a woman when you were studying at New York University, after an anonymous Twitter user claimed you forced yourself on her at a party in 2013. The user wrote, "I told him multiple times to stop, he wouldn't listen. By then I'm

in tears and gagging from the alcohol smell on his breath." You tweeted that "false accusations do tremendous damage to victims of actual assault." So, Cole, will you continue fighting against this kind of damage and help us free Cayden Chase?

5. Jamie Foxx: In 2018 *TMZ* reported that you were accused of sexual misconduct, by a woman who claimed you slapped her with your penis in Las Vegas 16 years before, in 2002, after she refused your request for oral sex. You said the allegation was "absurd," and your attorney Allison Hart added: "Jamie Foxx emphatically denies that this incident ever occurred, and he will be filing a report with the Las Vegas Police Department against the woman for filing a false police report against him." So, Jamie, we really hope you win another Oscar with your new movie *Back in Action*, but in the meantime, will you take action and help us free Cayden Chase?

6. Ryan Seacrest: You were accused in 2017 of sexual abuse and harassment by a former stylist, ranging from verbal harassment to slapping and groping. You released a statement to *BuzzFeed* and claimed that "Ultimately, my name was cleared. I eagerly participated in the investigation in order to demonstrate my innocence... This person who has accused me of horrible things offered, on multiple occasions, to withdraw her claims if I paid her millions of dollars. I refused." So, Ryan, we're not asking for millions; we're just asking you to post or tweet. Will you help us free Cayden Chase?

7. Michael Douglas: NBC interviewed a woman in 2018 who worked for your production company as a writer, and accused you of sexual harassment 32 years before, during a work meeting in 1989. In an interview with *Deadline*, you said: "She claims that I masturbated in front of her. This is a complete lie, fabrication... My kids are really upset, have to go to school worrying this is going to be in some article about me, being

a sexual harasser. They're scared... It has been a complete nightmare... It hurts a lot more than just one person." So, Michael, given your firsthand experience, will you lend your support to helping us free Cayden Chase?

8. Seal: In 2018 *TMZ* reported that you were under criminal investigation for sexual battery, after a female actress filed a complaint. She claimed you became friends while living near each other in Los Angeles, when one day, in 2016, in your house, you forced yourself on her, attempting to kiss her and grope her breasts. You vehemently denied the allegations. A few weeks later, the L.A. County District Attorney's Office rejected the case. So, Seal, you haven't really said anything about all this, and you probably never will. However, will you help us free Cayden Chase?

Dear Celebs: While you've all moved on from these events, we're afraid that Cayden Chase won't get that same chance. Some activists may claim that − for the sake of the greater good − it's okay to have a few innocent casualties. But you know firsthand the cost of false accusations.

Help us prevent an innocent man from facing life-altering consequences. Use your massive social media followings to raise awareness and demand justice for Cayden Chase. You have millions of followers on social media − please use your platforms to post, publish, add to your story, share, and tweet in support of Cayden's cause.

We pledge to share updates on every celebrity who responds to our challenge on www.freecaydenchase.com and on the social media accounts of this campaign. Subscribe to get updates in real-time. With your powerful influence, we can get justice for Cayden Chase.

I read this text three or four times. I had no idea about all of these falsely accused celebs, did you? Will they help me? I promise to provide updates here in the next chapters, about every celeb that responds to the challenge.

I had mixed feelings about the Free Cayden Chase campaign. On the one hand, it warmed my heart. But on the other hand – why now? What did these three mysterious women know that I didn't? Were they, like Marcel, concerned that the State Prosecutor's Office might indict me simply because of all the online fuss? And who were they, anyway? Anna said she didn't have a clue; she knew nothing about it or them. Did I know them? Were they even real?

I sat on the balcony while Anna made a few phone calls to find out. After about two hours she showed me a TikTok profile of a young actress named Alina. She had 250K followers and a blue checkmark.

"Listen, Cayden, I know of her, but I don't know her in person, and although I've tried to figure it out, I have no idea why she's running this crazy Free Cayden Chase campaign for you. Are you sure you don't know her?"

"I'm sure, Anna."

But suddenly it hit me. I did know who she was: Supercop's actress friend, the one she sent the voice messages on WhatsApp while keeping watch over me at the police station, a few weeks back. I watched a bunch of her TikTok clips, hoping that maybe I could find the answer there. Unsurprisingly, I couldn't; but I did find out she was a good actress, that was for sure.

After googling her name, I found the explanation for her acting skills and passion: genetics. In an interview with *Frogi* a few months ago, she explained that her parents had been actors themselves, and had met while studying at an acting academy in Russia. When Alina was 6 years old, 20 years previously, her mother died after battling a difficult disease. Her father was not part of her life, she said, but she didn't know why, and she didn't ask for many years. Alina didn't explain in the interview why she hadn't tried to find out earlier. Perhaps it was the survival instinct of a clever child.

Alina's character intrigued me. Why was she helping me? After her mother died, she left Russia with her grandmother, who raised her in a northern suburb of the start-up capital. Only when she was 16 did she dare to ask. And then she found out that she was a "secret" daughter, the one no one knew about, from her father's side, who still lived in Russia. Her mother was the other woman, and her father's family didn't even know that she, Alina, existed. Maybe actresses could hide things like cheating parents and secret affairs more easily than other people could, because they were actresses? I wondered if Alina regretted asking the questions she'd asked, and not listening to the survival instinct that I'd made up for her in my mind.

CHAPTER
FORTY-FOUR

*T*he rest of the country was celebrating yet another major holiday, Independence Day this time. Why were there so many damn holidays? I had never noticed this before, but now I understood how it felt to be a person who was an outsider, during holiday season.

I had been invited to several parties and social gatherings, but I'd learned from Memorial Day, that I would be better off staying at home, alone. Nevertheless, beginning at around nine in the evening, the sounds and smells of other people's happiness drifted into my apartment from parties being held on nearby rooftops. I quickly closed all the windows and shutters in my apartment and turned up the music in my living room, but it didn't help. Nothing helped. Other people's happiness was so fucking obnoxious.

The fireworks began at around ten. The loud booms from outside managed to drown out even my powerful speakers, and I could see that the cats were getting jumpy. I ran over to Ian and clamped my hands down over his ears, hoping to prevent another epileptic fit. I hated holidays!

CHAPTER
FORTY-FIVE

I loved holidays! It was exactly two weeks after my country's Independence Day when I got to celebrate my own personal Independence Day. Early in the morning, Marcel woke me up with the news.

"Cayden, my boy," he said, "the State Prosecution has decided to close the case against you, due to lack of evidence."

I jumped out of bed, literally. I took a deep breath, and collected myself. I had to make sure I wasn't dreaming; honestly, I had to pinch myself to believe it. Another cliché, I know, but can't I be forgiven? A dead man was being given back his life.

"Marcel?"

"Yes, it's me."

"Is this definite? Is this it? Is it official?"

"Indeed, it is," he said. "Your nightmare is officially over."

"But . . . I mean . . . tell me more! Give me details!"

"I don't really have more," he said. "But I'm assuming that Jade has also gotten the news by now. They would have informed her as well."

"Yeah," I said, "I mean, right; I mean, I would assume so." Then I thought about it for a second. Was there a reason Marcel was telling me this obvious fact? Was there yet another thing I needed to be prepared for? I asked him.

"This whole thing really has done a number on you," he said. "Do me a favor: Put your paranoia on hold and go out and celebrate."

So, then this was really it; I was not going to be indicted, and there was nothing else I needed to worry about. I was actually going to get my life back – for real. Yes, a cause for celebration, and I would do Marcel his favor too; I'd put my paranoia on hold.

That night, at around 9:30, I met several friends at the Jimmy Who nightclub, to mark the auspicious occasion. DJ Jenia Tarsol was playing. God, I had missed my life! Within the hour, those several friends had morphed into dozens, and we moved to Sheket, a nightclub on the other side of the boulevard. But they weren't the only ones to show up: two paparazzi came too.

—

Starting at eight the next morning, I began to get text messages telling me to look at a website that had covered the previous night's festivities. I didn't want to be plunged into darkness again, so I ignored the suggestions and closed my laptop instead. I paid a visit to my mom and picked up some cakes she had baked to celebrate the closing of the case. And then, for the first time in months, I went over to Channel 3. I could have gone over earlier before the case was closed, but I hadn't. I had been ashamed to walk in there as a rape suspect. But I wasn't one anymore.

Shouts of "Hey, Cayden!" and "Welcome back!" greeted me when I walked in, and people gave me such hearty hugs that I believed they were sincerely happy for me. I continued on my way until I finally reached my true destination. When I arrived, I closed the door, leaned back in the chair behind my desk, and just smiled. My office; my beloved office! Ordinarily, I shared it with another correspondent, but he was out on the streets today, interviewing, allowing me time and space, and privacy to soak up the atmosphere on my own. I breathed deeply, inhaling the old familiar aroma of work. Of course, I wasn't working yet, but I was at work. It was a start, right? Damn, I'd missed this place.

It wasn't long before the door swung open. People don't seem to knock in newsrooms, other than on the boss's door. My two young junior correspondent colleagues, Emma and Olivia, burst into the room, hugging me.

"Cayden," Olivia cried, "it's so good to see you back here again! You *so* did not deserve to go through all that shit. Fuck. Unlike lots of other guys, you're not even a douchebag."

"High praise indeed!" I said. I was reminded of how during the confrontation with Jade at the police station, I had made the same argument and used the same word – douchebag. It was a difficult flashback. I remembered her exact answer then: "Now we have a new nickname for you, Gentleman Cayden. And I hope for you that the other prisoners don't take it the wrong way. I bet they like the gentle guys there, in jail." And then she winked. I will never forget that wink. I swear to God I will never wink again, even in emojis.

"Touché," Olivia said, with a smile. "But listen Cayden, I was just telling Emma here before we knocked – "

"Actually, you didn't – "

"Cayden," Olivia interrupted. "Just shut up and listen; I want to tell you something. I was just telling Emma that if I didn't have a boyfriend, you would be the perfect guy for a rape fantasy."

She must have seen all the color drain out of my face at the word "rape," because she quickly added, "Too soon?" These two clearly didn't think it *was*.

"Well, the perfect guy might be just a wee bit taller," Emma added, "No offense, of course . . . "

"None was taken," I said, laughing. "I missed your stupid shit, girls!"

"We missed you too, handsome," Emma said, "but unfortunately we've got work to do. The Mason corruption case; you know."

"Sure, sure," I said, shooing them out of my office so they could get back to work. Anyway, I didn't want them to see that I had no idea what they meant by the Mason corruption case. I had become utterly self-absorbed since this whole Jade thing started, tuning out the world around me.

So I was alone again, in my office, my beloved office. And then, and then . . . well, it didn't take long for me to get myself in trouble. If only I could have left well enough alone. But I couldn't. I switched on my computer and opened the gossip website I'd been told to look at.

Last night, one of our photographers captured images of correspondents and employees from Channel 3 News who were out celebrating with Cayden Chase at the Jimmy Who and Sheket nightclubs, who disappeared recently from our television screens. For those who have missed him, Chase is expected to return to work in the near future.

The report didn't violate the gag order, since it didn't contain details of the case itself. But the comments on the article were painful.

"Cayden Chase didn't disappear – he was under investigation because he's a rapist."

"Disgusting! Violates an innocent woman and celebrates! Simply nauseating."

"Unbelievable! The justice system will never be on women's side!"

This wasn't enough for me. No: I continued searching for more, and of course I found it. On her Facebook page, a well-known activist for sexual assault victims shared the story's link and wrote:

"So this is what justice looks like. The rapist is free and out celebrating at a pub; the victim shattered."

And then, among other comments, a dialogue between two of the writer's Facebook friends, printed there for all to see:

If I wasn't so exhausted, I'd go over there right now. If I go, will you come with me?

No, I won't be able to control myself.

Same here. But I don't care anymore.

What the hell is he celebrating, anyway? His freedom?

Probably. Makes me sick. It's hard for me to digest. And physically, he's so like the scumbag who sexually harassed me for four years; I feel like throwing acid in his face! But I have no idea how to get it.

I know how to get a bottle of acid. But I don't know his address.

It's okay, I know where the scumbag lives.

I read these lines several times. What was I supposed to do if I looked through my peephole and saw a bunch of women standing there ready to fling acid in my eyes? Seriously: What was I supposed to do? Open the door and confront them? Ignore them and hope they give up? But how long would that take? And what would I tell the neighbors?

According to Facebook, the well-known activist and I had 69 mutual friends – most of them women. The phrase "mutual friends" sounded so neutral and balanced, but in reality, many of these were much more my friends than hers; in fact, they had sent me private messages, added screenshots, and advised me to go to the police and file a complaint.

And that was just what I did, making it my fourth time at the police station in just two months. The first visit was my interrogation; the second (the day after) was when I endured the polygraph and the Jade confrontation; the third was when I told them about Jade's miraculous ability to closely examine my hair-care products while being in a vegetative state; and now this. Four times in my life. I hadn't ever had any run-ins with the police before Jade, and I really wanted to bring these new relationships – with Heavy Metal, Supercop, Thug, Fingerless, and Leather Jacket – to an end. As much as I liked them: enough!

I showed Supercop the Facebook printout of the entire discussion. She examined them in silence, then looked up at me and said, "We'll call them in for questioning."

"Under caution?"

"Yes, I believe so."

"Do you think they'll be charged with anything?"

"Hard to say right now."

As she was typing the details of my complaint into her computer, I couldn't help noticing the fact that she was wearing a leather jacket and fingerless gloves. What were the chances?

"By the way," Supercop said then. "I see here that Jade's lawyer filed an appeal. Yesterday. You should tell your lawyer."

CHAPTER
FORTY-SIX

*F*uck, I didn't even know Jade had a lawyer. Unlike me, she hadn't required one originally, but obviously she wasn't going to let this go, she was going to pursue this to the ends of the earth, till one or both of us was dead. I swallowed two orange pills and called Marcel the second I got out of the police station.

"Marcel –"

"I know," he said. "Jade filed. I just got a message from the State Prosecutor. But I don't think they'll accept it; they usually decline these kinds of appeals."

"Usually?" I asked, that old familiar feeling of dread in the pit of my stomach. I hadn't had much of a vacation from it. "Define 'usually' for me please?"

"I don't know. 90 percent? Or in your case maybe 80, because of the online criticism. I mean the – "

"I know who you mean, Marcel. I read every fucking

word they post."

"Well, you shouldn't, Cayden."

"I can't help it. It's like staring into a fire. You can't stop, even when it's your house that's burning. So, 80 percent, you say?"

"Cayden. Come on, stop already with the statistics. And stop worrying so much. You know why I'm being so cautious: Complacency is a criminal defense lawyer's worst enemy."

And here we went with that damn line again. Before this, I thought I'd hit bottom and was on my way up again; now I realized that maybe it had only been a pause on the way down. I was sinking. Nothing had changed. And the celebration with my friends felt stupid, premature, and embarrassing.

About an hour later, I still feared what potentially awaited me, but the pills had taken effect, and at least I was calmer. Also, I really wanted to go to the gym, which I took as a positive sign. I hadn't been there in almost three months, but now I could hold my head up high, right? I wasn't a rape suspect anymore. *Not a rape suspect* wasn't really what I'd want on my tombstone, but I supposed it was good enough for going back to the gym.

My hands were clammy and my stomach clenched up again; lots of women worked out at my gym. What if some of them had read the articles? And what if some of them had read the story on the gossip website, with pictures of me celebrating with friends? They had probably read the comments as well. Who knew? Maybe they'd even written some.

Despite my anxiety, a plan started taking shape in my

head, and not long after, I put in a call to Brittany, one of the gym's two best personal trainers. The other was Brad, but for the purposes of my plan, Brittany was the one to call.

"Hey, Brittany!" I said, as casual and light-hearted as possible. "Listen, I haven't worked out in a really long time. Can you fit me into your schedule? Today? Tomorrow? Whatever suits you."

"Sure," she said in a friendly tone and suggested six o'clock the next evening. I couldn't let it go at that.

"Listen, Brittany," I said. "Before we hang up, there's something I have to ask you." I cleared my throat. "Do you, um, know?"

"Yes, of course, I know, Cayden."

"Oh."

"Listen," she said. "In general, I would say, Who the hell knows what really happened? I mean, yes, I've worked with you a few times over the last few years, and you've always been nice. But let's face it; I don't really know you."

"Okay, Brittany. I think that."

"Hold on, Cayden," she said, "I'm not done. Do you remember that about a year ago, you went out with a girl named Silvia?"

"Yeah ... "

"She's a friend of mine. We talked about you recently, and she told me that on your second date, she invited you back to her apartment, and when she suddenly changed her mind and decided she didn't want to ... you know ... you backed off right away. She said, and I quote: 'If Cayden Chase is a rapist, then I'm a serial killer.' That's exactly what she said."

Well, thank God for Silvia. Who knew, back then, how much I would need someone like her in my life? I loved her.

Brittany let me take in this news and bask in it for a second; then she confidently confirmed our appointment. "So, we're on for six o'clock tomorrow evening," she said.

"Great," I said. "But listen one more thing: Would it be okay if we met outside and walked in together?"

"Of course," Brittany said, "whatever you're most comfortable with. Though I have to say, I think you're being a bit paranoid."

"Unfortunately, I keep finding out that I'm less paranoid than I should be," I said. "Speaking of which, if someone approaches me in the gym, and starts cursing me – "

"Then I'll rip her head off," Brittany said.

CHAPTER
FORTY-SEVEN

*I*t was a few minutes after six, and Brittany and I entered the gym together. It was pretty crowded there at the entrance, with two receptionists working busily at the counter. One was giving an update to three gym members about a change in the Pilates schedule; the other was on the phone. In total, I was surrounded by five women, plus Brittany. The receptionist on the phone smiled at Brittany, and then whispered to her, loud enough for me to hear, "Hey Brit, sweetheart, take a look at the bulletin board."

Brittany and I both turned around to look. Among the notices and advertisements was a copy of a post that had been written by one of the bloggers, entitled, "The whole truth about Cayden Chase." This one was accompanied by a picture of me. Actually, this was the post I had read a few weeks ago, right after it had been published. Indeed, it contained some details that were totally true, some that were partially true, and some that were downright false, like the one claiming that Jade had been "hospitalized for an entire week after the rape." Particularly evil was the seemingly accepted mixing of truth with falsehoods, which gave these publications the veneer of truth.

Brittany pulled the article down from the bulletin board with a yank, held it up in front of her, and scrutinized it carefully. And we scrutinized her carefully. All of us – the two female receptionists, the three female gym members, and of course, me. She had set up a real drama, and I for one was eager to see the next plot point. What would she do now?

After a few seconds, she crumpled the article into a small paper ball, assumed form, wound up, and aimed to land it in the wastebasket. It was a tough shot; the wastebasket was actually behind the counter. She took her time, seeming to carefully calculate the best position, and then tossed it elegantly over the receptionists' heads. Even if she'd missed, she'd already earned my respect and admiration. But she didn't miss. What a gal! But who knew how many other articles were posted on bulletin boards out there, in other places?

Afterward, during our training session, Brittany took a selfie of the two of us, and told me that she would post it later on her Instagram.

"You're amazing," I said to her, as I toweled myself off. "Not all heroes wear capes; some of them wear sneakers like you."

She shrugged and said, "Thanks Cayden; you're adorable." Then she told me not to forget to schedule our next session and greeted her next customer.

I knew that a lot of people would see the picture; after all, everyone knew Brittany. On Instagram, she had 90K followers. I found myself wondering whether she really would post it.

CHAPTER
FORTY-EIGHT

I woke up to a deluge of missed calls and text messages. Twenty-one calls in all. Something had happened. Something bad, I assumed. I wasn't paranoid, I was a realist. And tired.

It turned out that Jade had compiled her own version of the events of that cursed night. And over the past several hours, her side of the story had gone viral. It had initially appeared on a mysterious website named "Jail Cayden Chase," containing nothing but Jade's story. It had spread through the web like wildfire.

I quickly discovered that Jade had a PR person, who had been hired for her by the National Women's Organization for Sexual Assault Victims, and that the blog post out there was their handiwork. Given my line of work, I was quite familiar with the way these PR people worked. They used their skills and connections to persuade media outlets to publish stories about their clients, who were looking for exposure and publicity.

When I thought about Jade's efforts to grab media attention, I got the sense that she wanted to make a name for herself and become a celebrity. I wouldn't have been surprised to discover that at some point in the past, she had applied to be a contestant on a reality show. And now here she has another chance. I found myself picturing the inside of her mind, dotted with detailed fantasies about her path to celebrity status. There she was, being escorted to the makeup room, then invited into the air-conditioned studio. One of the studio employees would hand her a glass of cold water, and thus it would begin: The host of the show would thank her for "agreeing to the interview," adding that she was sure "it was very difficult for you," and that she "admired your courage." And Jade would say that she was "doing it for all the other women out there who've been subjected to the same criminal treatment I was but can't cry out for help," and not just "for myself."

She would of course burst into tears at some point. And her sobbing would be heart-wrenching for all to see and hear. Who could remain indifferent? And it would probably be a live broadcast; a fantastic television drama. The ratings would go through the roof, and the interview would be on YouTube, Facebook, and Instagram. Jade would become a sought-after guest. Whenever a new rape case came to light, and the victim refused to be interviewed, they would invite Jade, who would always be happy to appear as the expert and tell everyone again about "the horrific experience" she had endured, and how "I shudder every time I hear of another incident." In no time at all, she would be a celebrity. They would talk about her in the gossip columns – sympathetically and sensitively of course. After all, she was a rape victim. They would probably write things like: "Jade, the courageous rape victim, who decided to go public with her story to raise awareness of sexual violence, was seen a few days ago at a restaurant near the beach with a new, handsome and mysterious partner, holding hands and kissing. Jade's response: 'No comment. I don't talk about my personal life.' We wish her the very best!"

CHAPTER
FORTY-NINE

*A*nd again, just as I had two days earlier, and the day before that, and the day before that, and I can't remember how many more days in the recent past, I woke up to yet another bunch of missed calls and text messages. Something had happened again. Something bad, I assumed again. I was a surrealist. And, again, getting really tired of all this. But what could I do?

I had become so used to the endless battle that this time I didn't even bother to check what all the hullabaloo was about. I took my time, made myself a cup of coffee, went out to the balcony, and lit my first cigarette of the day. I had left my phone in the bedroom; I didn't want to see it. I wasn't panicking at all. I just wanted to enjoy my coffee and first cigarette before diving into the latest bad news. It wasn't likely to get worse than it already was merely because I waited a few more minutes. I surprised myself with this calm attitude. It was something new. I had changed.

Fast forward 10 minutes: The sexual assault victims' organization had petitioned the court with an urgent request to lift the gag order. They wanted the court to publish not only the details of the affair, but also my full name, and thus reveal my identity. Now Jade had a powerful organization fighting for her, as well as a PR person and a lawyer.

—

I tried to get back to normal. The most important things right now were going back to work, earning a living, catching up on everything I'd missed. I had reactivated my Facebook and Instagram profiles a few days before, after having frozen them for over four months. There was something highly unnatural, counterintuitive, and downright dangerous about putting yourself back on Facebook and Instagram when you were a person who was trying to keep a low profile, but I had to get used to it again. I was pretty pissed at Facebook in particular; it had gotten me into a lot of trouble when it connected me with a complete stranger who almost finished me off. But I knew it would be unwise of me to close my accounts for good. Only fools tried to fight progress. Social media has become a part of life. And I wanted my life back.

"Filthy rapist."

"May you rot in hell."

"I don't believe you either."

These lovely messages, and many others, greeted me each time I logged in. I could have avoided them, by restricting my Inbox to "Friends Only," but I chose not to. I couldn't.

I had to be available and accessible; it was an occupational necessity. No reporter wanted to miss a good story, and I didn't either. So I suffered the blows in silence and moved on with my life. That was simply the way it worked – either your profile was blocked, or it was wide open. There was no "evil filter" for incoming messages.

But it wasn't only hate mail I received. Mostly, but not exclusively. There were other messages too – kind, supportive, encouraging ones – from people who had been following my story and concluded that I was the victim here. For some reason, the majority of these messages came from women. I answered all of them and thanked them, but when some of them – much to my surprise – expressed an interest in meeting me, I shied away. I knew it wasn't a good time for me to be meeting women. Some of them said that I was "cute," and also that not all women were evil. But I wasn't swayed. The dialogues embarrassed and emasculated me.

CHAPTER FIFTY

S o: I, Cayden Chase, was going to be the target of a protest rally. A real-live protest rally, with placards, megaphones, and all the other de rigueur accouterments. An activist in the National Women's Organization for Sexual Assault Victims had opened a Facebook group called "The Campaign to Get Sex Offenders Off the Air." The group's cover photo was a screenshot from a report about my going out to Jimmy Who and Sheket nightclubs to celebrate the closing of my case.

Cayden Chase, our Channel 3 Health Correspondent, invited a girl over to his apartment, drugged her, and raped her. But the Boys Club, you need to understand, protects its members, and so in no time at all, Chase was afforded something that no other thief/murderer/robber gets: a forewarning, which allowed him to get rid of the evidence and prepare for the investigation. When the police opened their inquiry into the complaint and began looking for evidence of a crime, they found nothing. And then, the case was closed on the grounds of a lack of evidence, of course. The rapist and his friends celebrated his release from house arrest at a party that was the talk of the gossip columns. The show of strength was widely publicized and achieved its goal of deterring other women from filing complaints. If a case falls in the Office of the State Prosecutor and no one hears, does that mean there was no rape? On Thursday, June 9, at six o'clock, we will rally outside the District Prosecutor's Office.

—

And yes indeed, at six o'clock on a beautiful Thursday evening in June, a protest against me got underway. I swallowed two orange pills and waited for updates. I didn't go anywhere near the place of course, but I had friends who kept me in the loop. According to the pictures, videos, and text messages I received, the crowd numbered around 150, and the rally itself – albeit not a very large one – was loud and stormy.

It feels pretty horrible to sit at home and receive updates while a protest rally is taking place against you. I felt hated. Despised. An outcast. People who didn't know me loathed me enough to take the trouble to make placards, to leave everything else aside, and to come out to demonstrate against me. I reviewed some of the videos that my spies had sent me, focusing on one particular video that had a lot of close-ups. Most of the protesters looked like good and decent women, making me wonder once again about the complexity of human beings. I took out my wallet, withdrew the printed picture of Jade receiving that fucking certificate of appreciation, and looked at it again, closely. Life was too confusing.

CHAPTER
FIFTY-ONE

*I*t was now two weeks after the protest rally had taken place, and I was getting ready for another tough day. The case against me was closed, but the war was not over. I woke up at eight-thirty and downed two orange pills. At a court hearing two and a half hours from now, Judge Benny would be handing down his decision concerning the petition. My presence at the hearing was not required, and I had no intention of being there. The women from the protest rally could be waiting there for me with their slogans and placards.

The courthouse was usually filled with press photographers in the morning, and they would be right there to document all the action. Water thrown into a stunned and mortified face: Now that was the kind of drama that made for a good shot. And then, of course, if the court decided to lift the gag order, the embarrassing photographs and videos would be published post-haste. I had no intention of making their jobs easier. I went to work as usual, as if my very life didn't depend on what happened next.

Work was tough these days for health correspondents. Thousands of angry doctors were threatening a mass walkout at the country's hospitals in protest of their employment conditions and the sorry state of the public health system. I was going with a friend and colleague, Kevin, the Channel 1 Health Correspondent, to cover the negotiations between representatives of the Physicians Association and senior Treasury officials. We were off to the capital, a one-hour drive. He was driving, and along the way, I told him about the court hearing that was happening as we spoke.

"Why aren't you there?" he said, glancing over at me. "Don't tell me you're afraid of those women."

"I'd just rather stay out of their way," I shrugged. I didn't like the implication that I was afraid of anything. "But, actually, if the circumstances were different, I'd be very interested in talking to them."

During the day, I received text messages with updates on the developments from Megan and Eddie, who had accompanied Marcel to court. The presiding judge was Judge Benny, again. At the previous hearing, he'd already come under fire for his decision in my favor about the gag order. I could only hope that he would be strong enough to ignore the inevitable backlash this time.

As for Jade, according to Megan, she was feigning a shy and frightened look – her eyes fixed on the floor. She arrived in court accompanied by a group of women wearing T-shirts with the slogan: "This is what a real feminist looks like." It reminded me that during the confrontation at the police station, Jade had said she filed the complaint against me not only for her own sake, but also for other women I may have raped, or might rape in the future. I had said that her false rape complaint was actually the height of anti-feminism, because it would only make it harder for real victims.

Megan sent me a picture she'd snapped with her cellphone, which revealed two of these women sitting beside Jade, embracing her. I looked at their T-shirts for a few seconds and then thought about all the women who had helped *me* along the way: Anna, Megan, Brittany, Judge Judith, and – of course – Alina, the actress and TikTok star who was running the "Free Cayden Chase" campaign, which was unfortunately still highly relevant given Jade's appeal. I wondered: who was actually a feminist? The women who protected Jade, or those who protected me? Could they *all* be considered true feminists? And if so, *how?* I suspected that ever since Johnny Depp's victory many people were looking for answers to such questions, but at this point I was just looking for a cigarette. I was nervous, and my pocket was empty.

At around four in the afternoon, I was notified that the hearing was over but that Judge Benny would only publish his decision the next morning. More agony. Marcel said he could have published it today, but he was taking his sweet old time, no doubt considering entities like the organization that had helped Jade.

Clearly, I had another tough night ahead of me. Although Brittany had told me she wasn't going to be available, I changed my clothes as soon as I got home from my "road trip" with Kevin and took off for the gym, the first time I'd shown up without my female bodyguard in disguise. I was scared, but I had to work out, I just had to. I was stressed, and I had already taken two orange pills.

Fortunately, the gym experience was uneventful this time, and I put myself through such a long and intense workout that when I got home, I could hardly move. I took a shower and then immediately hit the hay. About an hour later, the doorbell rang, so I got up to answer it, only to find Jade standing there in front of me. *What the fuck?*

She wore white heels, a short denim skirt, and a white t-shirt, and her hair was up in a ponytail. Her appearance reminded me of her outfit in the police confrontation a few weeks ago. Back then she wore white sneakers, not heels, and jeans instead of a skirt like now, but the rest was pretty similar - same colors, same style. But this time she smiled at me. And she smelled really good. It was my favorite feminine perfume, Chloé.

The combination of her smile and smell confused me, but surprisingly, I wasn't surprised. It was as if some part of me had actually been waiting for this moment, while having no conscious awareness of it. Was she here to apologize? And if so, was I going to forgive her? Should I forgive her? Was I supposed to invite her in now?

While I wondered what I should do next, Jade pulled a small knife from her purse.

"Shit!" I shouted, but I had strength on my side. She was obviously right-handed and was holding the knife in her dominant hand. I am left-handed, which served my purposes very well here: I could use my good arm to block her. I felt our bones smashing against each other, and then the knife fell to the floor, away from us. I spotted blood, just above my elbow, but felt no pain.

A fraction of a second after the block with my left hand, I slapped Jade across the face with my right one. It was my weak hand, but capable of delivering a powerful slap. She looked stunned for a moment, and I wanted to say, "See what it's like to be slapped against your will?" But of course, there was no time for that; instead, I made use of the moment to grab her by the ponytail and pull her down to the floor. She struggled against me, but she was no longer armed, and I was much stronger. I was also furious.

I knew that I had to tie Jade's hands together, call the police, and ask them to take her the fuck out of my life, once and for all. She was lying on the ground in a prone position, on her stomach, and I was sitting on top of her, pinning her down while holding tight to her ponytail. I could see one of my neckties, which must have fallen from the clothes rack near the entrance, on the floor. I reached my hand over to pick it up, and then used it to tie both of Jade's hands behind her back.

Only then, when her hands were securely tied, did I allow myself to release my grip on her with one hand. When I took my phone out of my pocket, of all the ridiculous things, I couldn't make the call: the phone was busy having its software updated—an uninterruptible process apparently—and wasn't even halfway through yet. I vaguely remembered having approved this update at some point – but really? Now?!

I looked down at the back of Jade's head. It appeared that she and I would now have some quality time together, till my phone was kind enough to finish its software updating. We were still in the same position – she on her stomach and me sitting on her hips, pinning her to the floor, my left hand holding her tied hands behind her back. *We've been in this position before*, I thought with a slight smile. She was no longer struggling against me. It seemed she realized she had lost the last and final battle.

I put my phone back in my pocket and, as I did, my cock unintentionally brushed against Jade's ass. Only then did I notice that at some point during our struggle, her skirt must have flown up, because now her entire ass was exposed. She was wearing a hot pink thong. I intensified my grasp of her tied hands with one hand, and then I slapped her right ass cheek with my other hand, as hard as I could. Twice.

"Guess what, Jade?" I said. "We're going to have some fun here together, before I call the police."

"No!" Jade said. "Please don't! I know the kind of guy you are; you would never do such a thing!"

That almost stopped me in my tracks. Almost. But not quite. "Oh, fuck you, Jade! Now you're saying this?! No, you fucking ruined my life, and now you're going to pay!" I shouted, punctuating my words with more slaps on her ass cheeks.

Jade renewed her struggle against me but she didn't stand a chance with her hands bound and lying beneath me. I had a powerful hold on her ponytail. In her futile efforts to escape, I could feel her bare ass rubbing up against my cock, through my pants, making me so hard I thought I might explode. Truly; it was the hardest I could ever remember being in my entire life. My whole body and mind were ready to tear into her. I pulled my cock out of my pants and slapped it against her ass a few times, like a tiger pulling his claws out right before he jumps on an unlucky doe.

"Let me tell you this, Jade, I didn't rape you when we met the first time, but I am definitely going to rape you *now*, and you fucking deserve it! And let me tell you something else: This is not *Fifty Shades of Grey*. I'm not going to send you gifts and ask you to meet my family; I am just going to fuck the shit out of you, whether you like it or not."

Jade made her last desperate attempt to fight me off, but it was useless. All she succeeded in doing with her pointless thrashing around was to make me even harder, her bare ass continuing to rub up against me. I looked down at my cock, lying there between her legs, waiting for my command to penetrate and complete this act of counter-revenge. This was a tough balancing act; very precarious indeed. In fact, if she kept struggling against me, things might not even be up to me anymore – my cock might just slide right inside her even before the command was ordered. I tightened my hold on her ponytail, and slapped her ass a few more times. I couldn't get enough of it. There had been so many slaps in this relationship, and yet this was the first time I'd enjoyed them.

CHAPTER
FIFTY-TWO

What woke me from this horrific nightmare was Jade's cry, a second before I'd been about to rape her. I sat up straight in bed. I was shocked, and shaking. It all felt so real that it took me a while to understand that Jade wasn't actually there with me in my apartment.

When I finally managed to get the shaking under control, I stood up and swallowed two orange pills. They helped, but I was still walking around under the effect of the nightmare, feeling dazed and unbelievably grateful that it hadn't really happened. Eventually, I made myself a coffee, lit a cigarette, and checked my phone. There was a text message from Marcel. I called him.

"A lot of good news for you, my boy. First, the court – I mean Judge Benny – rejected the petition. Meaning, you've still got your gag order; the media can't do any reporting about the affair and they can't reveal your identity either.

I'm talking about the mainstream media, of course, not social media."

"Oh, thank God," I said, suddenly religious.

"Second, Jade's appeal was declined."

"Really, Marcel? Do you swear to God?"

"I swear to God. This whole thing is really and truly over; the decision is absolute and final."

"I'm going to hold you to that, Marcel – I swear I am!"

"As well you should," he said. "And finally, not that it really matters now, but I thought you'd want to know that you passed the polygraph. You did have a problem with one of the questions, but they didn't care about that one. They only cared about the one asking if you'd put a date-rape drug in Jade's drink, and that one, my friend, you passed with flying colors."

I was quiet for a minute, taking everything in. And then, in a half-whisper, I said, "Marcel, I've got to say, now that we're at this point and I'm in the clear, there were times recently where I actually started to question myself. I mean, I started to wonder: Did I do it? Did I do what she accused me of doing? That's how crazy this whole thing has been for me."

"Shit, Cayden," Marcel said. "It's damn good you didn't say anything like that during the interrogation or the confrontation. You know, in a perfect world, she would go to jail for what she's done to you. But we're in the real world, and you should just be glad that *you* didn't end up in jail. Don't go looking for justice now."

"Don't worry; I'm not looking for justice now. I'm just looking for some weed to smoke."

"Great idea; have fun. You deserve it!"

I smiled. Yes, I was allowed to smile, goddammit. I had done nothing wrong from the very start, other than believing that people were basically good and that they wouldn't try to ruin your life for no reason. Damn, I couldn't rape even in my dreams.

—

For the first time since meeting Jade, I lit a joint. I had avoided cannabis for the last few months because I knew it would just heighten my anxiety.

So now here I was, with a lot of drugs in my system, something I had not intended. But honestly, I had really needed my two orange benzos after the almost-rape-nightmare; and then, after that great news Marcel told me, could anyone blame me for treating myself to some weed? I know physicians generally don't recommend mixing benzos and THC, but for me, at that moment, nothing had ever been quite so perfect. For the first time in what felt like decades, I had peace.

Once again, I took the picture of Jade out of my wallet. But this time I went out to the balcony, put it in the ashtray and set it aflame. I realized I had been using this picture to get in touch with my doubts, but now I didn't need it anymore. Having the polygraph results, there were no remaining doubts. Finally, I had tears in my eyes.

CHAPTER
FIFTY-THREE

A few days after meeting Brittany at the gym, for my first training session after the case against me had been closed, she posted our selfie on her Instagram, tagged me, and added the words:

My favorite TV reporter is back.

It made me feel good and gave me back some confidence. I browsed through the posts on Brittany's Instagram. I wasn't looking for anything in particular, but since I was already there anyway I took a look, and it hit me almost immediately, because here was another interesting picture, posted only a few days before. It was the three of them – Alina, Supercop, and of course, Brittany herself – and it was a selfie that Alina had taken. She was looking straight into the camera and smiling, while Supercop and Brittany kissed her: Supercop on her right cheek, Brittany on her left. I read the sentence that Brittany added to the picture, a few times:

With my two besties: My Supercop buddy Lara and my super TikTok hero Alina, celebrating something that we can't say anything about. Yet.

I already knew that Alina and Supercop were good friends, of course, but I'd had no idea that both of them were also close with Brittany. The first thing that came to mind was that when I'd told Supercop it was funny she had a superhero friend, she'd ordered me to shut up. It had only been a few weeks ago, right after my interrogation at the police station. Supercop had been guarding me while I was eating, and I'd been listening to the voice messages she sent to her friend Alina, because I'd had nothing better to do while eating. I wondered now if they were celebrating because Alina had done well at the audition and had gotten part of the protagonist, a TikTok star who discovers one day that she can make all the magic she makes on her crazy TikTok clips come true in the real life.

Discovering that they were three besties made me insanely curious. Maybe *they* were the three mysterious women from the Free Cayden Chase campaign? Alina, Supercop, and Brittany? I went back to the text on the campaign's website and read it again:

Dear Celebs: We need your help to liberate Cayden Chase! As three women united for a common cause, we ask you to support Cayden, a Channel 3 news correspondent facing a false sexual assault allegation. You've all endured the anguish and humiliation of false accusations:

They actually left a QR code and a link to the campaign's main website there. I'm subscribing, of course. You should too, it's real, just click the link www.freecaydenchase.com, or scan this QR code if you are reading a printed copy of the book:

Was it possible that Alina, Supercop and Brittany were the three mysterious women who ran this campaign for me? Nah . . . no way. Supercop was a chief inspector on the police force, and she was involved in my interrogation. There was no way she could be part of this. And anyway, I didn't even know if they really existed, these three so-called mysterious women. What I did know for sure was that Alina was the one actually running the campaign, but I still hadn't figured out yet *why* she was doing so. I remembered that her birth was the result of an affair that her father had with Alina's mother while being married to someone else. Was it possible that people who came into the world in such a way developed a stronger sense of justice than other people? Or maybe it was something much more practical, and Alina was just a young actress who was using this opportunity to promote her career? Was she getting paid for all this? If so, who was paying her? I don't have the answers, *yet*. But I'm still working on it, and I promise to update you, dear readers, in my next book.

In any event, Alina definitely represents a kind of fixed

pattern in my new post-Jade life. Whenever a woman tries to hurt me, another does something to protect me. One woman landed me in detention; another – Judge Judith - released me to house arrest. One woman pinned a shaming post to the gym's bulletin board; another tore it down and trashed it. A few bloggers ran an online "Jail Cayden Chase" campaign; a few days later Alina launched "Free Cayden Chase."

—

People ask me, almost every day, what this experience has done for me. They say: "Cayden, you must have learned some pretty valuable lessons from this whole thing."

The truth? I haven't learned any lessons, because women like Jade don't come with a warning sign. Maybe I've come out stronger and tougher: but wiser? Not so much. On the other hand, perhaps there is one thing I've learned: to be careful. And I am careful. I'm like a man who for years has been walking his dog through the fields near his house every evening, until one day he steps on a mine and half his leg is blown off. It turns out that the field near his house is an old minefield, from a past war, and he hadn't known anything about it. How could he have known? There was no fence, there weren't any signs. But he knows now, so now he's careful. He makes do with short walks in the yard of his home, hobbling on crutches or a prosthetic leg in his private, limited, and secure expanse. The yard isn't as much fun as the open fields, but it's still his best bet, because the yard is free of mines, and he can't afford to lose his other leg too.

I was saved by the recording of my phone call with Jade. Had it not been for that recording, I'd probably have been in prison now. The idea of recording the call could have escaped my mind at the time. I could have failed to consult with Marcel about it. I could have pressed the wrong icon and deleted the recording. A million things could have gone wrong with the recording. I thought about this a lot.

And I was thinking about it just last week. For the first time since meeting Jade, I had a stranger in my home. She was asleep in my bed, and I was sitting at the bar, writing this book. Her name was Linda, and we had met about six hours earlier at Cappella, a new nightclub with a perfect panoramic view of the city, located on the 14th floor of a tower in the center of the city. I arrived there at around ten with Eddie, and Linda walked in with a friend, Jennifer, a few minutes later. The two of them took the only two remaining seats at the bar, which happened to be alongside us. After a few smiles and a little flirting, we soon turned into a single happy group sharing drinks and appetizers, lots of laughter, and good conversation; and then, about an hour later, the one group turned into two, with Jennifer and Eddie engrossed in their own conversation and ignoring the two of us.

"So that's it," Linda laughed with a nervous little trill. "It's just you and me now."

"Yep," I said. "Just you and me."

"Are you – uh – single?"

"Yes," I said, realizing I was about to face my usual conundrum: "usual" since Jade, that is. What and how much to tell the unsuspecting woman who was about to get involved with the likes of me?

"Good," Linda said.

"I'm impressed with what you said before, about how you decided to go to medical school when you were twenty-eight," I said to her, both because I was, and also because I needed a stall tactic. I wasn't quite ready to enter the territory that I guess we had started to enter: her, me, relationships, dating, sex.

"Do you know what you want to specialize in?"

"Not yet," she said. "And by the way, I have nothing against being a teacher, which is what I was for a long time. There were even times I liked teaching."

So, she had also been a teacher once, like Jade. I tried not to think about it. We sat quietly then, both of us nursing our drinks for a while, until I finally decided to come out with it.

"Listen," I said. "There's something I want to tell you."

I told her. I had to. If she didn't hear it from me, Mr. Google would fill her in. I needed to beat him to it, so that she wouldn't read Jade's online version before hearing mine, from me. I told her everything. I knew she might retreat after hearing that I'd been a rape suspect, but I didn't care. I had just gotten my life back, and having overcome the whole false rape thing was an integral part of it, of my new life. I accepted everything, the whole package, wholeheartedly. I wasn't angry or frustrated. I would never forget the Plan B I'd once had, and so now I was just happy to be alive.

When I was done telling her everything, I ordered more drinks – a glass of wine for her and a shot of whiskey for me, downing mine in a single gulp. I guess we both needed the alcohol at this point. And then there were a few minutes of silence. I was awaiting the verdict: nothing new for me.

Linda looked at me, sipped lightly from her glass, placed it back on the counter, and reached out to caress my face. "I'm really sorry to hear what you've been through," she said.

"Yeah," I said, but I felt uncomfortable, and Linda apparently sensed my unease because she stopped caressing me. I ordered another shot of whiskey. And as I raised it to my mouth, our friends rose from their chairs to inform us they were leaving, together.

"I have a feeling you two will get along just fine without us," Jennifer said. Eddie placed several bills on the bar and whispered in my ear, "Looks like she likes you, my friend; I think you're back in business." Before they left, I could hear Jennifer thanking Eddie for paying the bill. Not all women said thank you after a man was treated. I remembered that Jade hadn't.

After a few more minutes, Linda turned to me and said, "Come on; let's get out of here too. I'm done with this place."

"Okay," I said, "but where are we going?"

"Do you live alone?" she said, a line I would have so enjoyed in my previous life. Fucking Jade.

"Yes," I said, "but I think."

"I didn't ask you what you think," she said.

"Okay, but, I mean, just don't forget. "

"I won't," she said. "Come on, let's get outta here."

I gulped down the remaining whiskey and paid the bill. Linda didn't say thank you, and I was bothered. Was it a sign? Was she just like Jade? Should I have made an excuse and sent her home? We walked to my place, hand-in-hand, without talking. I knew it was still too early for me to be inviting a stranger into my home, but I couldn't say no. I really did like her, the first woman I'd felt this way about since Heather, the one who got away, and the thought of a rejection that would send her off alone into the night made me feel shitty about myself. My wish to spare myself embarrassment won out over my fears.

We walked in and sat together on the sofa.

"Got anything interesting to drink around here?"

"Want a coffee?"

"Got any alcohol?"

"Beer? Vodka? Whiskey?"

"How about a vodka Red Bull?" she said. "Could you rustle up one of those for me?"

Really? She had to have the exact same drink Jade had had.

I went to the fridge. Lying on their sides in the freezer were two bottles of Grey Goose, an older one, half empty, and a brand new one, unopened and untouched. I took the new one and returned to the living room with the bottle, cans, and glasses, placing everything on the table.

"Feel free to help yourself," I said. "I'm going to run to the bathroom for a second."

I went into the bathroom and closed the door behind me. Okay, the bottle of vodka was brand new and unopened, the cans of Red Bull too, and she was pouring her own drink, with me nowhere in sight. She wouldn't be able to claim that I had spiked her drink with a date rape drug; and if she did, I'd sail through the polygraph once again. A good start, even though she could still claim that I had slipped the drug into her drink afterwards, without her noticing. I returned to the living room, joining her on the sofa, but kept a little distance between us.

"Let's watch a movie," I suggested brightly.

"A movie? Now?"

"Yeah, why not? A comedy. I feel like laughing."

"Are you serious?"

I understood what she wanted, and I wanted it too, but I was scared. So scared. And here it was: She'd been a teacher, she liked vodka Red Bulls, she hadn't said thank you back there at the bar. Maybe she was also a Jade kind of girl?

"It doesn't have to be a comedy," I said as if that were the issue. "I like action too."

"Sure, okay," she said.

I took the remote and flipped through the channels until I landed on a movie called *Mossad*. Beneath the title, it read: "After an American tech-billionaire is kidnapped, the Mossad rushes to save him while the CIA sends their best agent to help out. A film by: Alon Gur Arye." Linda had never seen it, and although I had, I didn't mind seeing it again, because it was one of the funniest movies I'd ever seen. If laughing was my goal, then this movie definitely fit the bill.

Before the opening credits had even finished rolling, Linda put her head down against my chest. I didn't respond. Then she began caressing me, slowly, lightly, and kissing my neck. Finally, she reached for the remote and pressed the Pause button, freezing the picture. She turned her back to the screen and straddled me.

Another woman threw herself at me. What luck, right? Actually, it was interesting. Ever since consent had become not enough for me to have sex with someone, this seemed to be the reaction: women wanting me. In my new life, there were only two options: *her move or no move*. And maybe they felt it – first Nicole, then Heather, and now Linda – and liked it. Ironically, my fear of sex seemed to promote it.

"So," I said, with a nervous laugh, "I take it you're not really into the movie then?"

"I have more important matters to deal with here."

"I'm just a little out of the loop since everything that's happened."

"Are you off sex completely?"

"Not exactly," I said. "If we had slept together before all this, it would be easier for me now."

"Oh really? And why is that?"

"Because I'd know you, and I'd feel more secure; I'd know that you weren't going to try to hurt me."

"Wow," she said, un-straddling me. "Look what she's done to you."

"Tell me about it," I said. "Now for the rest of my life I'll have to worry that if I don't want to go out with a woman again after we've been together, she'll get angry and try to get back at me."

"Well, what can I say?" she said, re-straddling me. "This is a first for me. But listen, relax. Who says I'll want to go out with you again? I want to have sex with you, not marry you. And anyway, you won't be able to call me, even if you want to. I'm not going to give you my phone number, I'm only going to take yours. And if you're good and I feel like it, then maybe I'll call you and come over again and take advantage of you."

With my mind still churning, Linda removed her shirt

and bra, grabbed hold of my hands, and placed them on her breasts, which felt great, but I was too uneasy to enjoy them. I tried distracting myself by wondering if they were natural, these beautiful breasts, but the only thing really going through my mind was: Here we go, I'm already knee-deep in the perpetration of an indecent act. I pictured myself facing the lie-detector eyes of Heavy Metal, and trying to convince him that yet another woman was the initiator again, and that everything we did was consensual. Again.

Linda took hold of my t-shirt and pulled it up and over my head, lifted herself off me, gently pushed me back, and began unzipping my jeans. I was nervous; she was going too fast for me, so I pulled her hands towards me and wrapped her arms around my shoulders. I suspected that men didn't generally do this kind of thing with potential one-night stands, and indeed it seemed to take her a few seconds to make sense of this surprising development. But then she hugged me tight and caressed my head. This was exactly what I needed.

"You okay?" she said. "I can feel your heart. It's pounding like crazy! I'm really sorry that you're so stressed."

I didn't answer her question. What could I possibly say? I mean, obviously, I wasn't okay, and furthermore, the random music playlist I chose was *again* playing the song "Stay," by the Kid LAROI and Justin Bieber, and now these two lines were messing with my head and freaking me out:

> *It's been difficult for me to trust*
> *And I'm afraid that I'ma fuck it up*

She continued to hug and caress me for a while, and

I started to relax. Then she finished unzipping my jeans and did something that in the context of a possible future investigation could definitely be considered another act of indecency on my part. That was it, there was no going back, and there was no point in stopping now. In fact, stopping now could create even more trouble for me: If I were to stop her, she could become angry – and ending up with another angry woman after a night out could land me in hot water again.

After a few minutes of feeling both the greatest pleasure and the sheerest terror, Linda removed the rest of her clothes, lay down on her back, and guided my head between her legs for yet another indecent act. Women did that sometimes. But try explaining during questioning that she had initiated this move too. When she was done with this stage of the proceedings, she asked me to get a condom, leading me to the most serious sexual offense of all – rape.

And so there I was, on top of Linda, inside her, thinking: Okay, as of now, there have been three indecent acts and one rape. This time, I don't have a record of any correspondence on Facebook, and I don't have a recorded conversation like the one I had with Jade, so if Linda were to file a complaint, I would be in even deeper shit than the shit I was in last time. And it would be the second complaint against me, and I wouldn't have any evidence to prove my innocence. Great, all I needed now was for her to ask for anal sex, and then they'd be able to throw in a charge of sodomy too.

—

I woke up slowly the next morning, trying to reconstruct

the events of the night before, a flicker of panic passing through me. I remembered us falling asleep in each other's arms, just as I had done with Jade, but – again, just like Jade – Linda was gone now. Somewhat agitated, I headed towards the bathroom, passing the front door on the way. There was a small note there. A note – again! I pulled it off to get a closer look, only to find that she'd pressed her lips to the page, leaving the lip-sticked outline of her mouth, in the form of a kiss. That was how she had chosen to say goodbye. No words on either side.

Naturally, I took a picture of the note with my phone, mailed the image to myself, and then immediately hid the note between the pages of my passport. A few minutes later, while brushing my teeth, I wondered whether lips could serve to identify someone the way fingerprints did: I mean, of course, only in the event that Linda was to deny leaving the note when she went ahead and filed a complaint against me.

A few hours later, I received the following text message.

Hi. It's me – Linda. I must say, it was a real challenge to break down your resistance. If you'd like a rerun, you're welcome to text me. You've got my number now too. And I'm reserving the right for myself as well. I hope you bounce back soon from the hell you've been through. Kisses.

P.S. Thanks for paying the bill at Cappella yesterday 😊

Yes! What could have been better? With the note she left on the door, my ass was covered. Everything was consensual. And I could prove it now too. I took a screenshot of her message, and saved three copies of the two images – the note and the text message – on a flash drive, the hard drive of my laptop, and as attachments to the mail I had sent myself. Life was good.

—

Want to Discover What Happened Next?

After the events of this book, unimaginable twists and turns took place—events filled with love, anger, passion, hope, and even Johnny Depp. Were they real? Dive in to find out.

To ensure you don't miss out on this incredible next chapter, subscribe now and receive a free PDF directly to your email. Get ready for a story you won't forget!

Visit: https://freecaydenchase.com/whatsnext

Or scan the QR code here if you hate typing.

Casey Harper is the pen name of an ageless author based in the start-up capital. Harper excels in crafting psychological thrillers so immersive that reading them feels like navigating in a literary adrenaline tunnel. Today, Harper stands as the foremost figure in interactive fiction for adults, having pioneered this intriguing genre. Harper is also famous for integrating real-time celebs' comments *to* the book - *in* the book itself. While single with no children, Harper lovingly raises two rescued cats that were adopted from an animal aid organization as abandoned kittens, named Ian and Amy, as well as three unnamed cannabis plants, which were bought from the local dealer as seeds. *Descent into Doubt* is the first book in a trilogy, of course. The next two books are almost ready to launch, and will be published as soon as Casey Harper writes them.

Printed in Great Britain
by Amazon

28494094R00185